One Breath at a Time

Tom turned sideways in the seat and kissed me. His mouth was warm and he smelled like sweat and leaves and gun oil. I remembered our first kiss. The memory would always be marked with that peculiar smell of oil on steel. How hesitant I was then, how uncertain – and what a difference a few days could make.

I kissed Tom hard, holding him by the hair to keep him from moving so I could delve deeper. He moaned low in his throat. Already I knew the difference in his reactions, and I knew what he wanted. If I decided to take this any farther, I would be the one in charge.

'Is this why you brought me out here?' I murmured against his lips.

'That's part of it,' he admitted.

'You're insatiable.'

One Breath at a Time
Gwen Masters

BLACK LACE

This book is a work of fiction.
In real life, make sure you practise safe, sane
and consensual sex.

This edition published in 2008 by
Black Lace
Thames Wharf Studios
Rainville Rd
London W6 9HA

Copyright © Gwen Masters 2008

The right of Gwen Masters to be identified as the Author of the Work
has been asserted in accordance with the Copyright, Designs and
Patents Act 1988.

A catalogue record for this book is available from the British Library.

www.black-lace-books.com

http://lustbites.blogspot.com/

Typeset by SetSystems Ltd, Saffron Walden, Essex

Printed and bound in Great Britain by CPI Bookmarque,
Croydon, CR0 4TD

The paper used in this book is a natural, recyclable product made
from wood grown in sustainable forests. The manufacturing process
conforms to the regulations of the country of origin.

ISBN 978 0 352 34163 1

Distributed in the USA by Holtzbrinck Publishers, LLC, 175 Fifth Avenue,
New York, NY 10010, USA

1

The old gate clanged against the post as I climbed into the truck and dropped it into drive. Gravel crunched under the wheels and dust rose up around my tailgate. This was an old utility road, one the government first forgot and then sold for more than it was worth. A casual driver on a lazy weekend afternoon would never believe that at the end of this dirt and gravel road sat a grand three-storey house looking out over the Tennessee River.

I took in a deep breath of dust as I closed the gate. A coughing fit ensued. I leaned over the tailgate and looked up at the trees as the dust settled around me. The leaves were almost full, growing into another spring. How could I have possibly missed that?

The answer was crystal clear, like a little voice in my consciousness keeping me up-to-date on my love life: perhaps because you've been heartbroken for the last six months. The man needs you and sometimes he wants you, but he damn sure doesn't love you. What was that old song? Two out of three ain't bad, baby.

I got into the truck and slammed the door behind me. I rolled up the window and gunned the engine, hit the gas hard, and tore down the driveway before the dust caught up with me. I didn't want to breathe that shit in, and I damn sure didn't want to think.

The extra set of keys jangled on the seat. My friend Ronnie was out of town for a family emergency and I was checking on the house for him. When I got to the end of the quarter-mile road, I came to a stop in the wide driveway and looked up at the mansion. Covered in fine cedar siding, the house tried desperately to look like a rustic cabin, but the sheer size of it belied the wealth of the man who had built it to his every specification. From the wide hardwood floors to the intricate ceiling fans and carefully chosen furniture, it was a home built for comfort and style.

I made my way around the wide porch, pausing once to move a pot of flowers closer to the protective railing – storms were forecast and that pot would tip over with the first strong wind. The dogs romped onto the porch, happy to see me and eager to be fed. I tried my key in the lock of the front door while I batted a Labrador away with my other hand.

The door swung open – it was already unlocked.

Unlocked?

A creepy feeling of fear and unease struck me. I swung around to look back at the driveway. My truck was the only vehicle there. The garage was closed up tight. Both bays were empty. Nothing seemed out of place.

I pushed the door open wider and let the dogs scramble into the house. I watched them as they made themselves at home. There was no sense of danger in their intelligent eyes. They were comfortable. No one here but us, their wagging tails said.

Satisfied, I made my way through the house. The floors were a mellow pine, covered haphazardly with rugs in every color imaginable. The kitchen was modern, filled with stainless steel appliances and slate countertops. I walked through it to the utility room, where the dog food waited in old-fashioned liquor barrels.

The dogs pranced happily at my feet. I set down bowls for each of them and then put more in the corner of the back porch, under the protective eaves. No matter how much it rained, they would have dry food for the evening if they chose to venture out of their backyard houses.

I listened to their low growls of satisfaction as I prowled through the house. I studied each window and each door, making certain everything was locked. The house was neat and clean, but in the bedroom the covers had been thrown to the floor, and the pillows were everywhere. I pushed one aside with my foot and smiled. Somebody had had plenty of fun before they left the house.

I pulled the covers back up and threw pillows on the center of the bed. I looked out the wide picture window at the blue water below. Boats kicked up wakes and, in those wakes, men and women rode on skis. Kids splashed near the shore. Gulls flew every which way, hoping for fish churned up to the surface by the boats.

Looking at the water made me think of Michael, and the pain took my breath away.

I sank down on the edge of the bed. The mountains of Tennessee seemed to be light years away, not just a few hours. If there were only miles between us, I'd be there in a day's drive – but there was more than that. There was her.

I tried to shake the images in my head, the ones that haunted me every night since he had said he wanted to sleep with her instead of me. Her, the woman who came before me, and the woman he might be seeing again now, for all I knew. He had told me so many things during those long nights while we made love until the sun came up, and soon I learned that the fantasies he weaved with his words weren't fantasies at all, but memories.

There was one image that never left my mind, no matter how much time had passed. The image of her tied to that weight bench he loved so much, the sordid things he described to me long before I knew it wasn't a fantasy at all. It was a memory that he held so sacred he let it taint everything about our relationship.

I could hear the voice of the man I loved so much, saying things I couldn't stand to hear: 'I fucked her so hard I moved the weight bench across the floor . . .'

Suddenly angry as hell, I kicked a pillow across the room. It bounced off the wall and lay innocently, alone on the carpet. Just as alone as I felt.

One of the dogs came up the stairs and sniffed at the pillow. I stared out the window and thought of other things, anything at all, until the images started to fade. I watched a man on a jet ski. I watched a boy on an inner tube. I watched the gulls pick up fish and then fight over them. I watched a Coast Guard cruiser make its way into the channel. By the time it was out of sight, my tears were gone – this time.

I went down the stairs. The dogs already wanted to go back outside, so I opened the back door and let them go. As I turned to leave, I noticed the basement door was ajar.

I pulled the keys out of my pocket and looked them over, then looked back at the door. The basement housed what was lovingly called the Jungle Room. Filled with mounted animals, pictures of safaris and guns big enough to bring down elephants, the room was definitely a man's domain, not the kind of place children or most women would go. The walls were lined with gun cabinets filled with every kind of weaponry imaginable, and I knew better than to ask if all of them came with proper permits.

That door was kept double-locked, for good reasons of both safety and security.

And now the door was open.

That creepy feeling hit me again; it was the same mixture of fear and anticipation that had assaulted me at the front door. This time I couldn't write that open door off as an accident. This time two happy dogs wouldn't be able to sway me into thinking everything was OK.

I was not alone in the house.

And whoever was there with me was much closer to the guns.

I stepped back into the shadows. The back door was right there, a quick escape route. But the whole backyard was visible from the wide windows of the Jungle Room, and someone with a mind to shoot would be able to pick me off without much effort. There was the phone, there on the kitchen counter. The front door was still open, and I could make a run for that.

So why was I still here?

There was no way I was going to be shot in the back while retreating. Something in me was determined that would not happen. Perhaps it was the image of Michael that came back to me, the way he had blindsided me on the day he said he would fuck that woman again. Perhaps it was the shock of knowing he had loved her all along.

I would not be blindsided like that again.

There were eight high steps between me and the basement door. I descended them one at a time, careful to keep my feet on the edges and avoid the squeaky centers. The insanity of what I was doing was screaming at me to run. One part of me wanted to listen to reason. And another part of me just didn't give a damn.

I reached out and pushed the door. It swung open silently on oiled hinges. Sunlight flooded the little space at the bottom of the stairs. It glinted from the metal and steel in the cases, from the leaded glass in the cases themselves. It was almost blinding, and I raised my hand to shield my eyes.

'Who the fuck are you?' a deep voice growled. He was there in the corner, standing by an open cabinet, reaching for a rifle with one hand and raising a pistol with the other. The business end was pointed directly at my heart.

I stared at the gun. The realization of what I had done slammed into me, along with a startling kind of peace. This man was going to shoot me. What frightened me was my lack of fear.

This man was going to shoot me, and I wasn't sure that I cared.

I slowly held out my hand and opened my fingers. The house keys tinkled in my palm. I held them up as if holding an apple up to a skittish horse. I opened my mouth to say something but nothing came out. All I could do was stare at the pistol and listen to the shocking mantra in my head.

I don't care. I don't care.

He slowly lowered the gun. The shot he hadn't fired seemed to echo through the house. We both listened to the roll of it in the silence. My eyes left the gun and traveled up a tall body, to a shadowed jaw and wary brown eyes almost hidden under an old battered baseball cap. He moved towards me and swept the keys from my hand. I watched him as he looked at them, then looked back up at me, his eyes still filled with shock.

'You didn't flinch,' he finally said.

We both looked down at the gun in his hand. He knelt and slowly slid it across the polished surface of the long low coffee table. It came to rest beside a mounted quail. His hand shook as he moved it away from the pistol. He stood up to face me.

'You didn't flinch,' he repeated.

'What good would it have done?' I asked him. His brown eyes were assessing every word and every expression, as though he could see right through me.

'None,' he said softly. 'I'm a damn good shot.'

The arrogance of the statement and the wry smile that accompanied it broke the dam inside me, but, instead of tears, what came out was a peal of laughter. I sank to the floor and buried my face in my hands, laughing so hard I couldn't catch my breath.

Soon the man was sitting in the chair closest to me, laughing as hard as I was. The nervous tension in the room was disappearing. By the time we were both done, the dogs had come in through the open front door to inspect the cause of the noise. I wiped tears from my eyes and looked up at the man who had almost shot me.

He was a bit older than me, but not by much. He had the shoulders and build of a well-muscled athlete. His brown eyes were and no longer wary. He had removed the cap and his deep-brown hair fell across his forehead, far too long and unkempt. His face could use a shave. But his smile was friendly and open, and I wondered how he ever could have pointed a gun at me.

'What are you doing here?' he asked.

'House sitting. I was supposed to come here every day and check on the dogs. Just keep an eye on the place. What's your story?'

'That is my gun,' he said, pointing to a rifle he had pulled from the open case. 'And that pistol is mine, too. Ronnie and me, we go hunting all the time. I have the same set of keys you do.'

'I didn't see a vehicle?'

'I rode the four-wheeler. It's out in the back by the patio. I live a quarter-mile down the river.'

We looked at each other, unsure of what to say. He went back to the thing that was still occupying his mind. 'You didn't flinch when I held the gun on you.'

'I am utterly without fear,' I said.

He eyed me suspiciously, unsure whether to take me seriously or laugh out loud. I took a deep breath.

'I'm hurting over someone,' I clarified. 'Let's just say a bullet to the heart might be easier.'

The man looked directly at me. 'You would rather be shot than lose him?' he asked. It was a direct question, blunt and to the point.

'No,' I said automatically, then considered my answer. 'Maybe a few months ago, I would rather have died than be without him. But maybe not today.'

He smiled, and his whole face again had that open

7

gentle look. 'Of course you don't want to die today – we already dodged that bullet, so to speak. Besides, how could you possibly die before you get to know me?'

I laughed. 'First you try to shoot me. Are you hitting on me now?'

'Depends. Is it working?'

I shook my head, still amazed at the audacity of this man and the circumstances under which we had met. 'To be honest, I'm not over my ex. Hitting on me might be a lost cause.'

'Tell me about him.'

I rose to my feet. The man stood up at the same time. He was a good five inches taller than me and much broader than I had first thought. He could have been a very intimidating man, but his attitude was more gentle teddy bear.

'Don't you have some place to be? The telling could take a very long time,' I pointed out.

'Good,' he said. 'A long time with you sounds very good.'

I laughed again, and slowly realized I hadn't laughed so much in months. Nervous tension, I reminded myself. Nervous tension does that. And being scared to death does that, too.

'What is your name?' I said.

'Tom.'

'Can I call you Tommy?'

'No.'

'OK. I'm Kelley.'

He smiled. He had one dimple in his cheek, which made him look suddenly years younger than he was. 'You were going to tell me about your ex, so we could get that out of the way. Then you were going to tell me about you. Remember?'

I looked out the window, deciding. The dogs nosed around our feet. The sun still glared from the line of gun cabinets, but my eyes were accustomed to it now.

Through the window I could see the sailboats moving like toys across the bay. The gun on the coffee table seemed to wink back at me as I looked at it.

'I wonder if Ronnie has any beer in the fridge,' I mused.

'Let's find out.'

Sure enough, there were beers in the fridge. We each popped one and sat down at the kitchen table. The dogs romped outside, happy again now that everything seemed to be under control. Tom draped his jacket over the back of his chair. His arms were lined with muscles, bulging under his T-shirt. His chest was like a barrel. It was the body of a man who loved the gym.

The horrible thoughts about Michael's weight bench and the things he did on it popped into my head again, taking me completely by surprise.

Tom saw me looking at his arms. 'I probably work out too much,' he said, almost in apology.

'There's nothing wrong with that.'

'You don't look like you believe that at all.'

Meeting his eyes was a struggle. I was sure he could see the pain in mine. 'It's a long story.'

'So you said. And I have a long time.'

'It's baggage,' I said. 'Why do you want to hear all that?'

Tom took a long sip of his beer. 'What is the first thing you do when you go on a long journey? You pack, right? What's the first thing you do when you get to where you are going?'

'You unpack.'

'That's right. You unpack, so you can enjoy your time there, however long that might be.'

I had to smile. 'Well, that's the most positive spin on baggage I've ever heard.'

'Consider this unpacking,' he said. 'That's what happens before you get to the good stuff.'

I started talking. Tom rose a while later to get more

beers from the fridge, but told me not to stop. I told him about Michael and how we broke up, and the reasons why. I told him about the nightmares and the visions in my head. When I explained the dreams about the weight bench, Tom glanced down at his arms and gave me an apologetic smile.

'That explains the look you gave me earlier,' he said. 'I'm sorry.'

'Sorry for what?'

'Sorry that I reminded you of something bad.'

I smiled and touched his hand. 'Talking about it helps,' I said.

'Then by all means, keep going. I'm listening. Can't you tell?'

Soon we were standing side by side at the kitchen counter, preparing a late and unconventional lunch of eggs and bacon and homemade biscuits, which Tom insisted on making himself. He asked questions in the blunt way I was already accustomed to, and I answered them with as much honesty as I could muster. He asked me about Michael. About my job as a writer. About my life and everything that made me who I am.

While we ate on the patio overlooking the water, I learned that he had been divorced for six years, that his kids meant the world to him, but he rarely got to see them. He loved his job, and it kept him busy instead of lonely. He had been a soldier for well over a decade, going wherever Uncle Sam decided to give him a free ride, but now he had settled into a more sedate lifestyle – somewhat. He was a security guard for a small but very exclusive firm. Occasionally he went on the road with a rock band or someone even more glamorous, carried a few guns, saw the world and made a living while doing it.

'I will never be a wealthy man,' he admitted, 'but I do what I love, and that matters more.'

He talked about his favorite hunting trips, about the new bow he bought the day before, and about the old truck that he had been working on forever. He told me about his family and his hometown and his plans for the future.

We carried the plates into the kitchen and started doing them by hand. He stood beside me and talked as he dried and put them away. We watched the boats out the window and listened to the dogs scuffling on the front porch.

I thought about Michael and the way we met, that first conversation that lasted for hours. I wondered how Michael would react if he knew I was here with Tom, talking about everything, including him. Would he care? Would he be angry that I had revealed so much about him? Would he be jealous about Tom? Or would he be relieved?

'Bullet for your thoughts,' he whispered in my ear. I smiled at the reference that had already crept so many times into our conversation.

'I was thinking about Michael. Wondering how he would feel about this conversation I've had with you. Wondering if it would bother him at all.'

'He would be jealous,' Tom said. 'Because he's not the one doing this.'

Tom took two steps towards me. His formidable body pushed my smaller one into the corner between two countertops. He slid his hand into my hair and, before I could take another breath, his lips came down over mine.

My hands were covered in soapsuds. He had a dishtowel thrown over one brawny shoulder. He smelled like gun oil and tasted like orange juice. His lips were cautious at first, taking their time, exploring, but not moving away far enough to allow me to protest. I pressed my hands against his chest and pushed, the motion fueled by instinct and indecision. He gently took my hands in his and pulled them behind me. His body settled comfortably against mine as he threw caution to the wind and kissed me for all he was worth.

Soon I was kissing him back, all thoughts of protest forgotten. The sweep of Tom's tongue against mine was maddening. He licked and sucked and nibbled on my lips before plunging deep again, kissing me hard enough to take away my breath. I slid my hands up his arms, memorizing every muscle. His hand tightened in my hair and those muscles moved under my hand, and I wondered what it would feel like to hold onto his shoulders while his hand was sliding all over my body.

Then I thought of Michael.

It took an effort to push Tom away. He moaned in protest. His hands didn't leave my hair, but he did stop kissing me. We stood together, breathing hard. Tom read my mind.

'You haven't kissed anyone since Michael, have you?'

I nodded. I was fighting the tears, but it was a losing battle. Tom pulled me hard against his shoulder and held me there while I got my emotions under control.

'Are you all right?' he asked me after a few minutes of silence.

No, I wasn't all right. I suddenly pushed Tom away and bolted for the bathroom, where I gave up everything I had eaten for lunch. The emotional upheaval was just too much. Images of Michael flashed through my head over and over and over, but this time they were interlaced with images of myself, standing in a kitchen and being thoroughly kissed by someone else.

Tom didn't come to the bathroom to check on me. I heard him pop open another beer. The guilt assailed me and I lunged for the toilet again. Nothing came up.

Michael was my ex. He wanted to stay that way. He had been given every opportunity to work things out with me, but he hadn't made any attempt to do so. Why did I feel guilty?

I washed my face and used the mouthwash. I looked at myself in the mirror and heard Michael's voice again in my head: 'The climax was a toy in her ass, while I fucked her so hard...'

'Stop it,' I said to my reflection. 'Stop it now.'

When I came out of the bathroom, Tom was outside on the patio. He put his arm around me and we stood together, watching the boats on the water.

'Was it the food?' he asked. 'Or the kiss?'

'It was the emotional turmoil.'

'How do you feel now?'

'I don't know what I feel,' I said. 'Other than lost. I feel completely lost.'

He handed me his beer and smiled down at me. His eyes said there was no reason to apologize. He reached into the pocket of his jeans and pulled out an old scarred compass. He flipped it around with the ease of an expert, lined it up with something on the waterline, and kissed my forehead with his warm lips.

'Good thing I'm a boy scout. You won't be lost for long.'

'I thought that was a Skoal ring in your pocket,' I said, nodding at the compass.

'No, that's the other pocket.'

'Ah.'

'My house is down there.' He motioned to the waterline. I took a few steps to the railing of the porch, and from there I could see the corner of a cabin with wide windows that looked out over the water.

'I see it. Is it as big as this one?'

'Almost. I want you there for dinner. I'll cook. Bring yourself and a good red wine.'

I didn't say yes or no. What I did say amused him greatly, and shocked the hell out of me.

'Tom. Do you have a weight bench?'

He smiled a low easy smile. The compass made a tiny click as he closed it up. He slipped it into the pocket of my jeans and let his hand linger there on my hip. This time when he pulled me close, I didn't protest. I melted into him as if he had touched me a thousand times. He whispered into my ear right before he started to kiss that sensitive spot right underneath it.

'Baby, I have a whole gym.'

His lips were playing along my throat. I sank my hands into his hair and he groaned against my skin. His hips pressed firmly against mine and I suddenly felt what I had tried to ignore in the kitchen, the evidence of how aroused he was. I ground against him and he suddenly sucked in a breath.

'If you do that much more, I won't be able to wait for the weight bench.'

His hands were hard on my hips, holding me in place without any effort at all. He was just as strong as he looked. The thought of all that strength unleashed on me set my body afire in places that hadn't been touched in far too long. I ran my fingertips over the muscles in his arms. Then across the muscles in his chest. Then down his belly, where he was a little softer, but still definitely carrying a six-pack. His back was strong and didn't give at all under my hands as I pulled him up against me.

'I don't know what I want,' I said. 'But I think maybe I want you.'

He chuckled against my lips. 'That's a damn good start.'

I kissed him. My tongue slipped across his soft lips and he took in a long breath. He let it out in a tortured moan as I ground up against him one more time.

'Be sure,' he whispered against my lips. 'Be sure, because, if you don't stop now, I'm going to fuck you right here on the picnic table.'

'Good.'

'Be sure you mean that,' he said again. He took my hands and pulled them away from his shoulders, locking them behind me in a grip that was impossible to break. 'You might feel guilty later. You might regret me.'

'Are you going to disappear after you fuck me?'

Tom snorted in laughter. 'Hell, no. You're fascinating and I want to get to know you. You know that already, or you wouldn't even be thinking about sex.'

He was right. If I had thought he just had sex on his mind, I never would have felt the urge to kiss him, much less let him do anything more.

'Aren't you glad you didn't shoot me?' I whispered into his ear.

He stood completely still, controlling himself with an effort, waiting for what I might do next. My hands were held tightly behind my back. My whole body was aching with need. It had been long months since I had been touched, and every last lonely moment was settling between my thighs in a raging fire.

'You are so gorgeous like that,' he said. He twisted his hand, and my shoulders burned with the pressure. He carefully watched my reaction, his eyes gauging the pain and pleasure in mine.

'I feel like a bitch in heat,' I gasped.

'You like it rough.' It wasn't a question.

'I like to be controlled.'

'Like this?'

Tom spun me around so quickly that I lost my balance, which was exactly what he wanted. He caught me around the waist and pushed me down face-first on the worn wood of the picnic table. He caught my hands behind my back. He was rough and gentle all at the same time, and the combination was explosive.

I wiggled my hips in invitation. The compass in my pocket dug into my thigh. Tom pulled my hair off my neck with his free hand and then laid a kiss on my nape. His teeth came next, biting me hard, marking me while I whimpered and put up a token struggle. He ground against me, moving his hips forwards and back, mimicking what he would love to be doing inside me at that very moment.

'Please,' I gasped. All coherent thought was long gone.

'Please, what?'

'Please fuck me, Tom. God, please. Please.'

'You have one last chance to tell me no. That chance is right now. If you tell me anything but no, you're going to get fucked good and proper, the way you deserve it. Do you understand?'

'Yes.'

'What do you want?'

I closed my eyes. Behind them I saw Michael, naked and standing over a weight bench.

But that woman tied to the weight bench was not me.

'I want you to fuck me,' I said out loud. 'Right now.'

He reached around my waist. My jeans opened with a fast snap, and the zipper came down even faster. I wiggled my hips to help as he pulled the jeans down. I wasn't wearing anything underneath them, and he groaned when he saw that. I kicked the jeans off my legs and away. Tom pulled me up against him and worked the buttons of my shirt one at a time, taking his slow and agonizing time with each and every one. Birds sang merrily around us. If anyone chose to look up at the grand houses lining the river, would they see us?

'The first time is going to be very fast,' he warned me. 'Because I want you so bad, and because it's been so long. And then I'm going to take you up to the bedroom and I'm going to fuck you in there. And then tonight I'm going to tie you to that weight bench and fuck you in every way humanly possible. Is that what you want?'

'That's just the tip of the iceberg.'

My shirt was open. My nipples were hard as rocks. He pulled the shirt back until it almost fell from my hands, and then he wrapped it around my arms. The expert way he did it told me that he was much more familiar with bondage than I had suspected.

'Boy scout,' I gasped as he pushed me down on the table and spread my legs with his hands.

'Always prepared,' he said. 'Do I need to use a condom?'

'No.'

The sound of his zipper struck both fear and anticipation in my heart. I could hardly breathe. I knew I might regret this later, but passion had pushed me past the point of all reason. I hardly knew this man but I knew he could give me what I needed, and that was enough.

Tom pushed the head of his cock against me. I gasped as the sensation rolled through me. My mind and body were a blank canvas. I was open to whatever he might want to do.

'Please,' I whimpered one more time, and that small sound was all it took to send Tom's control over the edge. He pushed into me with one long thrust. He filled me completely. I arched my back as he ground his hips hard against me, and I cried out loud when I felt him touch places that hadn't been plundered by anything but sex toys in years and years.

'Jesus Christ,' he growled. 'You're so damn tight.'

I bit my lip and pushed back against him. My nipples scraped against the wood, sending shafts of desire all the way down my belly. I trembled as he held very still, letting me adjust to the newness of him. I wanted to be able to see his face, to know what he was thinking by looking into his eyes. I had to settle for taking all my cues from his body. From the way he was throbbing inside me, he was enjoying every long second just as much as I was.

Tom tangled a hand in my hair. His other hand traced the curves of my ass. The first slap he brought down on me was gentle, testing me to see what my reaction might be. I bucked up against him and he let out a startled grunt as he braced himself. The second slap was harder, and the tingle seemed to settle right between my thighs.

'You like that,' he murmured.

'Yes . . .'

'I do, too.'

He ran his hand gently over the places he had just spanked. He brought his hand down again. And again. I knew my pale skin was turning red. His cock jerked inside me every time the sound rang out into the trees. I saw myself through his eyes: a woman almost completely naked, her hands bound behind her back, bent over a picnic table in what was practically the middle of the woods, exposed for anyone who might happen to glance up, his hand in my hair and my ass showing the marks he had put there. I moaned at the images in my head.

When Tom pulled halfway out and thrust back in, I was taken by surprise. I had been so focused on the picture in my head and the sensation of his hand on my ass, I hadn't realized that my body had adjusted to his size. He began to fuck me with slow deliberate strokes. But slow did not mean gentle; every one of them was hard, deep and punishing, and exactly what I needed. I told him so, with moans and whimpers and begging words that made him moan in response.

'I told you I wouldn't last long,' he said. 'I think maybe I overestimated myself.'

I laughed out loud, and Tom suddenly thrust forwards. His hands dug into my shoulders. His hips rose against me, forcing me harder against the edge of the table. He cried out and that's when I felt it, the pulsing of his cock buried deep inside me.

I hadn't been at all close to an orgasm, but his sent me over some invisible edge I hadn't even sensed was there. My scream echoed over the water. He groaned in surprise. I came hard enough to force him out of me. The juices of both of us slid down my thighs. He collapsed over my back, breathing hard.

Neither of us spoke for a long while. His hands were gentle on every inch of me he could reach. He slowly untied the shirt and pulled it off my arms. He massaged my back and my hips, smoothed my hair and kissed every inch down my spine. When he got to the cleft of my ass, I shuddered in delight. He slipped a finger deep into my pussy and my knees buckled.

Tom laughed against my back. 'OK, little one. Time to go inside so you can lie down.'

'Is that what you want?'

He turned me around and kissed me slowly. 'So eager to please,' he praised. 'How could any man let go of a woman like you?'

His words solidified the reality of what I had just done. Tom watched my eyes as the pain rolled through my very soul. He touched my face and kissed my forehead but said nothing.

Tom led me through the house and up to the bedroom. I looked out the wide picture window. The day was in full swing now; boats were all over the water. 'Lie down,' Tom whispered in my ear, and I crawled onto the bed. Suddenly shy, I pulled the covers up over my body. Tom smiled down at me while he took off every piece of clothing. I watched him. He was so handsome, in every sense of the word. An unaccustomed blush stole over my face.

'You look absolutely gorgeous when you blush,' he teased.

'I haven't done this in so long.'

'If I have anything to say about it, you will never utter those words again.'

Tom crawled into bed beside me, under the covers. We lay there quietly, looking at each other. He took my hand and pressed it against his chest.

'Touch me.'

I did. I explored every inch of his body. I straddled him and he gave me a wicked smile, then settled back to let me play however I wanted. His skin was soft and surprisingly flawless. He felt as solid as he looked. He was deeply tanned, and I enjoyed the contrast of that against my pale skin.

The thought of Michael's deep tan crept into my mind. I froze, my hands pressed against Tom's belly. I looked at the deepness of his tan against my hands and remembered doing that same thing with Michael.

'You're thinking of him, aren't you?' Tom's voice was slow and gentle.

'I'm sorry.'

'Don't apologize. I know it will take time. What reminds you of him now?'

'Your tan. He loves to tan. It's one of his favorite things.'

'My tan is from being outdoors so often. Not from a tanning bed. See?'

He pushed the blankets down and pointed to his waist. The tan line was clear. It made me smile to see that, and I knelt to kiss it. His hand tangled in my hair. I kissed lower, and his breath came faster. By the time I sank my mouth down over his cock, he was arching up off the bed, begging for it, just like I had begged him out there on the picnic table.

The feeling of power was an aphrodisiac. I took my time, teasing him right to the edge and then slowing down. His groans became louder, and I was thrilled to know he could make so much noise. I ran my nails down his chest while I took as much of him into my mouth as I could.

Tom let go of my hair and grabbed the headboard of the bed. He bucked up into me. When he couldn't take any more, he didn't bother to warn me. He came in my mouth. I swallowed every drop that he gave me, but took the time to taste him first. He was surprisingly bland.

'You don't taste like anything,' I blurted, and he laughed as he pulled me up to his side.

'Is that a compliment or not?'

'It's neutral. Like Switzerland.'

'I taste like Switzerland.'

'Sure.'

'I wonder what you taste like,' he mused, then grabbed the covers and threw them back. His eyes were bright with anticipation. 'Let's find out.'

I had rarely allowed a man to do that to me. It was something so intimate, so open, that I found it difficult to give that part of me to anyone. As a result, no man had gone down on me in years. But, when Tom gently pushed my knees apart, I lay back and closed my eyes, giving myself over to the exquisite sensations his tongue pulled from me.

His breath was hot and his tongue was rough, then gentle, then rough again. When he found my clit he wasn't careful, but teased the hell out of it, just the way I needed it. He took in every motion and paid attention to every moan. By the time he held my clit between his teeth and stroked it with his tongue, I was on the verge of exploding.

'I'm going to come,' I wailed. Tom let me move however I wanted. When I came it was with a loud cry. Tom immediately crawled up between my legs and took me into his arms. I was trembling and breathless. My arms felt like lead weights as I wrapped them around his shoulders. He was so big, so strong, and it felt so good to give myself over to him.

'You taste sweet,' he said after my body had calmed.

I opened my eyes and looked up at him. His hair was tangled and damp with sweat. His eyes were playful and his smile was real, genuine, and destined to stay there a while.

'I am sweet.'

Tom laughed as he settled next to me.

Long minutes later we lay together in the bed, his arms around me, my head on his broad chest. He played with my hair. Birds sang outside the window and from down on the water, a dog barked. I ran my fingertips along his arm. I thought about seeing his house, about watching him cook in his kitchen, about seeing him comfortable in his own space.

'I've known you for less than twelve hours,' I said. His hand slid lazily down my shoulder. 'We haven't even had our first date yet,' he teased.

I giggled and pressed my lips to his chest. He hauled me up for a long lingering kiss. 'I need to go to the grocery store to get stuff for dinner,' he said. 'I haven't had a woman in my house in so long, I'm sure all the fridge holds is soured milk and a case of beer.'

'We do have to eat. You need to have the energy to show me your gym.'

'Hmmm. My weight bench.'

'Yes.'

He gently spanked my ass and at the same time he pushed me towards the edge of the bed.

'Let's get up and get moving, little one. We've got a long night ahead.'

I watched him as he dressed. When he buckled the belt, I caught his eye. He glanced at my bare ass and actually blushed. It suddenly dawned on him why I hadn't started getting dressed, and with a bashful smile he headed to the patio to get my clothes.

I lay back on the bed and looked out at the water. The sun was starting to think about going down. From below, Tom hollered for the dogs. The screen door whacked against the frame. A speedboat roared, throwing a massive wake behind it. Jet skis raced for it, jumping over the water.

I thought about Michael and the pain was there, but

not as sharp as it had been before. I thought about the stories he told me, about the weight bench, about the things he hadn't done with me. I wanted to do all of them with Tom. Someone else might have called it revenge, but I knew better. It was what I needed to do to find myself again.

'Are you unpacking that baggage?' Tom asked from the end of the bed. He laid my clothes at my feet and looked at me with those understanding brown eyes.

'Yeah.'

'I don't know where we're going,' he said. 'But I'm ready to find out.'

'Let's start with steaks. And good wine.'

'And a weight bench,' he murmured, coming towards me for another kiss. I whispered against his lips, and he laughed out loud, a sweet and promising sound.

'I'm glad I didn't shoot you,' he said.

2

The road to Tom's cabin was rough. The dust swirled around my tires as I dodged one small pothole after another. I had found the gate hidden halfway down a utility road, like the one in front of Ronnie's house. After I opened it I stood there under the trees for a moment, breathing deeply of the spring dusk, wondering how I had come this far in so little time. Less than twelve hours and I had been fucked by a man I hardly knew.

And now I was going back for more.

The trees began to clear out, and suddenly I was there, coasting to a stop in front of a quaint two-storey cabin. It was made the old-fashioned way, solid logs lined with chinking, carried out to the ends in the traditional pattern. The porch was wide and deep, and the roof of that porch was weathered tin. Under the shadows a swing waited, and in that swing was Tom.

I climbed out of my truck. The sound of the door closing was loud in the little clearing. I made my way up the three steps and met Tom at the top of them. I handed him a bottle of wine. He didn't even look at the label. His eyes were on me and nowhere else.

'Hi,' I almost whispered.

'Hello,' he whispered back. 'I'm Tom.'

'I'm Kelley.'

'Now that we've been properly introduced . . .' he teased, and pulled me to him for a kiss.

My hands went around his neck and I melted into him. His body was already familiar to me. The strong lines of his shoulders and the firmness of his thighs felt like comfort, and the rhythm of his breathing felt like marking time, counting down the minutes until I would have him inside me again. If I had taken the time to really analyze what I was doing, I would wonder at the aphrodisiac of newness, at how good it felt to act so out of character.

Tom ended the kiss with a slow sucking on my bottom lip.

'How do you feel about all this?' he asked.

I laid my head on his shoulder and watched as a squirrel ran along the railing and picked up nuts that had obviously been left there by a deliberate hand. The squirrel chattered at me while he worried the nut around and around in his little hands. I blew him a kiss and the animal quirked his head at me.

'I feel comfortable,' I said, and it was the truth.

'Steaks are on. Want to help me with the salad?' he offered.

Tom's home was just as charming on the inside as it was on the outside. The furniture had seen better days, and so had the hardwood floors. Quilts hung everywhere, and were even used as curtains. The fireplace was glowing with embers of an almost-forgotten fire. The ceiling fan whirled lazily above us, and on every end table there was a stack of books.

I picked up a few of them. *Zen and the Art of Motorcycle Maintenance. Jurassic Park. Hurricane*, the story of Rueben Hurricane Carter. The collection of books was eclectic and interesting. I flipped through *The Little Book of Love* while Tom watched me from over the kitchen bar.

'Read much?'

'Every chance I get. I don't have your book here, though. I have to get that.'

'I'll autograph it for you,' I said. 'I'll make it very personal.'

'Personal, huh?' His eyes were bright with laughter. He tossed a tomato my way, and luckily I caught it before it knocked over the table lamp. 'Get over here and get personal with this set of knives. I'm starving, you know. Somebody tried to wear me out earlier.'

I wandered into the kitchen. There were slate counter-tops, just like in Ronnie's house. The kitchen table was big enough to seat eight, but right now it was set for only two. The obviously expensive china gleamed in the light from the tapered candles. Tom had buried the wine in a silver bucket full of crushed ice. The smell of steaks over charcoal drifted in from the open back-porch door.

I turned to chop tomatoes and lettuce. My mouth was watering. I had been hungry for him before I got here, but the good smells were making my belly rumble in want of food.

Tom kissed the side of my neck as I wielded the knife. I shook it at him with a stern expression. He ignored the warning and kissed my ear. When he reached my lips, the vegetables were forgotten. We spent a few enjoyable minutes there by the counter, until the smell of the steaks became too much for either of us to bear.

By the time he pulled the steaks and potatoes from the grill, the salad was ready. I placed the old wooden salad bowl in the center of the table. I watched him open the wine, his strong shoulders flexing under the cotton of his flannel shirt. I liked the fact that he didn't try to dress up for me. He was comfortable, and that was exactly how I already knew I liked him best.

'If I weren't so hungry,' he said as he poured the wine, 'I would have taken you on the front porch. And the living room. And the kitchen table.'

'That would be five times in one day. You sure you could do that?'

'Nobody says I have to come every single time,' he said, and the blatant way he said the words made me blush. After what we had done earlier and what was sure to come later, the fact that he could make me blush was incredible. He gave me a wicked smile as he settled beside me at the big kitchen table.

We ate from one another's fork. We drank from one another's wine. We fell into conversation on books, and debated the writing styles of biographers. He told me about the intricacies of hunting, and explained in detail how to choose a good bow. We discussed his stint in the military and his security job, but he never delved into too much detail. I asked him where he had been, and he simply shrugged and said, 'Everywhere.'

I pushed the steak around on my plate, hungry as a bear but too filled with anticipation to really eat much of anything. Tom, on the other hand, cleaned his plate and started stealing bites from mine.

'You really should eat,' he said. 'You're going to need your strength.'

'Feed me,' I murmured.

'I didn't hear you.' Tom gave me a look that said he had heard exactly what I said.

'Feed me. Please.'

Tom pushed his chair back from the table. He sat looking at me for a long while, until I blushed and looked away. As soon as I did that, he reached out and touched my jaw, turning my face back towards him. I was forced to look right into his eyes.

'We need to go to the basement,' he said.

I nodded. I knew what was down there. I thought of Michael – his weight bench was in his basement, too. Down in the bottom of the house, where no one could hear the noise. I realized that I was out in the middle of nowhere with a man I hardly knew, and I had already asked him to do wicked things to my body, in a place where no one could hear me scream.

The thought should have given me pause. Instead, I stood up and slipped my hand into his.

'Take me there.'

The basement was quiet, a tomb of steel and concrete under the earth. The lights were set into the ceiling and somehow muted. They cast shadows over the surprising array of equipment that filled the two large rooms. There were Nautilus systems and a Bowflex, just like the one I had seen on television during too many sleepless nights. There was a treadmill and a stair climber, both of them apparently professional machines. A variety of boxing bags hung in one corner. There was the weight bench, dwarfed by all the other things surrounding it. There was even a small hot tub in the corner of the back room. This was a space carved out by a man who took very good care of his body.

'I was a quarterback in college,' Tom said. I turned to look at him, but he didn't meet my eyes. 'We were playing 'Bama. The linebacker slammed me right under my knees. I heard the snap, and then I heard another one when I hit the ground. The first one was my knee, and the second one was my elbow.' Tom shook his head as he looked around the room. 'Glory days were officially over.'

'So you have a gym packed with more equipment than most people even know exists . . .'

'Yeah.' Tom shrugged. 'Old habits die hard.' He stood with his hands in his pockets, suddenly small and shy beside the massive machines. He reached to adjust something on one of them, but we both knew it was only a way to find more emotional space.

'Look at me,' I demanded.

Tom met my eyes, but it took a supreme effort. The power between us had suddenly shifted, and we both felt the unsteadiness of it.

'When we lose what matters, we have to find a way to reinvent ourselves,' I said. 'I think the way we remember while we do that is the true measure of what it meant to us. You remember well, Tom.'

'I've lost so much,' he said, and with those words I saw a new side of Tom.

I reached for his arm. He reluctantly came to me, his eyes downcast. I wrapped my arms around his shoulders and he returned the embrace with such force it became hard to breathe. He held me there for long minutes, and I didn't dare try to move. Somehow I knew that moving away from him would be a mistake on many levels.

Finally Tom took a gentle handful of my hair. He pulled my head back and gently kissed my lips.

'There's your weight bench, sweetheart.'

I turned in his arms and looked at it. The bar on the top held several large weights. The bar on the bottom was definitely more than I could ever think of lifting. The thought that Tom worked with that much weight on a regular basis gave me a new respect for the bulging muscles under his shirt.

'It's bolted to the floor,' I said in surprise.

'It has to be. With the amount of weight I lift, the bench would shift after too many reps.' He ran his fingers through my hair. 'But don't you worry,' he whispered. 'We might not move the bench across the floor, but you're going to wish to God we could. Because I'm going to fuck you so hard, you will beg for any kind of mercy you can get.'

I shivered. My nipples were instantly hard. My mouth watered. I stared at the weight bench and deliberately pictured Michael, pictured the things he had told me, the memory that he loved so much.

'I want you to tie me to it,' I said.

'Boy scouts are always prepared,' he said, and turned me towards the stainless steel cabinet in the corner. What I thought held workout gear wasn't used for that purpose at all. I gasped in shock when he opened the door.

Shackles. Floggers. Paddles. Blindfolds. Gags. There was a sampling of every sex toy imaginable. Leather and steel winked at me from the dimly lit corners. Some of it looked exciting, some of it curious – and some of it looked downright ominous.

I started to tremble, suddenly afraid for reasons I didn't understand.

Tom held me tightly against his chest. Together we stared into the cabinet.

'You still have the option of backing out,' he said.

'I never expected this.'

'Why are you so surprised? Lots of people are into this. You are, aren't you?'

'Yes. But . . .'

'But I'm not the kind of man you expect?'

I shook my head and reached out to touch a riding crop. It swung lightly on the hook. 'I know you were rough on the picnic table earlier today, but you were careful, too. You didn't strike me as the dominant type.'

'I'm not in the conventional sense,' he said. 'I think there is something deeply satisfying about power play. I'm just learning, really. I'm a novice in every sense of the word.'

I stared at the toys, thinking that 'novice' was probably not the word I would have used.

'There's something we need to do first,' he said. I nodded, still mesmerized by the array of toys and the wicked things we could do with them. Already my imagination was running rampant.

Tom gently turned me away from the cabinet and led me to the weight bench. Slowly he began to undress me, his hands reverent and careful. It was a heady contrast to the naughty things going through my head.

'First,' he whispered as he nibbled at my ear, 'you need to do something for me.'

'Anything.'

'You need to make love to me.'

The word hung in the air between us, weighting it down, making it hard to breathe. My leggings slipped down to the floor. My shirt went down on top of them. The rest of my clothing fell away and I was naked in more ways than one. Instinct begged me to drop to my knees in front of him, but I held my ground, uncertain of what I should do.

'You aren't the only one exorcising old ghosts,' he said softly.

I looked up at him, startled by the admission. The emotion in the room was becoming too much, too strong to deny any longer. Tears pricked at my eyes. I hadn't expected this when I had come to his home. Never had I expected any of this when I woke up in my lonely bed this morning. It seemed the normalcy of my life was a million miles away.

But Tom was here, standing in front of me. Waiting.

I opened the buttons on his shirt, one slow inch at a time. Even in the dim light, his tan was dark and exciting against my pale hands. He let me slide the shirt down his arms. Next came the jeans. He was wearing nothing underneath them, and that made me smile. I removed the unassuming gold chain from around his neck. I ran my hands through his hair and messed it up. I ran my fingertips over every inch of his body that I could reach, until he was trembling even more than I was. Exactly what he needed was slowly dawning in the back of my mind.

'I don't know what she did to you,' I said. 'But I will do whatever I can to make it go away.'

Tom shuddered under my hand, and I knew my instincts were correct.

'What are you afraid of right now?' I asked.

'I'm afraid that I won't be all the things you want.'

The words cut through the tension. Once the admission was out in the open, it wasn't as threatening. I kissed his ribcage, one rib at a time. I kissed his solid chest. His throat was covered with fine stubble, and I ran my tongue along it. I held him close, hiding my face against his body, giving him time to adjust to the newness between us.

'Tom, honey – you already are.'

He lay down on the bench and looked up at me. His eyes were dark, shadowed by things that he wasn't yet ready to tell me, and might never be able to say. I straddled him and settled the warmth of my pussy right over his cock. He was already hard and long. His hands rested lightly on the bar behind his head.

'Tell me exactly what you want me to do to you,' he said.

I slid back and forth on him. Within seconds he was slick with my own arousal. When I touched my hard nipples, he sighed in appreciation.

'I want you to shackle me to this weight bench,' I said. 'I want you to use most of those toys in that cabinet over there. I want you to put clamps on these,' I murmured, squeezing my nipples. 'I want you to put a gag in my mouth, except for the times you are fucking my throat with that long cock of yours.'

Tom groaned and shifted under me. The head of his cock pressed hard against my pussy, and I slipped down, letting him glide into me. He filled me completely, and I closed my eyes at the sheer thrill of it. It hurt a little, but I chalked that up to the long period of celibacy before Tom came along.

'I want you to spank my ass until my skin is red. I want to carry marks from your hands. I want to carry marks from your teeth. I want you to bite down on places where I can't hide it. My throat, under my ear, maybe even all over my body. I want you to mark your territory.'

I began to move on him, and Tom's hands weren't relaxed now, but tense, holding on tight to the bar above his head while he watched me with those wicked brown eyes.

'I want you to yank my hair and slam a toy into my pussy and call me names. Then I want you to fuck me. First with a toy, then with yourself. I want you to do it hard, and if I cry out I want you to gag me to make me shut up.'

Tom arched up into me. His powerful motion almost

knocked me off. I slid my hands up his shoulders and braced myself there, letting him take my full weight. I began to fuck him with long deliberate strokes.

'Then I want you to slip that toy into my ass. I want you to fuck my pussy while you do it. Fuck me so hard that you would move this weight bench across the floor, if it wasn't bolted down.'

I slammed down hard and Tom groaned. One hand came off the bar and reached for me, but with a deep sigh he gripped the bar again. He was letting me do anything I wanted to do to him.

'Then I want you to pull that toy out of my ass. I want you to put your own cock there,' I said, and I felt him jerk inside me at the same time as he groaned deep in his chest. 'I want you to fuck me so hard that it feels like my body will never be the same again. I want you to make me cry and make me beg and make me hurt for days and days and days.'

I ground down hard, and then suddenly sat straight up. Tom's eyes flew open. He stared up at me with baited breath.

'Then I want you to lay me down in your bed,' I murmured. 'And I want you to make love to me, so gently that it makes me cry.'

I began to rock slowly on him. Tom's face was etched with pure pleasure. His hands came down off the bar and he touched me reverently, his hands working across every inch of my skin. He touched every mark, every scar, every freckle. He ran his fingertips around my nipples.

By the time his hands reached my jaw, my own eyes were closed. His hands closed gently around my throat. He held me lightly while I rode him with slow tempered passion. My whole body was nothing but tingling sensation. That tingle ran up from my toes to my fingertips to every other inch of me, and I opened my lips in a silent cry.

The possessiveness in his hands was the perfect counterpoint to the delicious melting of my body. I was making love to him in a way that I hadn't made love to a man in years. There were no thoughts of anyone or anything else; the slate was wiped clean.

Tom's hands tightened around my throat. There was no fear, no hesitation. After a moment he dropped his hands to my hips and sat up under me, pulling me tight against his chest, rocking his hips in rhythm with mine.

'Come for me, come on me,' he chanted in a mantra of pleasure.

I came with a low moan and a shudder. My whole body went limp in his arms. His teeth settled on my neck and he bit down hard, the flash of pain sliding down my back and right to the core between my legs. His groan was muffled in that bite as he came. His cock throbbed deep inside me. I was flooded with the wetness of it.

His bite became gentle, small licks that eased the tender skin. His hands tangled in my hair as he brought me up for a kiss. His tongue lingered in my mouth, sampling every corner of it.

'Your mouth tastes different after you come,' he whispered. 'Isn't that odd?'

I nodded, too tired to speak. His broad hands were spread across my back. I cuddled into him, burying my face in the hollow between his chin and his shoulder.

Tom held me until I started to doze against him. I woke up, startled, as he rose from the weight bench, carrying my weight like it was nothing.

'What are you doing?' I asked.

He didn't answer. He gently placed me on my feet at the bottom of the basement stairs. With one hand on the small of my back, he pushed me ahead of him, turning lights off along the way.

'But –'

'Hush, little one.'

Tom led me up the two short staircases, and we wound up in the second-floor loft. Bookcases lined every wall. Photographs in sturdy frames mingled with the books. A battered football helmet sat in a glass case. The bedside lamp was on and the quilt was turned down to reveal soft cotton sheets. He gently nudged me towards it. As I crawled into the warm cave, I felt a drop of his wetness slide down my thigh.

'Tom –' I started to say, but he didn't allow me to speak. His lips stole the words as he kissed me.

'We're both too tired,' he said. 'We've had a long day. And there's no rush, Kelley. I'm not going anywhere and neither are you. Tomorrow I will give you all that you want. Tonight I want to sleep with you.'

Tom curled up beside me. He pulled me back against his chest and immediately my body was heavy with the need for sleep. With one hand firmly against my belly and the other wrapped around my shoulders, Tom kissed the back of my neck and settled in with a long sigh.

Long after his breathing was even and steady, he held onto me with surprising strength. The lights from the nearby dock cast an eerie glow over the windows. When the rain started I could hear it on the tin roof over the porch, a reassuring sound that seemed exactly like something that would appeal to Tom. The rain poured down and I watched the drops chase each other down the glass. Tom shifted once, pushing his knee between mine, and I let my leg drape over his. His breathing never changed.

I thought about Michael.

It had been six months since Michael and I had last made love. I remembered the confusion when I suddenly realized we hadn't had sex in a week, then the growing apprehension when a week turned into a month. The teasing and the innuendo, always so ripe and heavy between us, had simply stopped. No matter what I tried, nothing seemed to spark his interest in me. During those long months I wondered what I had done wrong. What had I done to deserve the loss of his affections?

The uncertainty of that time had scarred me in ways that I was just beginning to understand. I didn't know until months later that the real reason for his withdrawal was the love he felt for someone else. The pain of knowing that he was intimate with me while he wanted someone else was something I still didn't know how to deal with.

'Why didn't you just tell me in the beginning?' I whispered to the raindrops that rolled down the windowpane. 'Why did you make me wonder for so long?'

There would be no answer from the rain, just as there was never an answer from Michael. He dodged all of my questions and never once gave me a straight answer. It was a maddening thing, especially after all the months of stony silence whenever I brought up the subject of sex. Why was it impossible for a man to simply tell me the truth?

I wondered where he was right then, if he had called my number, and if he had been worried when I didn't answer the phone. Would he ever imagine I was lying in another man's bed, feeling the ache left by another man's body?

Tom cuddled into me, pulling me closer. I thought about the difference between want and need, and the undeniable momentum when they became one and the same. I wasn't in love with Tom, but I was definitely in lust with the man. And if I could want someone other than Michael, then maybe one day I could love someone other than Michael, too.

Tom's breath was warm against my neck. I found the hand that was wrapped around my belly. I linked my fingers with his. Even while sound asleep, he squeezed back. It was the last thought on my mind as I drifted off to sleep.

3

When I woke up the next morning, the rain was falling in sheets outside the window. It rang merrily on the tin roof of the porch. The ceiling fan swung lazily above the bed. It was the kind of day made for staying in bed.

That's exactly what we were doing.

Tom was between my legs, watching me as I shook off the daze of sleep. His hands were on my open thighs. His tongue was working wonders between my legs. Every now and then he would rise up to watch me, and that's when he used his fingers. One at first, gentle and slow until I was good and awake, then two. Now he was up to three and I was arching off the bed every time he pushed deep and touched that oh-so-perfect spot.

'You like being so open to me, don't you?' he almost hissed. 'You like being a little slut for me, don't you?'

Slut. The word tumbled through my head and ricocheted through my body and settled right between my thighs. I arched up to him and he pushed me back down. His hand was tight on my hip. I would have bruises there for days if he kept that up.

'I like it when you call me names,' I gasped.

Tom blinked at me once, seemingly surprised by my sudden admission.

'Really.'

'Yes.' I knew I was blushing, but I stared right at him anyway. A slow grin played over Tom's lips. I watched him as he weighed the options.

'Slut,' he said again, then paused. 'Whore. Bitch. Which do you prefer, you little cocksucker?'

Every word was a direct stroke to my libido. I moaned

with each caress of his voice. I grabbed for the headboard of the big four-poster bed. Tom pressed his fingers deep and flicked his tongue across my clit.

'Answer me, damn it! Which do you prefer?'

'Anything,' I gasped out.

'I think whore sounds mighty good,' Tom said, finally getting into the idea of calling me names. 'That's what you are, isn't it? You're my whore and I can do whatever I want to you. Isn't that right?'

Tom was leaning over me, putting more force behind the thrusts of his hand. I cried out loud as I came. My pussy throbbed hard around his hand, almost to the point of pain, and I gasped aloud as he twisted his fingers a little deeper.

He watched my face as he moved. He was searching out every inch of the hidden parts of me. His fingers explored, sometimes rough, sometimes gentle. Every now and then he hit that spot at the very core of me and I gasped involuntarily, as if there was a string tied from that point to the center of my chest, affecting my whole body with one small touch.

'What is that?' I finally whispered.

'Your cervix. Do you like that?'

I shuddered as he did it again. 'Sometimes it hurts. Sometimes it feels really good. It is almost like a switch inside me that I can't control.'

'But I can.'

The muscles in his arm flexed as he pushed his hand deeper. The burn of it was delicious, licking at my aching thighs like a tempting fire.

'How far do you want to go?' he asked.

'As far as we can.'

He bent to kiss one nipple, then the other. I raised my hands to his head and gently pulled on his hair. It was deep brown, and in the early morning light I could see the strands of gray that had begun to creep into the dark. He pushed harder against me and I closed my eyes, took deep breaths, and tried to relax against the invasion of it.

'Maybe we should save this for later,' he suggested after long moments of riding the line between pleasure and pain.

'I want you to do that to me,' I said. 'Maybe not now. But soon.'

Tom lay beside me and kissed my shoulder. He brought his hand to my mouth and I sucked on it slowly, pulling my own juices from his fingertips. It tasted like me and somehow like him too, a wildness that reminded me of running streams and fallen leaves.

'You even taste like the outdoors,' I teased.

'I should. I might as well live up a tree.'

'How often do you hunt?'

He shrugged. 'As often as possible, which actually isn't that often. Most of my weekends are spent on the road somewhere. This one is an exception.'

'I just wondered how busy you were going to keep me.'

Tom crawled over me and turned the light off. He reached down to the floor for an old pair of jeans and a discarded shirt. I watched as he shrugged it on, then grabbed another one and threw it at me. I slipped my arms into it and slowly rose from the bed. The antics of the night before made me sore, and I winced as I walked across the hardwood floors beside him.

'It's Sunday morning. Are you a churchgoer?'

'Not since I was a kid.'

'Southern Baptist?'

'Yeah. How did you figure that?'

Tom winked at me when we got to the bottom of the stairs. 'Because Southern Baptist girls are really wild in bed, that's how. All those years of fire and brimstone have to come out somewhere.'

I laughed as I sank to the kitchen chair. 'Sounds like you've known a lot of us Southern Baptist women,' I commented.

Tom slowly closed the refrigerator. He set the gallon of milk on the table. Every move he made was controlled, and he refused to meet my eyes. He pulled the cereal from the cabinet with such deliberate slowness I began to believe he wouldn't answer.

'Tom, I didn't mean –'

'I've known too many,' he finally said.

The silence in the room was heavy. I was slowly realizing that I wasn't the only one with baggage, and that Tom might even have more than I did. I sat quietly as he found bowls and spoons. He poured two tall glasses of orange juice. As he set mine down in front of me, I touched his arm. Tom flinched and started to pull away, but stopped himself with an effort.

I stood and wrapped my arms around him. I kissed his lips. He was unresponsive at first, but when he did kiss me back it was with a desperation that told me how badly he was hurting.

'It doesn't matter, Tom.'

'Is that true?' he asked, challenging me with flat brown eyes.

'Yes.'

He sank down into the chair. I moved with him and crawled into his lap. Tom smiled despite the seriousness of the conversation. I played with his hair and laid my head on his shoulder while he poured a bowl of Rice Krispies. I kissed his neck.

'My legs are probably as stubbly as your face is,' I said.

'I don't care.'

'Want to get a shower with me?'

'Depends. Do I have to shave your legs for you?'

'No.'

Tom swirled the dry cereal around in his bowl. 'I wouldn't be as kind as you are.'

'What do you mean?'

Tom sighed and pushed his bowl away. 'You remember that old saw about musicians, right? A woman in every zip code? It's like that for their security guys, too. We're just quieter about the whole thing.'

'Tom –'

'No. You know this already, but I need to say it. I've never said it before.'

'OK.'

'There have been more women than I can count,' he said. 'I've been with women and I haven't known their names. I've been with more than one woman at a time. Frequently. It was always a good time and nothing more than that, but when it was over I really hoped they didn't feel as empty as I did.'

I felt a sudden welling of jealousy, something that caught me completely off-guard. I rested my lips against his jaw and felt him speak, even as I heard the words.

'At first all the women are exciting, and you think you are the king of all you survey, and so you have one or two a night. And then the nights turn into weeks and the weeks into months and pretty soon it is an assembly line of pussy that means nothing at all. And then you meet someone who does mean something, even if you don't know quite what that *something* is, and not only do you have to look at yourself in the mirror again, but you have to look at her, too.'

I linked my hand with his, silently telling him it was all right to go on.

'It's a horrible double standard, Kelley. If you were the one telling me this, I would be showing you the door. But I know you aren't that kind of woman, you never have been. Our first conversation, the way you talked about Michael – I knew then that you not only know the names of every man you have ever been with, you remember everything about them. You probably loved every single one of them. Didn't you?'

'Yes,' I whispered.

'But here I sit, telling you about hundreds of women, maybe even thousands of them, and you aren't getting up to leave. And I don't think you will. Why is that?'

'Because they really don't matter. That was then. This is now.'

'How can it not matter?'

I sat up and thought about that for a moment. 'Do you still do that?'

Tom sighed and looked away. 'Sometimes. Yes. Sometimes I get too lonely.'

What could I say? Tom and I had known each other less than 24 hours. Incredible sex didn't make a relationship. Our time together had not been discussed beyond what we might do on that weight bench in his basement. We hadn't talked about what would come later.

So I said the only thing I knew was true. 'I guess we will cross that bridge if we get to it, Tom.'

'We will get to it,' he said.

'What?'

'You heard me. Do you think I'm going to go anywhere? Do you think you're just one of those women out on the road?'

I took a deep breath. 'I'm trying to be realistic.'

'I can't promise you much, little one,' he said. 'But I can promise you this: I can be the faithful kind. I just need a woman to make me want to be that way. And you might be that woman.'

I shook my head in amazement. 'It's been less than twenty-four hours.'

'It's been long enough to know you're different,' he said softly. 'Don't you feel it?'

That was the problem. I did feel it. And, given the emotional turmoil Michael had kept me in for months and months, I didn't trust the way I felt. I knew that I wanted Tom – there was no denying that, no way – but I knew little beyond that.

'I know I'm willing to see where this goes,' I said.

'Is that the truth?'

'Cross my heart and pinky swear.'

He uncapped the milk and poured it into his cereal. It made the familiar sounds: Snap. Crackle. Pop.

'You're wonderful,' he said.

'Please.'

The paddle came down hard on my ass. I knew that was only the least of what I was going to get. I had seen the floggers, the cat-o'-nine-tails, the riding crop and the cane. The cane had given me a sharp moment of fear when it caressed my heated face, a gentle warning of what was to come.

'Breathe deep,' Tom said. 'Even breaths. Focus on the sensation. And don't panic. Panic is the absence of trust. You know the words to stop me, and you trust me.'

'Yes.'

Those words came back to me now, and I took slow and even breaths. I could stop him in an instant. How I trusted him so much in such a short period of time might always be a mystery, but the underlying reasons didn't matter much. The trust did.

The tingle spread through my thighs.

'Please.'

The paddle came down again, this time whistling through the air before it hit. I bit my lip hard to hold in a startled cry. It wasn't hurting, not yet, but I knew it would soon enough. I wasn't sure how much I could handle, but I had told Tom to make sure we found out.

I was shackled to that weight bench, right where I had wanted him to put me. In this physical position, there was nothing in the world I could do to prevent the blows. If I told him no, he would spank me harder. If I moved too much or tried to get away, he would spank me even harder than that. I was at his mercy, tied down with my legs spread on the lower bar and my arms on the upper bar.

'Please.'

This time the blow came from the other side. I was startled by it and moved slightly. That was a mistake. The paddle whistled through the air and this time the smack was much harder. It echoed through the basement.

I gasped in surprise. Tom didn't speak.

'Please.'

This time he braced himself; I could see him out of the corner of my eye. Then I didn't have to ask again, because each blow came down in rapid succession, a carefully orchestrated dance. With only a few seconds between each paddling, he worked my ass from top to bottom, grazing my thighs and my lower back with the paddle, and a few times hitting almost dead-center, making my pussy jump only inches below the punishing leather.

By the time he was finished, we were both breathing hard.

'Please,' I whispered.

Tom stood behind me in shocked silence. I could almost hear his mind working, weighing what to do, wondering how serious I really was, and if I was doing it for his benefit or for mine. I watched as he deliberately reached over my line of vision and picked up the cat-o'-nine-tails.

I opened my mouth to speak, but thought better of it. I had asked for this. And, from the look on Tom's face and the rock-hard arousal he wasn't trying to hide, I knew he wanted it even more than I did.

So, instead of doing what my fears told me to do, I did the exact opposite.

'Please,' I said again.

He didn't give me an opportunity for second thoughts. The cat-o'-nine-tails came down on my ass, and this time I cried out. Each little leather strap stung like a bee.

'Did you know,' Tom asked conversationally, 'the cat-o'-nine-tails was originally a form of punishment on naval vessels?'

I closed my eyes. Naval vessels were the farthest thing from my mind.

The whip came down again, harder this time.

'A man was flogged by the quartermaster. The whole vessel voted on whether or not a man was to be flogged for some crime. It was necessary sometimes to keep honor among thieves.'

Tom hit me three times in rapid succession. I cried out with each blow. Tom yanked my head back by the hair. He whispered into my ear, even as he brought the whip down again.

'Then they poured salt water over the wounds. Should I do that to you? Should I punish you for being such a naughty little comeslut?'

I was shaking in the restraints, frozen in place even if they hadn't been there to hold me down. Panic threatened to rise up within me and I pushed it down with the mantra in my head: panic is the absence of trust. I trust him.

I slowly opened my fingers. I had dug my nails into my palms. My hands throbbed. So did my body. I was throbbing everywhere, and I could no longer find the line between pleasure and pain. They were one and the same.

'Please,' I murmured through the tears.

Tom didn't make a sound, but he abruptly dropped the cat-o'-nine-tails. It clattered on the floor. It looked so benign, so unlikely to inflict this kind of pain. It looked just as benign as Tom usually did.

He stood beside me. His cock was so hard, I could see every vein throbbing with his heartbeat. His breathing was just as ragged as mine was.

'Fuck me,' I begged in a whisper.

Tom didn't pause. He didn't say a single word. He straddled the weight bench behind me, wrapped his hands around my hips and plunged into me with a single thrust. I screamed at the sudden invasion, at the burn of his hands on my tender skin, at the new things I had learned. It was a howl somewhere between joy and rage.

'Accept it,' he demanded. 'Don't anticipate it. Don't fight me.'

I pushed back into him, deliberately offered more of what he was already taking. He fucked me hard, rising off the bench with every thrust, pushing me forwards so roughly that I had to concentrate to keep my head from slamming into the bar. The weight bench was groaning with every thrust, straining against the bolts on the floor. The pleasure was turning into pain and still I couldn't stop it.

I wouldn't stop it.

Tom's cock was hard and solid inside me, like a steel bar pushed deep into my belly. He yanked my hair and slapped my ass with his free hand. The pumping of his hips was relentless. The welts on my ass burned from the sweat. The shackles were hard on my hands and my ankles, leaving red marks I could already feel.

It was a medley of thrill and agony.

'Please,' I cried out. Tom pushed hard enough to make the bench rock against its mooring, hard enough to send a jolt of pain straight through my spine. When he came it was with a shout ripped from deep inside him, primitive and vicious. His semen actually burned, and no sooner had that registered in some deep part of my brain than the whole slate was wiped clean.

I hadn't expected to orgasm, but I did. The warmth of

his come spurting inside me was the final push over the edge. I screamed with the unleashing of both pain and pleasure. Every part of me collapsed with the intensity of it. I slumped on the bench, no longer able to hold myself up.

Tom's strong arms were around me in an instant. He unsnapped the shackles on my wrists, then pulled me back so he could reach my ankles. I had imagined being left in the shackles until I was able to come back to myself, but Tom's actions told me he was just as deeply affected by what we had done as I was.

He cradled me back against his chest. My ass burned when it touched the leather of the seat. Sweat dripped from his forehead and landed on my shoulder. It rolled a tickling trail down my breast.

'I'm taking you upstairs to bed,' Tom said.

'No, I'm OK –'

'You're not. Neither one of us is, Kelley. Let's go lie down, OK?'

Anger flashed through me. 'I can handle myself,' I said. 'You didn't hurt me.'

'Bullshit,' he shot right back. 'If you can let me fuck the fear of God into you, you can also humor me while I try to take care of you.'

I stood up from the bench and turned to him. He didn't wipe the look of concern off his face quite fast enough.

'You're red as a Coke can,' he said. 'We should go upstairs.'

'I want to see.'

There was a mirror on the far side of the gym. I walked to it and gasped at what I saw when I turned around. My ass was red as fire, from the waistline to the top of my thighs. There were welts across each cheek, and a few of those were an angry red. My ankles and wrists were chafed. There was a bruise in the perfect shape of Tom's teeth, right there on my neck. My hair was hopelessly tangled, my face was flushed, my eyes were red, and my lips were swollen from biting them.

I looked like a woman who had been thoroughly fucked.

I smiled at my reflection. When I began to laugh, Tom moved up behind me. My breasts were the perfect size to fill his broad hands. His shoulders were much wider than mine, and he towered over me by a good six inches of height. His hair was damp with sweat, and so was his chest. Every muscle was primed and ready. His face was as flushed with passion as mine was. We faced the mirror and looked at ourselves together for the first time.

'My God, Kelley,' he breathed.

'We're beautiful.'

We were. My pale skin was the perfect contrast to his dark tan. My blue eyes were wild when seen beside his sedate brown ones. My red hair was rich and thick, and his too-long brown waves were the perfect complement. I looked small and vulnerable next to him.

'Come to bed with me,' he whispered as he kissed my ear, all the while never looking away from the mirror. 'Let me take care of you.'

Tearing ourselves away from the mirror was difficult, but not nearly as hard as climbing the stairs. My body was tired. My mind was exhausted. Tom led me into the shower, where the water was far too hot for my skin, but I didn't protest. I knew it would be good for the soreness. And if I was this sore now, I was going to need a lot of hot showers before the weekend was over.

Tom insisted on washing my hair, an endearing gesture that made me feel closer to him. He washed my body with soap that smelled deliciously like him. I reached for his razor and he gave me a strange look.

'No woman *ever* uses my razor,' he warned.

I gave him a sultry smile. 'The next time you use this, don't you want to think about this razor being against these legs I wrap around you? And think about this razor being between my legs, keeping me nice and smooth for you?'

Tom licked his lips. He was suddenly seeing things in a very different light. 'I can see the advantages. Want me to do it for you?'

I let him watch instead. Every time I ran the razor over my skin, his hand was right behind it. He watched every move I made. Then his tongue followed the path his hand and his eyes had taken. By the time he delved between my legs, my knees were weak. His tongue played with my clit for long minutes. The water turned cooler and I finally had to make him stop before I fell to the floor of the shower.

'I love the way you taste,' he whispered against my lips, and I could taste myself when I kissed him.

By the time I crawled on top of the covers of that big four-poster bed, I was yawning. It was only mid-afternoon, but I was as exhausted as if it were midnight.

I lay there while Tom gently traced the welts on my ass. Soothing cream covered his fingertips, and he wielded his touch as lightly as a flock of butterflies landing on flowers. Stretched out across his mattress, I watched the world outside the window. The rain had stopped but the clouds were ominous, ready to open up and pour at any moment.

Tom hummed a low tune as his hands worked. Every now and then he dropped a kiss on my bare shoulder. I ran my fingers through my damp hair, casually working out one tangle after another. The silence between us was comfortable and easy. When his fingers trailed up and down my spine, I shivered, and heard him chuckle.

My thoughts turned again to Michael. I wondered if he would ever know what we had done down there on the weight bench. A part of me wanted to call him and tell him every detail, especially how the bench groaned and protested against those bolts in the floor. But the new part of me, the woman who had been awakened with the touch of leather and steel, simply wanted to keep the new knowledge to myself. There was nothing I needed to share with the world. All the things I needed were either inside me or right here with me.

I thought about the unlikely trust I had handed over to Tom. I hardly knew him, but already I had let him shackle me to a weight bench in a basement so far out in the wilderness that no one would ever hear me scream. I had let him do things to my body that I hadn't trusted with anyone in my past. I was lying there on his bed, perfectly content to stay right where I was.

Michael was no longer the only one with a secret. He wasn't the only one who had a memory that seemed untouchable. I knew that, no matter what happened in my future, I would remember Tom as the man who had opened up a whole new horizon for me, the person who had shown me another side of myself that was there all along.

Maybe that was what that woman meant to Michael. Maybe that was what held him so strongly to her, so much so that, when it came down to a question of her or me, there was never any contest.

Now I was finding myself in the same boat. It wasn't love – not yet – but it was special.

After a weekend like this one, would I ever go back to Michael? If he asked?

The question popped into my head and I shook it away, unwilling to deal with it just yet.

Tom pushed a pillow under my head. I took it gratefully and smiled as he curled up beside me. His hands trailed up and down my back in constant soothing motion. He flipped on the television and turned to the Weather Channel. I listened for a while.

'Going hunting?' I asked.

'In the morning. You can come with me, or you can stay here and clean up the house like a good woman should.'

I snickered at the idea, but I secretly liked the thought of having breakfast ready for him when he came back to the house.

'Hunting for what?'

'Quail. It's that time.'

'Tell me more.'

Tom kissed the nape of my neck. 'About what?'

'Do you always kiss like that?'

He laughed. 'Yes. I'm a very physical kind of person, if you hadn't noticed yet.'

'Tell me about your time in the military. Tell me about those guns you have hidden around here someplace. Tell me about your job. Tell me everything?'

Tom began to talk. His voice was low and soothing, even when it filled with excitement as he talked about a mission in some foreign land. He told me about hiding in a bombed-out building while he tried to determine where the snipers were. He told me about jumping out of a plane and realizing you were far out of your safe drop zone, you were in the middle of enemy territory, and the near-panic when that magazine emptied out and you realized it was just you and your knife.

'Were you ever hurt?' I asked.

Tom was quiet for a moment. 'I got shot once.'

He lifted his leg over the covers to show me the scar. It marked both sides of his calf, as if a bullet had gone straight through.

'What happened?'

There was a long pause before he answered. 'Everything went wrong.'

Before I could say anything, Tom suddenly changed gears and told me about flushing a covey of quail, about bringing down one or two or, if you were lucky, three birds at a time. He had only done that once, he said, and it was a thrill. There were other things he had done over the years. He had hunted for almost everything you could possibly buy a license to hunt for and a few things, he admitted, that he never should have gone after in the first place. He had traveled all over the world to bring down big game.

I wanted to talk about his time in the military, but obviously he had changed the subject for a reason. So I went with the hunting instead.

'Do you ever feel guilty about hunting?' I asked.

'No. There are a lot of reasons why not.'

'Why.'

'Hunting is perfectly legal. It helps keep the animal populations down to manageable numbers. The animals are killed very quickly, with very little pain. Of course there is the occasional mistake, and those are horrible, as anyone would suspect – but the majority of hunts are good and clean.'

'Do you eat what you kill?'

'Have you seen my freezer?'

'I haven't seen half of this house,' I mumbled. 'You've kept me in the sex rooms.'

He laughed, a deep and content sound. 'We'll remedy that situation soon.'

I listened as he talked. He described stalking a wild boar through the deep Florida woods. His story was so vivid I could almost see it, as if I were dreaming it.

Sometime much later I woke up, startled by the fact that I had fallen asleep. I immediately felt guilty. When exactly had I nodded off? Tom was right there beside me, but he wasn't sleeping. He was running his hand through my hair and looking at me with wide brown eyes.

'Tom?'

Tom climbed out of the bed and stood over me. He looked down at my face. His cock was hard, jutting out at an angle from his body. He was slowly stroking it with his right hand while his left hand pulled at my hair, urging me closer to the edge of the bed. When my head fell back over the edge, I realized exactly what he wanted from me.

I braced myself with my hands on his thighs. The muscles under my fingers were hard as steel. 'Don't fight me,' he said. 'I'm going to fuck your throat, and you're going to take it, and you aren't going to fight me, are you?'

I shook my head.

'Have you ever deep-throated a cock?'

'Yes,' I whispered.

Tom's hand tightened in my hair. He stroked himself a little faster as he pressed the tip of his cock to my soft lips. 'Did you like it?'

'Yes.'

'Have you ever deep-throated a man who was bigger than me?'

I smiled. Why did men always think size mattered? 'No.'

'Good. I want you to gag on this cock. I want to feel you do that,' he hissed. His hands slowly massaged my throat, and I fought hard to relax. He pushed the head of his cock into my mouth. He was already slick with arousal. I licked in circles as he stroked his shaft. I sucked at him gently and he rewarded me with another inch. Then another.

I took a deep breath as he touched the back of my throat. The gag reflex welled up in me, and my belly jerked. Tom saw it – and felt it – and his hands tightened on my neck.

'Don't fight it,' he warned.

He pulled back enough to allow me to recover, then he pushed in again. Relentless this time, he didn't give me time to control the urge to gag. He pushed into my throat and, when I did gag, he pushed farther. Suddenly there was no air, and I was struggling against the panic. I pushed hard on his thighs until he pulled my hands away.

'Relax into it,' he ordered.

He pulled out of my mouth and I took great gasps of air. Tears, the result of the gag reflex, ran down my temples. Tom stood over me and watched while I got myself back under control.

'Thought you said you had done this before,' he said in an accusing tone.

'I have!'

'So why are you acting like a goddamn virgin?'

Anger sizzled through me. 'I've never had a man of your size, OK? Does that make you happy? To know you've got a big cock I can't fucking swallow?'

Tom chuckled. Then he laughed. Then he laughed even harder, and within seconds he was roaring with laughter, his hands on his hips, his penis bobbing in front of him like some puppet on a marionette's string. It looked absolutely ridiculous. I was angry as hell but I had to smile at the way he looked. The man's beautiful body was suddenly more like a caricature of something obscene.

His laughter eventually tapered off into breathless gasps. I reached up to stroke his cock. My hand circled around it and my fingertips almost touched. I jacked him slowly as I licked at his balls. Tom moaned in approval and spread his legs wider. I explored with my tongue, slowly licking down the inside of each thigh, then delving between his legs and finding the most sensitive places. Once I sucked his balls into my mouth, one at a time, and he groaned with the pleasure of it. All the while my hand moved slow and steady.

'When you feel like you need to gag,' he murmured, 'Swallow. It won't feel natural at first. But, once you do it a few times, you'll get used to it. It works.'

I stopped what I was doing long enough to shoot off one smart-ass remark. 'How would you know that, huh?'

He chuckled but said nothing.

Finally Tom pulled away from me. I opened my mouth

and he slid into it, gliding back and forth, every now and then pushing deeper than before.

'I like knowing I'm the biggest you've had,' he murmured. 'That makes me feel like more of a man than anything else we've done. It might be immature, but it's one hell of an ego rush.'

I tilted my head back and swallowed. This time when he pushed forwards, I tried to swallow every time I felt the urge to gag. It didn't work every time, but it worked enough. I took a deep breath while I still could.

Within three strokes he was buried completely in my throat, the base of his cock settled right against my lips. He slowly massaged my throat with his broad hands. When Tom pulled his cock back, I had a brief second to take another breath. Soon the gag reflex was gone and he was fucking into my throat with every thrust, carefully timing each motion to allow me to breathe. From the tension in his legs and the pressure on my throat, I knew he wouldn't be able to keep that steady pace for very long.

I was right. Tom suddenly grabbed my hair, spread his legs wider for more leverage, and began to fuck my mouth in earnest. I could do nothing but hold onto his thighs as he did it, struggling for air when I had a chance to draw some in. His thighs trembled and his breathing was ragged. His cock throbbed against my tongue.

'Oh, God – take that cock, every inch of it, take it –'

When Tom came, he pushed deep into my throat. My tongue pressed hard against his shaft. Each burst of come made his cock swell in my mouth. The warmth of it slithered down my throat and I tried my best to swallow. Only when Tom was finished emptying himself into me did he pull away and let me take a long tortured breath.

He collapsed onto the bed beside me. Tom's hand settled on my neck. The possessive weight of it made me feel small and vulnerable beside him. The need for reassurance became impossible to ignore.

'Was that good?' I asked him timidly.

Tom pulled me close to him. He kissed me slowly, letting his tongue explore my mouth in the same way he had during our first kiss. That first time felt like years ago. I had learned so much, given so much of myself to this man, that I didn't remember who I had been before he came along.

'That was absolutely incredible,' he praised.

I shocked myself when I burst into tears.

Tom didn't say a word. He didn't ask me what was wrong. He simply cradled me against him like a baby, letting me cry it out against his broad shoulder.

'I feel safer than I have ever felt,' I said through the tears.

'You are safe, Kelley,' Tom whispered against my forehead. 'You are.'

4

When I opened my eyes, Tom was gone.

I stretched in the early-morning light. My whole body ached. I touched my buttocks carefully with my finger-tips and felt the welts there. Tom had whacked me a few good ones, and we hadn't explored the whole cabinet of toys yet.

His pillow was soft and smelled like him. I pulled it up to my nose and lay there for a while, looking around the room. A mounted deer head looked down at me from over the bed. I stared at it for a while, wondering why in the world I hadn't noticed it before. The glass eyes looked down at me with a non-judgmental air.

'Howdy,' I said. The deer didn't answer.

I looked around the room. The bookcases covered almost every available space, with the exception of the small dresser in the corner. The man had more books than I did. As a writer, I thought I had a massive collection of works, but Tom's eclectic array put mine to shame. He had books on everything from hunting to astronomy, from music to do-it-yourself projects, from literary classics to dime-a-dozen paperback romance.

I raised an eyebrow at the shelf of those. Tom read romance novels?

I tried to picture him in a deer stand, covered in camo and packing a lethal rifle, slowly flipping through a bodice-ripper with a man like Fabio on the cover. I couldn't quite manage to see that in my head, but Tom was full of surprises.

Where he was this morning wasn't a surprise – I could very well guess where he was. I was sure I would find a note of some kind on the kitchen counter, or even stuck on the bathroom mirror, telling me that he had gone hunting and would be back sometime during the late morning hours. I had his whole house to myself.

I started with a shower.

I looked around the bathroom as I stood under the water. Now that Tom wasn't in here with me, I could explore everything at leisure.

His towels were mismatched, but all of them were in a shade of cream or blue. One toothbrush stood in the holder. He used Crest, and I smiled at the tube that had been squeezed from the middle, not neatly rolled like mine. The soap smelled like sandalwood and the shampoo was something from a salon. It smelled professional, not feminine but not masculine either. I used it and watched the white suds swirl down the drain. The washcloth on the bar was still damp, and I guessed that was the one he had used before he went out hunting. I pulled it off the bar and used it myself.

In his medicine cabinet was every kind of first aid imaginable. I found ibuprofen and took two. There was a bottle of Valium in there behind the ibuprofen. I looked at it curiously, and saw that it had been refilled about two weeks ago. I put it carefully back in the cabinet. My face burned, as though I had been caught peeping at something that was entirely none of my business.

His closet was filled with more camouflage than a military barracks. I chose a camouflage sweater. It fell almost to my knees. I found my black leggings folded neatly on the dresser, and pulled those on. The hardwood floors were cool against my bare feet as I came down the stairs.

It felt strange to be in Tom's house without him in it, but he certainly didn't mind. If I had any doubts about that, the note on the kitchen table erased those from my mind.

'Kelley – Do what you want! Just be here when I get home? xoxo. Tom.'

I poured a glass of orange juice and set out to explore.

I had already seen the kitchen and dining room, and spent some brief time in the living room. I ambled back in there now. The furniture was pine, and looked to be handmade. Pillows were everywhere. There were mounted animals on the walls, and a huge framed photograph of an eagle in flight. The television was hidden in an armoire in the corner, and when I opened it I found a cache of hunting films, nestled in alongside such gems as *Die Hard* and *Star Wars*.

He also had an interesting porn collection, hidden behind the more sedate titles. The porn consisted mostly of intense blow-job scenarios. I wasn't surprised in the least.

There was a pair of boots next to the door, caked with mud. There was a handsaw, painted with a wilderness scene, hanging near the staircase. There was a horseshoe above the door. I wandered into the other side of the house, down a short hallway. There were the photographs of his children. There was a little brunette girl with big blue eyes. She looked nothing like Tom, so surely she must be the image of her mother. The photos of his son looked more like the father. The smiles on the faces in the family pictures made me smile right back.

There were other photographs. There was a man who looked exactly like Tom, and I could see what he would be like when he was twenty years older. That man had to be his father. His mother looked happy as she held her husband's hand.

I went into the spare bedroom. There was a big sleigh bed in there, a dresser, a few odds and ends. Nothing of interest in there.

The room across the hallway was Tom's office.

I stood at the threshold and stared, almost afraid to

go into the space. It was thoroughly lived in and comfortable. There were two computers. The first was a simple laptop, now closed, that lay in the center of the wide oak desk. The other was a sophisticated, state-of-the-art desktop model. I had no idea why he would need two computers but, from the paperwork on all sides, it looked like they got a great deal of use.

There were papers everywhere, but in surprisingly neat order. There were bookcases in here too, but they held very different books than what I had found in the rest of the house. Books on weaponry, military history and civilian law were neatly pushed into every available inch. He had a whole collection of books on business and entertainment law. There were files clearly marked in his bold hand: *Attorney. Contracts. Extended Contracts. Stats.* There was even a file that made me laugh out loud when I read it: *What The Fuck Ever.*

There wasn't a single piece of hunting memorabilia in sight. Instead, there were plaques and shiny awards here and there. There were all sorts of memorabilia heralding various military units. There were notations of bravery – and, just as I was about to turn away and look at something else, one of those caught me dead in my tracks.

A commendation of bravery. From the CIA? That one got my attention. I looked at it more closely.

'I'll be damned,' I breathed. 'You've been holding out on me, Tom.'

I closed the door and looked at it for a moment. I touched the wood with my fingertips. Here it was splintered, not quite broken, but damaged. That damage was obviously not done by something sharp, but something blunt – and it looked suspiciously like the indentation of a man's hand.

What would make Tom angry enough to put his hand into a door?

I told myself that I was reading too much into things. What did I really know about his life?

I wandered out onto the porch. There were squirrels all over the place, and they seemed to be completely comfortable around humans. Piles of nuts were here and there on the porch railings. Bird feeders hung from the outer beams of the porch. A birdhouse hosted a family of sparrows. Flower boxes hung on each windowsill, and from the black soil small green shoots had started to show themselves. I stared at those shoots for a long time.

Then I went back to the kitchen and started breakfast.

By the time Tom came in through the back door, smelling of wood and soil and morning dew, the omelets were almost ready. Pitchers of orange juice and milk were waiting on the table, along with orange and apples slices in a silver bowl. Tom wrapped his arms around me from behind and kissed the side of my neck.

'I love coming home to you,' he said. We rocked back and forth together while the eggs bubbled in the pan. The stubble on his jaw rubbed harshly against my face.

'Good morning.'

'Did you miss me?'

'Yes. But I had the squirrels to keep me company.'

'I want you to go out there with me today. On the four-wheeler. I want to show you some of the places I go all the time. So if you ever wonder where I'm at or if you ever need to find me for some reason, you can.'

I turned the fire off under the pan and scooped the omelets onto plates. Tom dropped his hat onto the table and his jacket onto the back of the chair. I watched as he sat down and started to eat.

'We're permanent, aren't we?' I asked quietly.

Tom looked up from his breakfast. The morning sun cut through the window and turned his brown hair a deep shade of red. The old chair creaked when he sat back in it. I don't know what I expected; perhaps some discussion, some remark that wasn't really an answer, maybe a question in response to my own. What I got was certainty.

'If you want to be.'

I sat down beside him. His hand found my thigh under the table and for a few moments we could have been a painting, a still life illuminated by a sunbeam.

We stared at each other. A smile slowly started at one corner of his lips, and I could feel myself smiling back.

'Where did you go today?' I asked, and the tension of the moment was broken. We were simply two people eating breakfast on a chilly spring morning.

He talked about hunting while we ate. He cleaned his plate and half of mine. We devoured the oranges and apples. Thirty minutes later we were on a mud-crusted four-wheeler, headed along a trail through the trees.

I wrapped my arm around his middle. Tom's whole body was solid and unyielding – except for that little spot above his belt. I massaged his belly while we rode. I discovered his ribs were ticklish. I cuddled right up next to him and pressed my breasts against his back.

The sun was high over the trees now, and cast shadows over us. I could suddenly see how his camo would blend in perfectly with the surroundings. Even the ATV was covered with that same subdued print. If not for my red hair catching the wind and blowing back away from my face, we could have drifted into the woods and disappeared.

When we came out onto a high bluff overlooking the Tennessee River, I tightened my arms in fear. The drop was sheer and steep, a good fifty feet straight down.

Tom cut the engine and we sat together, looking out over the water. The engine ticked a melody as it cooled. Birds sang and in the underbrush some small animal chattered before scurrying away. The leaves above us barely swayed on a light breeze. A fallen log sat in front of us, the only thing between the tires of the four-wheeler and that deadly drop.

Tom turned sideways in the seat and kissed me. His mouth was warm and he smelled like sweat and leaves and gun oil. I remembered our first kiss. The memory would always be marked with that peculiar smell of oil on steel. How hesitant I was then, how uncertain – and what a difference a few days could make.

I kissed Tom hard, holding him by the hair to keep him from moving so I could delve deeper. He moaned low in his throat. Already I knew the difference in his reactions, and I knew what he wanted. If I decided to take this any farther, I would be the one in charge.

'Is this why you brought me out here?' I murmured against his lips.

'That's part of it,' he admitted.

'You're insatiable.'

We were covered in frustrating layers of clothing. Jackets, long-sleeved shirts, pants and even boots. I flipped Tom's baseball cap from his head and it landed on the ground, where it was almost invisible in the shadows. I started to unzip his jacket.

'In a hurry?' he teased.

I answered by kissing him again. Soon he was helping me with the jacket, and I had moved on to more interesting parts, like the zipper of his cargo pants.

He was wearing camouflage underwear.

'You have got to be kidding me,' I blurted in surprise.

Tom had the grace to blush. It wasn't long before the camouflage underwear was forgotten. I was much more interested in what was rock hard and waiting underneath. When I circled my fingers around him, Tom lay back against the handlebars to allow me more access to what I wanted. He closed his eyes while I stroked the length of him. I let my fingers slip down lower, and he groaned when I started to play with his balls. One drop of precome appeared at his tip, and I bent low to lick it off with one quick flick of my tongue.

He pushed his pants down lower, kicked off his boots on either side of the four-wheeler, and soon there was nothing on him but an old T-shirt, which quickly did a disappearing act. He was lying naked on the four-wheeler, his head resting on the wide space between the handlebars, his arms resting on the fenders. I sat back against the rack on the rear of the machine, watching every move he made.

I pushed his thighs wider apart. A ghost of a smile flashed over his face, then disappeared when I surprised him by sliding my mouth down over his cock. He bucked up into me. I held him down with both hands on his knees.

'Don't you move,' I ordered quietly.

Tom lay still underneath my wandering hands. I remembered how it felt to be so exposed on the picnic table, hardly clothed while he was still wearing his, the thrill of knowing someone might come along and see what was happening. I wondered if he felt that way now. I wondered how many people used this trail. I wondered if anyone on those boats down below had binoculars, and if they might see a flash of something moving up there, something they wanted to investigate. Did Tom think about the fact that he might be seen, lying there naked on his four-wheeler?

He seemed calm, but when I ran my fingertips over his chest his heart was drumming hard. I traced his sides, smiling at the way he reacted to every touch and stroke. I breathed cool air across his chest, then warm. Then cool again. He chuckled deep in his throat. I picked a green leaf from the closest tree and ran it over his arms, his chest, his belly. The ticklish spots made it difficult for him to lie still, but he did an admirable job.

'My exhibitionist,' I murmured.

The leaf trailed down between his legs. He arched a bit when I ran it over his balls. When I trailed it a bit lower, he shuddered. I lingered there a while, teasing that little hole and the sensitive spot right in front of it, until he started to squirm all over the seat. It made me feel wickedly in control of him, to watch such a formidable man reduced to whimpers and moans at the lightest touch.

I replaced the leaf with my fingertips. Tom stopped moving. Instead he lay perfectly still, barely breathing, waiting for what I might do next.

I slipped my lips over the head of his cock. Tom jerked under me and let out a long breath. I swirled my tongue around the tip, teased that sensitive button right underneath it, and sucked gently while I slid my hand up and down his shaft. I traced every vein and ridge with my tongue. My free hand was playing low between his legs, touching every inch of him, until his hips rose up from the seat and he murmured the one word that had become our personal mantra of pleasure.

'Please.'

I gently probed with my finger, stroking between his cheeks with it, feather-light touches that made him shiver. His hands went up over his head and he held onto the handlebars. I gently pushed forwards with my fingertip, and was surprised to feel the tight muscle sucking at my finger, as if trying to pull it in.

I took half of his cock into my mouth. His eyes were closed and he was breathing hard, whimpering with pleasure. I pushed my finger deeper as I swallowed his cock, and he cried out for the first time.

'Please, oh God, please.'

'Say my name when you do that,' I ordered.

'Kelley. Kelley.'

I pushed that finger in another inch, and he rose from the seat, pushing into my hand. He wanted even more. I began to fuck him with my mouth, keeping it soft and supple around him, not giving him enough friction to let him come. I slowly pushed my finger in to the hilt and began to move it in and out, fucking his ass like I was the one with a cock. He gasped for air and gripped the handlebars so hard his knuckles turned white.

I abandoned his cock and moved down. My tongue

lapped at his balls. My other hand wandered up his belly until I found the tiny nubs of his nipples, rock hard and sensitive in the cool air. When I squeezed each of them in turn he moaned and soon he was helping me, fondling them himself, freeing up my hand for more interesting things.

I stroked his cock as I sucked both of his balls into my mouth.

The effect on Tom was electric. He shuddered. There was no holding back the groans now. They were pouring out of him, much louder than I had expected him to be out there in the wilderness. He was completely lost in a world of pleasure. I smoothed my tongue along his sensitive skin. My hand moved faster. When he arched up into me, I pushed my finger deeper and sucked on his balls. The steady pressure was almost too much, but I wasn't giving him that same firm touch on his cock. He needed that to come.

I had him, literally, in the palm of my hand.

'Please,' he begged, and this time the word had a different quality. This time it was the plea of a man who was riding the fence between pleasure and pain.

I sucked harder. I squeezed his cock roughly, making it pulse harder under my fingertips. When I pushed a second finger inside with the first, there was no question of whether or not there was enough friction to make him come – he came anyway.

His balls jerked in my mouth. His ass clenched on my fingers. His cry of ecstasy echoed through the trees. He bucked up into my hand as the first shot of semen hit his collarbone, then his chest. Then some of it landed on me as I licked my way up his shaft. By the time he was done my lips, my hand, and his chest were covered with the milky cream.

'Kelley,' he panted.

I slowly pulled my fingers out of him. I stroked his

cock lightly, carefully, wary of him being too sensitive to handle it. I dipped my head to his belly and licked up what had shot out of his cock. Tom watched me and groaned, and he groaned even louder when I climbed over him and gave him a kiss. He wrapped his fingers in my hair and held me tightly against him, kissing me hard, showing me that he liked the way he tasted, too.

He fell back on the four-wheeler with a satisfied sigh.

I sat up, fully clothed, straddling him. My whole body ached with need. I wanted it exactly that way. I wanted to deny myself until he had me down in his basement again, until he was fucking into me as hard as he could.

'I want you to take my ass,' I said deliberately.

Even as Tom laughed, his eyes were dark with passion and intent. 'You'll get more than you can handle tonight.'

'Oh, I know I will.'

I watched Tom get dressed. It was more intimate than watching him undress. I giggled as he searched for the camouflage hat in the underbrush. When he was fully dressed again he sat on the four-wheeler behind me. He pulled me back against his chest and together we watched the lake come to life. Boats danced across the water; from this height they looked like toys in a child's bathtub. Birds flew below us, dipping into the water. We kissed like teenagers. Tom whispered in my ear, things that didn't matter in the least, while the sun tried to find us through the canopy of fresh spring leaves.

On the way back, he taught me how to use the four-wheeler. I stalled the engine twice before I figured out how to use the gears. All the while Tom held me tight, his arms around my middle. By the time we came back into his clearing, I felt as though we were one and the same, a single being on the back of that machine.

I cut the engine and, for a long time, he didn't let me go. We looked at the cabin, watched the squirrels and the birds, and after a few moments Tom pointed out a rather brave deer in the distance, moving like a silent ghost through the trees. A crow called out overhead. Somewhere in the underbrush, a small creature moved.

'I could keep you here forever,' Tom said.

5

I crept to the doorway and watched Tom as he worked. Both computers were fired up. He had a few pamphlets open on the desk in front of him. One of them looked like a schedule, with yellow highlights all over it. He ignored the laptop and instead wrote the old-fashioned way, with a sharpened pencil and a yellow notepad. It was just like Tom to have so much technology around him, yet ignore all of it.

I went back to the kitchen and stirred the chili. The whole cabin smelled like warmth and comfort. I was going through the cabinets to find crackers when the sound came from outside, louder and louder, the unmistakable rumble of a well-tended Harley-Davidson engine.

'Seems we have company,' I said as I turned off the heat under the chili.

Tom walked out of the office. His eyes were shadowed. The usual ease of his body was gone, replaced instead by a tension that made me dread seeing whomever it might be on that motorcycle.

The Harley roared to a stop in the clearing. The silence was absolute for a long moment before the birds began to sing again, the interruption forgotten. Tom walked in his bare feet to the front windows. He shoved his hands into his pockets and took a deep breath.

The door swung open without a knock. A young man stepped in. His dark hair was long and in a ponytail. His jeans were ragged and his jacket was black leather. A tattoo ran up one side of his neck. Both ears had two sets of earrings. A diamond stud flashed in his nose. His boots were leather, studded with silver beads, and had seen many better days.

The scowl on his face said he wasn't happy to be here. When he whipped off his dark sunglasses and looked at me with wide brown eyes, I realized who he was.

Tom stepped towards him.

'Hello, David.'

The boy looked at his father and then looked back at me.

'So you're the flavor of the month, eh?'

My face burned with surprise and indignation. My first instinct was to defend myself, but this was Tom's son. A long moment of silence, pregnant with the tension, stretched out between us while he waited for my response. I chose the civil route.

'My name is Kelley.'

The kid snorted and looked back at his father. 'You don't waste much time between pussy, do you?'

Tom's face flushed, but he held his ground. 'Why are you here?'

'Do I have to have a reason to see my dear old dad?'

'Yes,' Tom said simply, and I realized there was much more between these two men than a bit of teenage insolence.

David looked back at me. His eyes trailed all the way down to my toes and then back up, deliberately pausing at my chest. The scrutiny made me feel dirty all over.

'Nice,' he drawled.

'Why are you here?' Tom asked again.

'Money,' David said bluntly. 'Mom says you haven't paid enough for my tuition this semester. I'm here for my share of your cold hard cash, Daddy-o. How 'bout taking care of your responsibility?'

Tom took a deep breath. 'I gave your mother more than enough money to cover the tuition, plus the extras. Like that goddamn Harley out there. I suppose that came out of your college fund?'

David smirked out of the other corner of his mouth and said nothing.

'You're not getting another dime. You'll spend it on women and cocaine and God knows whatever else you're into.'

David shrugged and glanced over at me again, shooting daggers with those otherwise beautiful brown eyes. 'The apple doesn't fall far from the tree, does it?'

'Get out.'

The words were low and dangerous, a rattlesnake of promise. His jaw was set in a hard line. He stared at David with a mixture of hurt and confusion but, most of all, there was rage. Not anger, not disdain, not even fury – but the kind of rage that results in violence.

David saw it, too. He didn't drop his eyes or the challenge in them, but he did take a step back towards the doorway. The two stared at each other for what seemed like an eternity. David reached up and pulled the cap low over his eyes. He glanced at me, that same sordid look, then walked out the door. On the way down the steps, he kicked over a flowerpot. The black soil tumbled out over the boards of the sidewalk.

'Let him go,' Tom said out loud, though neither one of us had made a move for the door.

David kicked the Harley to life. We watched as he tore out of the yard, knocking over the small rocks that lined the driveway, throwing gravel all over the wide front porch and blowing up a tail of dust in his wake. Tom stood watching him out the window until the sound of the Harley faded into nothing.

I looked at Tom. He refused to meet my eyes. Knowing he needed to be alone, I quietly took the broom from the kitchen and went to the porch. I heard Tom moving around in the house, then a loud bang. I swept the gravel from the porch, focusing on one wide board after another, thinking about the young man I had just met.

David was a firm departure from the happy teenager

in the family pictures that lined Tom's walls. He was filled with a simmering anger that wasn't anywhere near the surface in those smiles captured by the photographer's lens. I wondered whether he really had used the money for his college tuition to buy that shiny Harley. Somehow I had the feeling David would do whatever he pleased.

My mind kept coming back to the way he had looked at me. The kid was undressing me with his eyes. He might be nineteen, but his attitude was like that of a thirteen-year-old with a chip on his shoulder and a complete disregard of respect. How did he get so bold? Was it something he got from his father?

That father came out of the front door a few minutes later. He sat in the swing and watched me as I swept the porch. I kept my eyes on my work, giving him the space to say what he wanted when he felt the time was right. The swing creaked in that comforting way as he rocked back and forth. His eyes were on me as I stepped off the porch and cleaned up the driveway. By the time I was done, all evidence of the incident had been erased, but the words between them still hung in the air.

I sat down beside him. He put his arm around me. Together we watched two birds squabble over the best spot on the feeder.

'He wasn't always like that,' Tom said.

'What happened?'

'The divorce, I think. It was hard on him. He blamed me for all of it. He had reason.'

'He had reason?'

'It was my fault. She never should have married a man like me.'

'Why?'

Tom shifted in the swing, and it took a moment for the momentum to even out again. 'I got her pregnant. That's why we got married. I was definitely not marriage material. Hell, I was traveling all over the world, sometimes on a moment's notice. I was a die-hard military man. That doesn't leave time for a home life. And, to be honest, she wasn't the only girl I was seeing. But I was the only guy she was seeing, and she held that over my head all through our marriage.'

'There's no doubt David is yours. His eyes are exactly like yours. He stands like you, too.'

'And he fights like me,' Tom said. 'Dirty.'

I didn't know what to say, so I said nothing at all.

'The women didn't stop after the marriage started,' Tom said. 'I knew damn good and well it was wrong but I did it anyway. There was a woman in every port – literally. And, when there wasn't, there were whore-houses. I went to more than my share. I hoped she would never find out. I guess I'm not any better at lying than I was at being a husband.'

'She left you?'

'Yeah. She held on for the kids but I didn't give her much to hold onto.'

I rested my hand on his thigh. 'You're really honest about this.'

'There's no reason not to be. A few years ago I might have lied and told you I was Prince Charming, but, honestly, I'm just too old for that shit any more.'

'I'm glad you don't lie to me about it.'

'But you're also not glad I tell you the truth about it. Are you?'

I sat forwards and plucked a handful of nuts off the porch railing. One by one I threw them at the nearest tree and watched them bounce. 'It frightens me.'

Together we rocked on the swing. I laid my head on his shoulder and he kissed my forehead.

'More bridges to cross,' he said.

'One at a time, baby. One at a time.'

Tom pushed the empty bowl across the table. He leaned back in the chair, took a long drink of his soda and burped loudly. I shot him a smirk from across the kitchen, and he had the good sense to look contrite.

'Compliments to the cook,' he said sheepishly.

The confrontation between Tom and David was almost forgotten. After our talk on the porch, Tom had retreated to his office and closed the door. The occasional slams and curses made it very clear how badly his son had pissed him off.

I had found cleaning supplies and went after the living-room floor, even moving furniture around in order to clean underneath it. I found spots that hadn't been touched by a mop in years, and attacked them with vigor. By the time I was done, his floor was spotless.

Tom had walked out of the office hours later with a spring in his step and a smile on his face. The shadows in his eyes told the tale of more than a few tears shed.

'Let's go out for dinner tonight,' he said now, even as he munched on another cracker.

'My food isn't good enough?'

'It's excellent. But I can't show you off while you are here in my kitchen.'

'Good point.'

'You have to go home and get some other clothes. Can I come with you? I want to see where you spend your time when you're not under me.' He gave me a charming smile and I blushed.

'Only if you fuck me while we're there,' I shot back.

'In that case, let's go right now.'

Within minutes we were in my truck, headed down the driveway. The house had been locked up tight, just in case David came back and decided to make himself comfortable. Tom had even locked the windows. I felt very uneasy as I watched him do it. How badly did a relationship have to deteriorate before a man locked his own son out of the house?

Then I remembered the lewd way David had looked

at me, and thought that barring every single opening into the house was a very good idea.

Tom opened the gate and I drove through. I watched him in the rearview mirror. His jeans were slightly tighter than they should have been, perfect to show off that toned rear and thick thighs. His shirt was button-down, an expensive designer number that fit across his shoulders as if it had been tailored especially for him. I had been very surprised to see the tag, and silently calculated what that shirt must have cost.

'Considering I only have three shirts that are suitable for going out like this, I think the expense was worth it,' he teased. And he wasn't kidding. The dressy clothes in his closet were few and far between. This was a man who was comfortable in his own skin, with his own style, and no need to answer to anyone but himself.

'You are gorgeous in that,' I said to him now as he climbed into the truck.

'Maybe I should buy designer clothes more often.'

'You're gorgeous in anything. And out of anything.'

'Somebody's horny.'

I smiled and turned the truck towards my house on the other side of town. The sun was going down; street-lights were flickering into life. Tom rode quietly, his hand on my thigh, watching every move I made. At the first red light, he unbuckled my seat belt.

'Hey,' I breathed in mock protest.

His hand slipped between my legs.

Tom's fingers pressed hard against my crotch, pushing the cotton of my leggings against my pussy. I was already wet. I spread my legs a little and leaned back in the seat. Tom took the opportunity to push harder between my open legs.

The light changed to green and I drove on. Tom moved his hand away, leaving me aching for more. He gently flipped the compass hanging from the rearview mirror. He opened my glove compartment and leisurely explored the papers and CDs he found in there. He studied my registration. He turned on the radio to see what station I had been listening to, then turned it off again.

We came to another light.

This time Tom wasted no time. His hand slipped down the front of my pants. I opened my legs and he slid a finger deep into my pussy. Slowly he began to slide it in and out, fucking me with it while I bit my lip and tried to look as though nothing was wrong. The man on my left wasn't paying any attention, but the woman in the turn lane was looking our way. Tom gave her a wicked smile and slid two fingers into my pussy, pushing up hard on that magic spot that made me horny as hell. I leaned my head back against the seat.

A car honked from behind me. My eyes snapped open, and Tom's hand disappeared. The light was green.

'Fuck,' I murmured, and hit the gas.

Tom busied himself with picking my purse up from the floorboard. He unzipped it and started looking through it, completely ignoring me. He pulled out the lipstick and twirled it up and down. A notepad, a tube of lip balm, a few pens – all seemed to be of interest. He pulled out a wrapped tampon and grinned before pushing it back down to the bottom. He studiously ignored my wallet but pulled out photographs that he found in a side pocket. He flipped through them slowly but didn't say a single word.

When I came to a stop at the next light, he was on me.

His tongue slipped into my mouth, hungry and punishing. He bit hard on my bottom lip. One hand went under my shirt while the other went between my legs. He pinched one nipple hard while two fingers slammed into my cunt, lifting my hips off the seat. I let out a squeal of delight. His lips trailed back to my ear, where he bit down again before he whispered, 'I'm going to fuck you in public. You know that, don't you? This is just a warm-up. One day I'm going to strip you down and spread your legs and give complete strangers a damn good show. You would do that for me, wouldn't you?'

'Fuck, yes,' I growled.

His hands disappeared, and I was left dazed.

'Drive,' he ordered.

The last quarter-mile to my house was an exercise in torture. He sat right next to me. The heat of his body was driving me insane. I could smell my own arousal on his fingers, and when I glanced over at him he was casually sucking the taste from them. I bit my lip to keep from groaning aloud. He seemed so calm and cool about the whole situation, but I was already trembling with desire.

We pulled into my subdivision, then into my drive-way. I killed the engine. Tom and I were on each other in an instant. I reached for the snaps of his jeans while he unbuttoned my shirt. His mouth came down on one nipple at the same time I pulled his cock free from his boxers. We groaned in unison.

'We need to go inside,' I begged.

'No,' was all he said.

My leggings came down. I kicked my shoes off. One of us hit the horn, a brief peal of noise that surely got the attention of the neighbors. He pulled me across the seat underneath him and pushed his jeans down. I lifted and he thrust, and I cried out when he impaled me on his cock.

'Hard?' he asked.

I held onto the steering wheel with one hand and his hair with the other. Tom pushed one of my legs up on the back of the seat and lifted the other to the dashboard. Spread as wide as possible and exposed for anyone who might happen to investigate, I lay under Tom and looked up at him through a haze of passion.

'As hard as you can,' I begged.

Tom went at me hard enough to rock the truck on its wheels. Already his forehead was covered with a fine sheen of sweat. I reached up to brush it away and Tom caught my hand in his. He led it down between us and let me feel the slickness of his cock, the way our bodies slammed together.

'Jack me off while I fuck you,' he said.

I circled a finger around the base of his shaft. When he pulled out, I stroked him. When he pushed in, my finger landed right against my clit. I was working us both at the same time, and the combination was sexy as hell.

Just as I was close to coming, Tom pulled out.

'Hey!' I protested.

'Jack me off,' he demanded.

Anger sizzled through me. Born of sexual frustration, it was sudden and deep.

'Fuck you,' I said.

His quickness caught me offguard. One hand tangled in my hair and he yanked hard. His other hand came down over my mouth. He rammed his cock into me again, this time without any ounce of mercy. The force drove me up the seat, and my head slammed into the door. Tom yanked my hair again and this time I hissed in pain, even while his hand tightened over my mouth.

'You said you wanted to do whatever I told you. Isn't that what you said?' he growled. He looked down at me until I slowly nodded.

'Then you will do whatever the fuck I tell you to do. If I tell you to jack off my cock, you will do it. You know the word to stop me, don't you?'

Again I nodded.

'Jack me off,' he said again, and his hand lifted away from my mouth.

'Fuck you,' I spat at him.

I knew the safe word. I knew what to say to make him stop anything he might be doing at any particular moment. He knew that I knew, and a glimmer of a smile passed over his lips. There was no way in hell I was going to say that safe word unless I really meant it.

'You are going to pay for that,' he promised.

'What about me?'

'What about you?'

'I want to get off, too.'

Tom sat up. He didn't let go of my hair. I squealed as he opened the passenger side door and started to back out of the truck. He pulled up his jeans with one hand and yanked me along with the other. He hauled me out onto the driveway and slammed the door hard behind us.

I was standing there with an unbuttoned shirt on – and nothing else.

'Tom!' I yelled in indignation.

'If you're so worried, shut the fuck up and get in the house,' he hollered back. He pushed me towards the front door but I yanked away from him and went around the side of the house. There were fewer neighbors to see me that way. As I ran along I heard him right behind me. I grabbed for my keys and realized they were still in the truck.

'No,' I groaned, and Tom caught up with me.

'This looks just fine,' he said, and picked me up like I was nothing. He deposited me not-so-gently on the picnic table there in my backyard.

The neighbor's outdoor light came on.

'Tom, they will see . . .'

Tom straddled my waist. He pulled his jeans down. He wrapped his hand around his cock and started to jack himself slowly, right in front of my face.

'So let them see,' he murmured.

I pulled my knees together.

'Don't you dare,' he said.

I glared at him.

'What's the safe word?' he asked.

I spread my legs wide.

'Good girl,' he said, and closed his eyes as he started to jack himself harder. He laced his fingers through my hair and pulled my head up off the picnic table.

'Open your mouth,' Tom ordered.

I was mesmerized by the sight of his cock. It was hard and throbbing in his hand, almost an angry red and slick with my own juices. A drop of precome slipped down the head. I opened my mouth and Tom kept jacking himself, only now his hips were moving into his hand, fucking the tight circle of his fingers. His motion became jerky and his breathing became harsh.

The first shot of come landed right underneath my right eye. The next one covered my upper lip and slid down the side of my face. The third hit my chin and trailed down to my throat. Tom milked the last drops out of his dick while holding it right over my nose. By the time he was done I was covered with him.

Tom climbed off the table. He pulled up his jeans and looked at me for a moment.

'I'll get the keys. Don't you dare wipe that off.'

He stalked around the corner of the house, but I didn't miss the little smile.

I rolled off the table and darted for the back door. Hidden behind the screen, I scanned the backyards and saw no one. I hovered there near the door until Tom came back with the keys. When the door closed behind us, I breathed a sigh of relief.

'Where is your bedroom?' he asked.

I walked through my kitchen and down the hallway. His come dripped down my face and landed on my collarbone. When I got to the bedroom, Tom stopped me by pulling on my hair.

'Where are your sex toys? A good whore always has a cock or two hanging around to fuck whenever she wants.'

I pointed to the small box underneath the bedside table. It appeared to be a quaint, benign wicker basket.

Tom pulled it out and opened the latch. Inside he found an array of toys – dildos, vibrators, anal beads, nipple clamps. He also found lubes and a stash of condoms in a small box tucked into the corner of the basket. After a moment of thought, he pulled out the longest dildo I had.

'Get on your knees on the bed.'

I got on my knees.

Tom stood behind me. I couldn't hear him, but I could sense him. He was watching every move I made. I already knew what he would want, and so I did it. I got on my knees, lowered my shoulders to the bed, and stretched my arms out in front of me. I spread my legs wide so he could see everything.

He touched the crack of my ass. His fingertip gently ran down between my cheeks. Then there was the cold plastic of the dildo, slipping slowly through the wetness between my legs. The dildo was a few inches longer than Tom. He pushed it in all the way, and then put more force behind it, making sure every inch of it was as deep in my pussy as it could go. The deeper it went, the harder it was to breathe.

I laid my head on the blanket underneath me. His semen had cooled and now it was a fine sheen of wetness across my face. I closed my eyes.

Tom climbed on the bed behind me. He pushed against the end of the dildo with the palm of his hand. I cried out as it went deeper than I had ever felt it.

'Good little whores can take big cocks, can't they?'

Tom pulled the dildo halfway out and the pressure was gone; he pushed it in again, and this time he went even slower. There was a flash of pain as the toy slid against my cervix. My clit throbbed.

'Hold that there,' he ordered. 'Reach down and hold that toy right there.'

I did as I was told. Tom took my hand and pressed hard against it, making sure I understood that I was not to remove that toy. Within seconds a cascade of cool lube slid down the crack of my ass.

'Oh, God, Tom –'

'Grind against that toy. That's it, move your hips like that. Push it in good and hard. Move that cock around in you. Do you like being full of cock, Kelley?'

I took a deep, shaky breath. 'Yes.'

'Keep that cock up your hole, you little bitch. Keep that hole full for me.'

Tom climbed off the bed. I listened as he slowly removed his clothes, one piece at a time. When he got back on the bed, I whimpered in anticipation. His broad hands settled on my ass.

'Tell me you want it.'

Sudden fear welled up in me. The dildo in my pussy was making me crazy with desire, but that didn't change the fact that I knew how much it was going to hurt when Tom shoved his cock up my back door. I didn't know if he would be gentle. He might choose to thrust straight in, punishing me for being disobedient when he wanted me to be submissive. Whatever he chose to do, I was at his mercy.

The safe word crossed my mind, but I wasn't ready to say it.

'Fuck me,' I whispered.

He pulled my cheeks apart. I wiggled against the dildo in my pussy. The lube ran down across my ass with ticklish intimacy. I shivered as he blew cool air across my back.

'I should get you ready,' he said. 'But I'm not going to.'

I tensed up, and he trailed a hand down my back, gentling me. 'I'm going to push my cock into that tight little hole. I'm going to open you up with my cock. And it's going to hurt, but you want it to hurt, don't you?'

I shivered under his hand. I held the dildo deep in my cunt and closed my eyes. My entire being was focused on the tight rosebud of my ass. My heart was pounding and it pulsed with every beat. I thought about that throbbing around his cock, how tightly he would stretch me, how it would feel when he started to fuck in and out.

'Do it,' I whispered.

'You want me to open you up with my cock?'

'Please.'

'You want me to fuck you hard?'

'Please.'

'Are you mine, Kelley?'

I could hardly breathe. I knew what he was really asking.

'Make me yours,' I said.

Tom pressed the head of his cock between my cheeks. He braced himself on the bed behind me, spreading his knees until they touched the insides of mine. He slowly pulled my cheeks apart, until the slightest pain ran through me, until I was stretched so tightly that his cock could impale me as hard or as gentle as he wanted.

Tom began to push. I tensed against him at first, and the pain shot through me, little slivers of fear that shimmied their way down my thighs. I took a deep breath and pushed back against him. Slowly that tiny hole opened up for his hard cock. A burning sensation filled my belly. My ass stung as he pushed relentlessly against it. The pressure of his cock opening me up was almost unbearable.

'Scream, Kelley. I want to hear it. I want to hear you while I do this to you.'

I took another deep breath and, when Tom pushed a little harder, he got what he wanted. I couldn't hold in the small scream. Suddenly my sphincter gave under the pressure, and the head of his cock pushed inside. The pain slithered down my pussy and deep into my womb, where it throbbed in time with my heartbeat.

Tom slowly slid his hands up my hips. Over my waist.

To my breasts. He found my nipples and pinched them hard. I cried out again, this time begging him to stop. He leaned over me and whispered into my ear.

'Do you really want me to stop?'

I nodded.

'Do you know the safe word?'

I nodded again.

Tom paused for a long moment. Then he slid his hands up to my shoulders, holding me tightly against him. He moved his cock in gentle circles. Only the head was inside, and the burn just wouldn't go away.

'What kind of person does it make me,' he said, 'if I like hurting you with my cock?'

My pussy jerked at the confession. My hand trembled on the base of the dildo.

'Kelley.'

I fought for enough breath to speak. How odd that he wanted reassurance at a time like this, but that was exactly what he needed.

'I am yours,' I said. 'If it pleases you to hurt me, then I want you to hurt me.'

Tom groaned. I felt the sound just as well as I heard it. He rose up on his knees a bit more, and his fingers clenched hard on my shoulders.

'Mine,' he said.

Tom impaled me with his rock-hard cock. He shoved it all the way in, fast and hard. I screamed into the mattress. He pulled out almost immediately and then thrust back in again. He drove deep, slamming his cock to the hilt. His balls slapped against my hand. Tears sprang to my eyes and the safe word was a mantra in my head. It was on the tip of my tongue.

I called his name instead.

Every thrust was long and deep, and Tom's groan of pleasure rang out with each one. I was shaking too hard to keep my hand on the dildo, and it slipped halfway out of my pussy. The next time he thrust, it was forced out of me. Without the added pressure, Tom's cock reached deeper.

'I came all over your face,' he said. 'So I'm going to last a long, long time.'

The pain of it was starting to recede, replaced by a deep ache and a near-numbness. I bit down hard on the blanket below me. His cock slammed into me over and over, until I lost track of time and space.

It was more than a physical taking; it was an emotional and mental one as well. I completely surrendered. I belonged to him, and the power of that made me weak all over. All the while he pumped into me with long and steady strokes, motions designed to claim what was his. I was somehow grateful for the pain that came along with it, the forever reminder of what it felt like to give myself wholly over to Tom.

Near the end he leaned down over my back, holding me up with his arms around my waist, fucking into me with a vengeance. His whole body was trembling. Tom buried his cock inside me one last time, as deep as he could go. This time when he came, it was without a single sound. His cock throbbed hard against my tightly stretched hole and, though I didn't come with him, it was perhaps the most satisfying sexual moment of my life.

Tom collapsed on top of me. His weight pushed me down into the bed. After long moments he moved to my side and turned me to face him.

Tom took the corner of the blanket in his hand. He cleaned my face with it, wiping away not only the evidence of him, but the tears that had covered my cheeks. He pressed his lips against mine but he didn't kiss me – instead he took deep breaths against my skin, taking my own breath into his body. He laced his fingers with mine.

Neither of us said a word.

6

I woke to the sound of running water. I was in my own bed, my head resting on my own pillows, covered with a thick quilt that smelled like lavender. I didn't look at the clock, but from the darkness outside the window I knew it had to be late. We had missed the chance to go out for dinner.

I listened to Tom moving around in the bathroom. He hummed a happy tune as the tub filled up.

Having him in my house was a comforting thing. Heaven only knew how long he had been wandering around while I slept, but I knew he was just as curious about my life as I was about his. He had probably peeked in cabinets and peered into a drawer or two. I didn't mind because I had nothing to hide. In less than a week I had told Tom more about my life than most people had learned about me in years. It felt good to be so open with someone.

My medicine cabinet opened. Tom's hum changed tune for a moment, then started up again. The cabinet closed.

I thought again about the prescription Valium I had seen in his cabinet. Then I thought about David. I was starting to see how something like that might come in handy.

I carefully rolled to one side. My whole body protested. I was sore and tender in places that hadn't been touched in years. I stifled a cry of surprise when I finally settled on my back. Everything hurt, and some things hurt much more than others.

There was a thin line of light coming from the

bathroom door. I studied it like a child studies a crystal on a windowsill. Tom was in there, in my bathroom, doing heaven-knows-what, and I loved having him there. I loved the sound of a man in my space. That hadn't happened in so very long, but I remembered how it felt.

I remembered sitting on the lid of the toilet in the bathroom, watching Michael as he shaved. He thought it was amusing that I would be so enthralled by something so simple as a man with a razor, but it was much more than a daily ritual happening in my bathroom. It was something profoundly intimate, something he allowed me to share by opening the door and letting me watch. The thrill was not in the act, but in the fact that he was willing to share that act with me.

Tom swirled the water in the tub. There was the snap of a towel, and then the unmistakable sound of a match scraping to light. I smiled in the darkness of the bedroom. He was running that bathwater for me. Or better yet, for both of us.

A flicker of light touched my closed eyelids, and then I heard the linen closet open. He was getting more towels. He turned off the water and the faucet made that usual drip-drip, as if it wasn't quite ready to give up yet. Soon he settled on the bed beside me.

'Baby,' he whispered.

I could have opened my eyes and looked at him, but I was too curious about what he might do next.

His fingertips trailed over my arm. He traced the line of the quilt where it crossed my chest. He pulled it down slowly. Goosebumps covered me and my nipples grew hard in the cool night air. He brushed my hair away from my face and touched my nose with one finger. He bent to kiss my forehead, and not only could I smell my shampoo in his hair, I could feel the smoothness of his cheek. I hadn't seen – or felt – Tom clean-shaven before.

He lingered over me for a long moment, his lips pressed against my forehead, breathing deeply of my skin. Then he kissed his way down my nose, skipped over my lips and planted a kiss on my chin. He licked a sensual trail down my throat. He traced my collarbone with his fingertips, even as his lips delved between my breasts.

He found both nipples with his fingertips and gently squeezed. He kissed all around my belly button and gently pushed one of my legs to the side for better access to what lay aching and waiting there between them.

He looked up at me and, in the dim light coming from the bathroom, we could barely see each other. He smiled that wicked smile.

'You didn't come with me earlier,' he murmured.

'No.'

'I have to make up for that.'

His hands were gentle as he spread my legs wide. He licked all over my mound until he found the slickness of my lips. His tongue ran over each of them, tasting every inch, then he slowly delved inside, licking his way into me. I spread my legs wider, and he murmured in approval. His tongue dropped lower, until he found that small bruised spot that he had taken so roughly hours before. I jerked in surprise when his tongue flickered over it.

'Easy,' he whispered.

No one had ever done that to me. Tom massaged my thighs until I relaxed under him. His tongue touched me again and this time I gave myself over to it. The sensation was exquisite. By the time he pressed his tongue against my ass and gently pushed, I was beyond coherent thought. I gripped the headboard and stretched into him, lifting my knees to allow him better access. All the while his hands were moving, wandering between my wet lips, smoothing my thighs, even massaging my feet.

'Tom,' I said, and it sounded absolutely right, so I said it over and over.

His tongue stayed right where it was, now delving as

deep as he could reach. His fingertips found my clit and he pinched it gently, then massaged it up and down, around and around, pulling me deeper into the vortex of pleasure. I reached down to help him, showed him how best to move his hand, let him feel me do it to myself while his hand rested on top of mine.

'I'm going to come,' I whispered.

Tom held me down. His tongue never left me. The feeling of his hands on my thighs, holding me open, the thrill of his tongue, the way he moaned right along with me when I came, all served to make the orgasm so much harder. I suddenly understood what it meant when a woman said she had seen stars. I saw whole nebula.

I was trembling and on the verge of tears when Tom crawled up beside me. He gently ran his fingertips over the insides of my thighs.

'You're shaking,' he murmured into my ear.

'I can't handle much more,' I admitted. 'These last few hours . . . they've been . . .'

'I know.'

Tom pulled me close to him and kissed my nose. I could smell my own arousal all over him. His face was baby smooth when I touched his jaw. He slowly pulled me to a sitting position, and both of us winced when the discomfort set in through my hips.

'Bathtime, sweetheart,' he murmured. 'We've got to make amends for that pounding you took.'

I laughed out loud. Amends was the last thing I wanted. It had been the kind of experience that made me feel like a completely different person. I felt liberated and somehow more mature for the moments I had spent in complete submission there on our bed.

Our bed? The words, and the ease with which they had popped to mind, surprised me. I was already comfortable with Tom being in my home, in my bed and in my life.

'I'm yours,' I said to him as we walked towards the bathroom.

The way Tom's arm tightened around me was answer enough for both of us.

The bathtub was surrounded by candles. There were candles on the window ledge, on every corner, and on every shelf in the bathroom. The water was piled high with bubbles, fragrant with my favorite lavender. Big fluffy towels were in stacks everywhere.

'Climb in,' he encouraged.

The water was hot, almost steaming, and perfect for my sore muscles. The bubbles came up over the side of the tub as I sank down into the water. My long hair tumbled down, the ends of it instantly wet. The bubbles came up to my chin.

Tom squeezed the water out of the sponge and ran it over my shoulders, my neck, and my chest. I sat up to let him do the same thing to my back and there he lingered for a very long time, cascading water down my skin in long sheets, rubbing my spine with the softness of the sponge and following that with his wet fingertips. I laid my head on my knees and blew bubbles away from my face with every breath. Tom's ministrations were like nothing I had known before, and I told him so.

'No one has ever done this for you?'

'No. I like it. It makes me feel safe.'

'You put a lot of emphasis on feeling safe. Why?'

That was a good question. I played with the bubbles while I thought about my answer. Tom was running his hand over my lower back, massaging me with an expert hand. My whole body felt as though it were melting from the inside out.

'Feeling safe is something I haven't had that often,' I said. 'I've been hurt so many times.'

'Physically?'

'No. Emotionally.'

Tom pondered this while he worked the sponge over

my belly. He wrung it out and a cascade of bubbles slid off my chest. 'We've got plenty of time to talk about all of it,' he said, as if a serious decision had been made. 'Right now, I want you to lie back and get comfortable.'

The aches and pains of my body were easing, and I was a bit saddened by that. The rough-and-tumble sex we had been having made me feel more like myself than anything else I had done in the years past, and feeling the marks of Tom's hands was a delicious reminder of naughty things that made me blush with the thrill of new experience every time I thought of them. The soreness was welcome.

I mentioned this to Tom and he laughed, the sound bouncing around loudly in the little bathroom. 'Oh, you think you like it, wait until the morning!' he teased.

'Are you going to fuck me again before then?'

Tom froze with the sponge in mid-air. 'Are you serious?'

'Of course I am.'

'Baby,' he stumbled, searching for the proper words. 'There's only so much a man can do.'

'Are you at your limit?'

Tom blinked at the challenge and slowly nodded. 'Well . . . yes.'

It was my turn to laugh. 'I love a man who is man enough to admit that.'

He blushed in the light of the candles. The bubbles made their light crinkling sounds and the candle flames sputtered. A knock came at the front door, and Tom grinned at me while he rose from the floor.

'Dinner,' he said.

We hadn't eaten anything since lunch and, at that one simple word, my stomach started growling. Being with Tom made me forget about everything but the two of us.

Tom swept into the bathroom with a tall glass of wine in one hand and a pizza box in the other. I had already seen his cooking skills, which were more than up to par;

now I was seeing his ordering skills, which were just as good. It was a super supreme pizza with everything but the anchovies. I was suddenly starving. I snatched a piece of pizza as soon as he opened the box, wet hands or not.

Tom drank the wine and watched me while he picked peppers from the pizza and slowly ate them, one at a time. I put away three slices and lay back in the tub with a contented sigh. Tom smiled.

'That's the most I've seen you eat since we've been together,' he said.

'You had better eat some before I finish the whole thing.'

The water grew cool. Tom and I drank the wine and he went to pour more. Somehow he poured it over the edge of the glass onto my bare shoulders, and then found that the perfect excuse to lick it off my skin. We fed each other pizza and he avoided the onions while I avoided the peppers.

A long while later Tom pulled the plug in the bathtub and we both watched the bubbles swirl down the drain. The shower made its usual loud roar as he turned it on, hotter than I was accustomed to, and he climbed under the water with me. His hands were immediately in my hair and he was kissing me, his lips sliding wetly against mine.

'Onion breath,' he whispered.

'It's better than peppers,' I whispered back.

When he reached out of the shower curtain and grabbed my toothbrush and the tube of Crest, I laughed out loud. I had laughed more in the last week than I had in the last six months. Everything about Tom seemed to make me happy.

Brushing my teeth in the shower was yet another new experience in a whole host of recent ones. Then Tom found the shampoo and started working it through my long locks. He hummed a low tune as he combed his fingers through my hair. He whispered every now and then, but mostly just let me enjoy the feeling of what he was doing. I leaned my forehead against his chest and let my hands settle around his waist. Together we stood under the water, steeped in the newness of each other.

'I think I could fall in love with you,' I said.

Tom's hands stopped moving for a moment. He chuckled, the sound low and deep in his throat.

'I want you to fall in love with me,' he whispered.

He took two steps and then my head was under the water. I took a deep breath and looked up into the spray, while the shampoo rinsed away down the drain. Tom's hands followed the bubbles all the way down my body, running his hands down my torso, down my legs, down to my toes. He worked his way back up and cupped my breasts in his hands. The motion was not sensual; rather, it was a touch of reverence. I lifted my hands to cover his, and together we rocked under the water until it became too cold to stand.

Minutes later we were in the bedroom, tangled in towels and sheets and covered with a quilt, snuggled up together. The candles had been moved from the bathroom and now sat on top of the dresser, reflecting in the mirror and casting a lovely light across the room.

'Tell me your fantasies,' Tom murmured.

'We've fulfilled a lot of them.'

'Tell me about the ones you are afraid to tell me about.'

I thought for a long while about things that I might be frightened to tell him. I hadn't shared my fantasies with other partners. Most of them had been too jealous to handle the things I harbored in my secret heart, even if those were simple fantasies that I would never try to make a reality. Tom didn't seem like that kind of man. But were there fantasies in my head that were too extreme? I thought about the things that always worked to get me off when I was alone, the things that seemed too unrealistic to ever become my reality. Someone else's, maybe, but not mine.

I decided to start with something relatively safe.

'I like the thought of having more than one man in bed with me,' I said.

'Tell me more.'

'I think about two men, most of the time. About them taking turns with me, or taking turns with my mouth while the other had whichever hole he wanted. And sometimes I think about more than two men. Sometimes I think about a whole room of them.'

'Doing what to you?'

'Anything. Everything. Mostly fucking me, one after the other. I like the thought of being filled up by them, one at a time, and letting them all come inside me. I'm not sure I could ever do it, though.'

'Why not?'

I shifted under the blanket and Tom's hand drifted down between my legs. I spread my legs for him, and his hand slipped between them.

'I don't think I could do that,' I said. 'I'm a one-man woman. I'm not the kind who shares well. But the thought of having more than one man, and pleasuring all of them, makes me feel wanton. The very thought makes me feel like a sexual vixen.'

'I like that you are like this,' he said.

'Like what?'

'That you like to be used. But, at the same time, you are a one-man woman, like you said you are. I like knowing what a slut you can be.'

The whispered words were like lighting a match. My body went all wet and supple. Tom sensed the change and took advantage of it. He slipped two fingers deep into my pussy.

'I've never felt comfortable enough to be like this before,' I said.

'You trust me.'

'Yes.'

'Would you trust me if I said I wanted to see you with another man?'

My whole body responded to the words he had uttered. My nipples grew hard, my pussy got even wetter, and my heart sped up. Anticipation lit a fire in my belly.

'Do you?'

'I've always wanted to see a woman of mine take on other men. To watch her enjoy it. And then to punish her for enjoying it, even while I know that we are both getting off on every last second.'

'Punish her?'

'Imagine,' he whispered into my ear. 'Imagine being on top of one of my friends. Riding his hard cock. Rocking back and forth on him. Letting him suck your tits. Letting him kiss you. Feeling his dick throb inside your cunt. And then imagine me behind you, spanking your ass with that paddle and making you count each and every time. Spanking you for fucking him.'

Tom slid his fingers deeper. I spread my legs wider. I turned my face towards him but he held me steady, whispering in my ear. 'Imagine doing that. You would, wouldn't you?'

I nodded, my hips moving up against his hand.

'You would let him come inside you. You get off on it.'

'God, yes.'

'And then you would climb off and start to suck him until he was hard again. Maybe I would pull out the riding crop and let you have it while you worked him over. And you know what?'

'What?'

'I would fuck you. I would ram my cock into your snatch so hard you would taste us both. I would fuck you after he had come inside you. I would feel how hot his cream was. That would turn me on and it would make me jealous and it would make me want to punish you some more. Would you like that? Would you like to turn me on and make me jealous?'

'Yes,' I whispered.

'I think you just like to be punished. I think you like to be a bad girl. Good girls always have that desire deep down, don't they? And you have been a good girl way too long.'

It was my naughty conscience talking, a little devil sitting on my shoulder and whispering into my ear. I had always been so predictable. I wanted to be unpredictable.

'Would you want to watch me fuck another woman?' I asked.

Tom went silent. His hand was still moving, but slowly, exploring every last inch of me.

'Yes,' he finally said.

'Is that a fantasy of yours?'

He nodded against my shoulder. I was surprised at his reaction. He seemed shy, suddenly uncertain, and that was not a side of Tom I had seen that often. And it was one I hadn't seen when it came to sex, not since that night on his weight bench, when he was the one who needed reassurance. But I knew from the way his breathing had changed, from the urgency in his body, that it was a fantasy he had harbored for a long, long time.

'Have you ever done that before?'

'Yes,' he said promptly. 'But not with someone who was my woman.'

'You've done it with women while you were on the road, you mean?'

'Yeah. It's different now, though.'

'Why?'

His fingers moved smoothly into me. He pushed as deep as he could, until his fingertips swept over my cervix. He knew I loved that. It took my breath away.

'Because you are mine,' he said.

And I was. I knew it just as surely as I knew the sun

would rise in the morning. It would find both of us here on my bed with some part of us touching, even if it was simply our hands linked together or my leg thrown over his. Part of my heart was still aching over Michael, and a small part of me wished things were different – but I knew they weren't, and never would be.

And I knew, if things did happen for a reason, Tom was the reason.

7

Tom was absolutely right about how sore I would be the next morning. When the sunlight came streaming through the window, I stretched in his arms and woke us both up with my sudden shout of surprise. My whole body hurt, but especially my ass. The kinky abuse it had taken was just a bit too much.

Tom climbed out of bed and made his way to the bathroom. He came back with a bottle of ibuprofen and a glass of water.

'This makes me hate you a little less,' I growled. I downed four of them while Tom watched me with sleepy eyes.

'Better be careful how many of those you're taking.'

'I need the whole bottle.'

Tom crawled back into bed. 'You can't hate me. You wanted it.'

Indeed I did. I wanted things now that I hadn't dreamed of asking for in the past, things I hadn't even considered sharing with anyone. I reveled in knowing Tom would accept whatever thoughts were in my head.

I thought about the way he had fucked me on my bed, the rollercoaster of emotion that came along with it, and the fact that my safe word had been right there on the tip of my tongue, but had never been voiced. I knew he would have stopped instantly if that word had ever fallen from my lips. I had let Tom do things to me that I never thought I would allow a man to do and, though my fears had caused me some hesitation, I hadn't once tried to stop him.

How had I come to trust him so much?

The phone from the living room. I considered ignoring it, but I had been away from home for days, and friends were probably starting to wonder exactly what had happened to me. My publishers might be wondering the same thing. I carefully climbed out of bed and grabbed my robe. Tom chuckled as he watched me walk out of the bedroom.

'You're walking funny,' he hollered.

'It's your fault,' I hollered back from the hallway. I got to the phone just as it stopped ringing. The touch of one button showed me the caller ID, and my heart started to pound when I saw the name.

Michael.

All the strength went out of me and I sank down into the nearest chair.

'Honey?' Tom's voice came from the bedroom.

'It was a wrong number,' I called to him. The lie tripped out of my lips without a moment's hesitation. I picked up the phone and erased the listing, then listened to the message Michael had left on my voice mail.

'Hey, I was just wondering how you were doing. I wanted to check on you. But you're busy or out or something. I'm on my way to tan and thought I would give you a call. I hope you are OK and having a good day. Bye.'

Busy. Or out. Or something.

I pictured Michael behind the wheel of that truck, his deep tan showing off the colors of the tattoo on his arm, the way his eyes always hid behind sunglasses while he drove. I tried to picture him in a tanning bed, his whole body bathed in light.

Did he ever think of me like I thought of him?

Tom came out of the bedroom and looked at me. His body was naked, stocky and muscular. I reached for him and he took the phone from my hand. My head rested perfectly on the softness of his belly.

'I lied to you,' I admitted.

'I know.'

'Sometimes it still hurts so bad,' I said. 'Then I get so angry. I wish he knew what it was like to hurt in the same way he hurt me.'

'You don't really mean that, Kelley.'

I dried my tears on his skin. 'I think I do.'

Tom tipped my head up with a finger under my chin. 'I'm going to go pick up some lunch so neither of us has to cook,' he said. 'Why don't you give him a call while I'm gone?'

'No –'

'Yes. I trust you, Kelley. I know there are things you still need to do.'

Tom walked down the hallway. I watched his ass as he walked away and, despite my best intentions, I started comparing his body to Michael's. I caught myself wondering which one had the tighter ass and chastised myself for it. I listened to Tom get dressed and, when he came out, he was wearing the same clothes as yesterday, plus a confident smile. He dropped a kiss on my forehead.

'I'm going to get a change of clothes and come back here. Tonight we're going out to dinner. Think you will feel up to it?'

'Yes.'

'Make that call, Kelley. Then let's forget about him for a while. OK?'

A minute later Tom was gone, the door closing softly behind him.

I stared at the phone. I could call Michael. I could tell him that there were things we needed to talk about, and then I could blurt out what I had been doing these last few days. I could tell him that he got what he wanted, he got rid of me, and now I had done the same thing concerning him.

But that wasn't the truth. I wasn't free of him. If I had been, I wouldn't be hesitant to make that call. What stopped me, more than the fact that I wasn't quite over him, was the fear of what he would say. I wasn't afraid of his anger, or even of his sadness. I was really afraid that he just wouldn't give a damn. I could handle any reaction except one of indifference. If he didn't care that I was moving on, that would leave a hole in my heart that might never heal.

I had told Tom I would call. And so I did, dialing the number from memory, the same one I had dialed every day for so long I could remember it in my sleep. My heart pounded until the answering machine picked up, and I breathed a sigh of relief. My message was short and sweet, to the point, and I didn't ask him to call me back. I simply wished him a good day and hung up.

Michael probably wouldn't call me back. He had become notorious for calling when he had a brief moment, then being unreachable until late at night, right before he fell asleep. I often felt as though he was avoiding me, though he swore up and down he wasn't. How ironic that now I was the one doing the avoiding.

I slowly dressed in my bedroom, looking around at the things I had always known. They seemed to have changed, to have taken on subtle nuances, just as I had. I remembered the way Michael moved there on that bed, and then I remembered the things Tom had done to me on it. I remembered wrapping myself in the sheets long after Michael had gone, steeping myself in the scent of him, and now I did that very same thing, lay down on the bed that was rumpled with sleep and still smelled of sex. I breathed deep and closed my eyes and again imagined Michael lying in that tanning bed, his cellular phone in the console of the truck, his eyes closed while the lights baked his body and the light on the little phone blinked, announcing my message.

It was all the same as it had been days before, but it was all different.

I was different. I touched the headboard where Michael's hands had been. I touched the quilt, the one I had bitten down on hard while Tom took me from behind. I thought about their voices, both deep and melodic, but so different when taken over by orgasm. Michael was always loud, almost had no idea how to be quiet. Tom, well, it depended on his mood.

'You really need to stop this,' I said out loud to the ceiling.

I wondered if Tom made any comparisons like that. I wondered if he compared me to other women. How did I measure up?

That was a whole new concept, and one that made me forget all about Michael for a while. I rose from the bed and looked in the closet. I had been wearing leggings or jeans for days, but now I pulled out a sundress. Deep blue with white checks throughout, it was a pretty and demure outfit, but my body filled it out well. I took off the clothes I had planned on wearing – a simple T-shirt and shorts – and slipped the dress over my head. I turned to the mirror and looked at myself with a critical eye. Were my breasts too big? Were my hips too wide? I knew I turned Tom on, but what did he prefer? Was I the kind of woman he would have stopped on the street, or had he only noticed me because of the unusual circumstances of our meeting?

'Just because Michael didn't want you doesn't mean Tom doesn't,' I murmured to the reflection in the mirror. A pretty redhead looked back at me, her eyes somber yet alive, her body filled with urgency. I watched the blush rise higher on my cheeks and thought: that was Tom's fault. Entirely his. Him and his passion for me.

'For me,' I whispered to the mirror.

Suddenly I spun around on my toes, suffused with the joy of the new person I was finding, and thrilled at the fact that the man I wanted most would be coming home very soon.

Michael didn't cross my mind for the rest of the day.

Tom came in with a massive spread from Kentucky Fried Chicken. I took one look at the food he was setting out on the table and laughed out loud. 'That's going to put five pounds on each of us, you know that, don't you?'

Tom looked up at me and froze with his hands full of Styrofoam containers. His eyes trailed all the way down my body and then back up.

'Wow,' he breathed, and the heat of another blush stole across my cheeks.

'Do you like it?'

Tom looked me up and down again, the food completely forgotten. 'Baby, you're gorgeous.'

I looked down at the floor, uncertain of where to rest my eyes. I was a little puzzled by how much his approval meant. I had always been the kind who could accept compliments gracefully, but, when it came to Tom, the need to please him was greater than it had ever been for anyone else.

'Thank you,' I said softly.

Tom set the food on the table and walked over to me. His hands were cool on my face. He guided me to look right into his eyes.

'You are perfect,' he whispered.

I blushed harder.

'I want to be good for you,' I said, but Tom wasn't paying much attention. His lips had found that tiny mark on my throat, the one that looked so much like his teeth, and he was licking and kissing and sucking there for all he was worth. I giggled when he hit that ticklish spot right underneath my ear. Tom's hands were scoping out the back of my dress, searching for a zipper.

'There isn't one,' I whispered.

Tom responded by running his hands down my thighs and finding the hem of the dress. He pulled it up over my hips. I tried to push the dress down, to slow things a bit, but he growled low against my throat.

'Don't.'

He took me right there. Against the wall. He pulled my silk panties aside while I wrapped my legs around his hips. One long thrust and he was deep, moving hard and fast. There was no foreplay, no discussion, no playfulness. He fucked me with utter abandon.

I reached down between us to play with my clit. If he was going to get there that fast, I was going to need some help. He growled in approval and angled his thrusts to give both of us the most out of my stroking fingers. I thought again how good he was, how experienced, how he knew just what to do and when to do it. Right as my orgasm hit and my pussy spasmed hard around him, Tom thrust deep and came.

The tumult was over as quickly as it had begun. We were left breathing hard, wet and sticky from the passing storm of passion. Tom pulled out of me. The wetness seeped out of me and soaked my panties instantly.

'Leave them on,' he said hoarsely.

'Yes.'

'Sit down and eat lunch.'

I looked at him through a daze of stunned pleasure. How did that happen so fast?

Tom finished putting the food on the table. He put straws in the sodas. His hands shook while he did it.

'Sit down,' he said.

I watched as he picked a piece of chicken out of the box and slowly pulled the breading off. He ate in slow bites. We didn't speak while we dug into the chicken, but I was certainly hungrier than he was. Finally Tom dropped the chicken to his plate and put his head in his hands.

'I saw David today.'

I reached across the table to touch his arm.

'Where?'

'He was on that Harley. I saw him at the intersection of Main and Wood. He didn't recognize me at first, since I was in your truck. But I could tell when it dawned on him. He looked right at me until traffic started, and when he passed me he spit at the truck.'

The flash of anger was surprising in its force. I pictured in my mind slamming on the brakes of the truck, hearing tires squeal, hearing that rumble cut down until it was a low hum under the simmering of my own fury. I could imagine climbing out of the truck, right there in traffic, and giving that boy what-for after what he did to his father. I imagined him removing the helmet and, as soon as he did, slapping his face so hard it rocked back on his shoulders.

One look at Tom's eyes said he had the exact same thoughts.

'I'm sorry,' I said.

He shrugged and looked out the window.

'What did you do?'

'What could I do? I stopped but he kept on going. I couldn't have chased him down. And, even if I had, what would have happened?'

'It would have come to blows,' I said, remembering the dent in Tom's office door.

'I have a temper,' he said. I was surprised at his candor.

'Is that how your office door got damaged?'

Tom nodded and pushed his plate away from him with a disgusted air. 'I was angry with her.'

'Does she have a name?'

'Melissa.'

'Why don't you say it?'

'Would you want to?'

I shrugged and started to eat again. The mashed potatoes were too thick. The gravy was just right. I dipped a piece of chicken into it and watched Tom as I ate. He picked at his food and his eyes wandered all over the kitchen, taking everything in. I knew he was trying to think of other things, anything other than David.

'Tell me what we are going to do today,' I said, changing the subject.

'Do you need to work?'

I thought about my deadlines. I was fortunate in that I had always worked ahead of schedule, in case an emergency came around and I needed to be away for a few weeks. But, after spending several days with Tom, I was starting to feel a bit uncomfortable about keeping that safety cushion of time in my professional life.

'I should get some things done,' I said. 'Are there things you need to do?'

Tom smiled. 'I need to go to the firing range. You keep me sharp in the bedroom, but I still have to take care of skills everywhere else.'

I laughed and watched the life slowly come back into his eyes. The incident with David was moving to the back of his mind like a bad dream, and I was glad for that.

'You go do that, and I'll write, and then we'll go out to dinner.'

Tom reached over and took my hand. He licked crumbs from my fingertips. 'You choose where we go. But make sure it is the kind of place where you would be expected to wear a dress.'

'This one?'

'No. Something much more formal than that.'

I raised an eyebrow at him, and he gave me a wide-eyed look of innocence. 'Hey – I can clean up real good. I can also behave myself to some extent. You'll see.'

'Seven,' I said.

'You're on.'

8

Tom looked sexy as hell in a suit.

I had a moment of sheer lust when I saw him emerge from the truck wearing those pinstripes. His shoes were polished to a high sheen. He wore a gold watch on one wrist. His hair had been carefully brushed back from his forehead. He was clean shaven. He wasn't wearing a tie, but that was his only nod to the man he usually was. He looked like a stranger, albeit an extremely sexy one.

I stared at him from the porch. He took three steps away from the truck before he saw me in the shadows. His response was gratifying.

'Oh, my God,' he blurted out.

My dress was long and green, chosen specifically to set off the red flame of my hair. It had a dangerously high slit up the side, but the rest of the dress was demure and showed nothing inappropriate. My hair was styled into curls, and I had makeup on, the first Tom had ever seen me wear. My heels were high enough that, when he stood before me, I could look directly into his eyes. They were dazzling with desire.

'I want you right here,' he said.

He leaned forwards and brushed his lips over mine. I kissed him back. He pulled away and licked his lips in surprise. 'You taste like strawberries,' he said incredulously, and I blushed.

'Strawberry-flavored lipstick.'

'You definitely need to buy more of that.'

That surge of feminine power ran through me. His mouth descended over mine again and a shiver ran all the way down to those high heels. We stood there in the waning sunset, only our lips touching. His breath came softly across my cheek.

'You are going to have to put on more lipstick,' he whispered.

'You didn't get it all yet,' I protested. His hand slid along my back.

'You're going to kill me by the end of the night, looking like this . . .'

'You make me want to ditch the whole thing,' I admitted. Who needed dinner at a nice restaurant? Seeing him in a suit with that look in his eyes was more than enough.

'We can be late,' he suggested.

I smiled back at him, a couple of co-conspirators.

'Will they hold our reservations?'

'A place like that always holds reservations.'

I grabbed the lapel of that suit and pulled him into the house.

The top of his silk shirt was open. The jacket slipped down his arms and pooled on the floor behind him. I was surprised anew to see that the suit was of the old-fashioned variety, not to be worn with a belt, but with suspenders. They were the same color as the pinstripes. I trailed my fingers down the suspenders, marveling at how they contoured against his chest. The buttons of his shirt fell open one by one. When he sucked in his breath as I trailed my hands over his belly, I had to smile.

He touched my hair. Reverently, with the kind of touch that Tom only bestowed in the moments when he was feeling completely out of his depth. I looked up at him in surprise.

Tom stared back at me in the waning sunlight coming through the windows. We both smiled at the sound of his dress slacks opening.

He wasn't wearing anything underneath that suit.

'Make me taste like strawberries,' came the whispered plea.

The hardwood was cool under my knees. Any other time I would have played with him, teased him mercilessly, but this seemed different. I didn't hesitate. My lips slid over his cock and I sucked half of him into my mouth. His fingers twined through my hair. A hairpin pinged as it hit the floor.

Tom groaned loudly. The sound echoed through the house, bounced on the floors, shot right through me with a thrill of desire. I took him in as deeply as I could and Tom held me there a long moment, his hands on the back of my head. When he released me, I took a deep breath and looked up into his eyes.

'Again,' I murmured.

Tom guided my head down. I swallowed all of him with some effort, and then I couldn't breathe. His hands were on the back of my head, holding me steady while he slowly ground in circles. I concentrated on my heartbeat, on the feel of his strong thigh muscles under my hands, on the way his breathing sped up and up. Tom finally let me go and I pulled back as slowly as I could, breathing heavily all the while.

'You're so good at that,' he praised.

The compliment made me bold. I took his hands away from my hair and Tom chuckled. I went at him in earnest then, bobbing up and down on his cock, letting my tongue mimic every motion of my lips. Tom shuddered when I licked that sensitive spot just under his crown. His hands clenched into fists, then relaxed, over and over again, as I sucked him deeper into the wet cavern of my mouth.

By now I knew exactly what would make Tom come. I didn't do it. I licked him one last time, then slowly stood to my full height and stared right at him. His cock was glistening, hard as a rock, and straining in the air between us.

Tom's eyes were hazy with desire and confusion. He slowly smiled as it dawned on him that I had really stopped. He shook his head.

'I could make you finish, you know.'

I nodded, and Tom shook his head again, this time with a chuckle.

'So this is how the night is going to be?' he said with a smile.

'Yes.'

'Two can play at that game, sweetheart.'

With all the dignity he could muster, Tom tucked his erect cock back inside his pants and zipped up. I couldn't help but laugh at the very serious look on his face. He shot me a frustrated smile and pulled up the suspenders. I helped him button his shirt. Before we turned back to the door he pulled me to him, and kissed me hard enough to take my breath away.

'You're beautiful,' he whispered in my ear as we headed out to the truck.

Things had changed. I could feel it just as well as he could, and neither one of us was trying to stop it. There was a certainty between us that usually comes only with long-term lovers. I wondered if this was what came along with the sexual explorations. Was this something I was always capable of having, but only now discovering?

The road to the restaurant was hidden and narrow, the kind of road that leads to out-of-the-way places that many people discuss but few ever really find. The last of the sunlight poured through the canopy of trees and left a dappled carpet on the ground, guiding our way to the tall, elegant plantation-style house at the end of the road.

Men dressed in full tuxedo stood ready to open our doors. Tom and I were whisked up a small flight of steps and through an ornate entrance. The lighting was dim, mostly cast from oil lamps on the scattered tables, and the music was low, understated. The delicious smell of the place hit me as soon as I entered. The woman at the front desk did not smile.

'Good evening, Tom,' she said, and the fact that she called him by his first name was jarring, out of place in this proper atmosphere.

His hand tightened on my elbow.

'We apologize for being tardy,' he said properly. His voice was hard and clipped. 'Is our table ready?'

The woman held out a hand, gesturing to the spiral staircase. She carefully avoided my eyes, but I saw the look she shot at Tom. It skewered right over my shoulder, filled with the heat of anger and indignation.

'Your usual,' she said.

I climbed the staircase with him right on my heels. The tip of my stiletto caught in the grate and I would have pitched forwards if not for his hand on my elbow. I looked back at him when we were safely on the second level.

'Tom?'

He shook his head slightly, a quick motion.

The waiter was cordial and seemed quite happy to be there. He brought water and a wine list. Fresh bread was placed in the center of the table. It had been baked in a terracotta pot. On the walls was an eclectic collection, all by local artists, all tremendously expensive. Tom's face was lit handsomely by the flicker from the oil lamp.

'She detests you,' I said.

Tom nodded and sipped his water. 'Any idea what you might like to eat tonight? I'm not sure what wine to order.'

'I won't be drinking tonight.'

Tom put down the wine list and sighed heavily. 'I told you I wasn't an angel.'

I nodded and took an interest in a painting of a broken pitcher. 'Is this how it will be?'

'Meaning?'

'A woman sending you messages with her eyes everywhere we go?'

'Perhaps,' he said.

I was startled by the admission, and I didn't do a good job of hiding it.

'You know my history. I haven't held anything back from you. I was honest about the women.'

I nodded.

'So, if you have a problem with it, Kelley, you tell me now. I don't want to fall in love with you and then lose you because of the things I did before I met you.'

I closed my eyes. The room seemed to sway. The waiter arrived back at the table and asked what we would like to drink. I hardly noticed as Tom ordered for both of us. His hand was warm when he reached over the table and touched my arm.

'Kelley?'

I placed my hand on top of his.

The waiter came back. Menus were placed on the edge of the table. We were left alone.

Tom was right. I knew his history. He had been honest with me about that. Was I now going to reward his honesty with distrust, when he had done nothing at all to deserve my anger?

I picked up the menu. Tom studied me over it. I was aware of his eyes but studiously ignored them.

'I believe I'm in the mood for steak.'

Tom reached under the table and took my hand. 'I want you,' he whispered.

I smiled.

'You're going to make me work for it,' he said.

'That's the best way.'

Tom leaned back in the chair. The suspenders stretched and the buckles winked at me in the lamplight. He slid his hand down the front of his shirt, all the way down to his slacks. He squeezed the bulge there. I watched every move he made. He didn't move his hand away until we heard the waiter coming up the stairs to take our order.

The steak was served sizzling hot on a plate of greens. The vegetables were in wide variety, obviously fresh from some local farmer's garden. The wine was beyond excellent, and by my second glass I was decidedly giddy. I suddenly didn't give a damn about the hostess who had made her feelings about Tom so clear.

I watched Tom's hand on the wineglass. He swirled the dark liquid while he watched me finish my steak. He had been shifting in his chair all evening, obviously uncomfortable. His erection would not go away. I took my time eating, fully aware that his body was protesting every long moment.

'You keep looking at my hands,' he said quietly.

'Yes.'

'That's because you want them on you.'

'Yes.'

'Or better yet, you want them in other places.'

I looked up at him, surprised that he had read my mind.

'Do you have any idea how much I want you?' he murmured.

The blush on my face wasn't just from the wine. I looked at Tom over the lamplight. He reached forwards and caught my hand in his. He kissed every knuckle with his warm soft lips. I shivered once, as though a cool hand was teasing its way down the small of my back.

'Tell me,' I whispered.

'I want you so much I can't think about anything else. You're constantly on my mind. I can't concentrate until I've sated myself with you, and then I need you again just hours later. I'm a junkie, and you're the drug.'

He paused, thinking.

'The way I feel – it's absurd.'

He took my fingertips into his mouth one by one, and licked the flavor from them.

'Sometimes I find myself wanting to push myself into you so hard – into your mind and your body and your soul – that you can't forget me, either.'

Maybe it was the wine that loosened his tongue. Whatever it was, it was making one hell of an impression on me. The tingle of emotion settled right between my thighs.

'I will never forget you,' I assured him.

To my surprise, Tom looked away. He blinked hard. The waiter came by and took our plates, but neither of us noticed.

'Tom?'

'Let's go home,' he said in a voice that was suspiciously rough.

The restaurant had definitely lived up to its reputation, even as we were leaving. Somehow the waiter had alerted the valet and, when we stepped out of the front doors, our truck was already waiting. The hostess was nowhere in sight, but, even if she had been, it was doubtful either Tom or I would have noticed.

Once in the truck, the console between us was maddening. I found myself longing for my truck instead of his, for it was an older model with a bench seat. My hand rested on his thigh. The muscles tensed and relaxed as he worked the gas and the brake. We looked at each other almost as much as he looked at the road.

Something had shifted before we left the house, and that something had shifted once again while we sat at that table in the restaurant. My jealousy, his possessiveness, our pasts and the way we felt about each other – it had finally all settled into one vital emotion that seemed to be breathing in tandem within us both.

We drove in silence. At a stoplight I watched the color play through his hair. Without any discussion, he turned down the road that would take us to his house.

Once we were there, the exercise in restraint wasn't over. Tonight already felt like something special, and I didn't want to rush it. Tom had the same thoughts; he pulled me close to him and spread his hand wide on my belly, a possessive gesture that took my breath away, but he didn't attempt to touch me anywhere else. His breath was hot against my ear.

'Why don't you go run a bath for us,' he murmured. 'Put in lots of bubbles.'

Tom's bathtub was quite different than mine. His was an enormous old-fashioned thing with taps that squeaked and pipes that whistled. It was also big enough for three, if the mood ever struck. Tonight it would be more than wonderful for two.

The bubble bath smelled like sandalwood and oranges. I found candles on the high shelf and there, beside them, an old pack of matches that were covered in dust. The candles flared and flickered across the bathroom counter, casting a golden glow. I carefully hung my dress on the back of the bathroom door. I peeked out into the bedroom, and what I saw made me smile.

Tom was getting undressed. He stood in front of the dresser and carefully took off the cufflinks, little mother-of-pearl ovals surrounded by glittering gold. The watch came next, that one I had never seen before tonight, the one that was so expensive. The suit jacket slid down his arms. Tom closed his eyes as the fabric worked its way over his shoulders and down to his hands. He threw it on the bed behind him.

With his eyes still closed, he pushed the suspenders off his shoulders. He worked one button on his shirt, then another, then another. He took a deep breath and ran his hand into his open shirt, down his belly and back up to his throat.

That's when I realized what he was doing. He was enjoying those few moments when the thought of me was just as strong as the reality of me.

Suddenly I felt guilty. This was far too intimate, something not meant for me to see.

I watched anyway.

By the time he was completely naked, I had forgotten about the water running in the bathtub. I wasn't thinking about the dinner or the women or the plans for the evening. Everything was in suspension, and the only thing that mattered was that man standing in the bedroom.

'Turn off the water,' he murmured without turning around.

I should have been startled at the words, at the fact that he had known I was there all along, but this was Tom. Observing everything was what he did best.

The pipes whistled in protest as I turned the taps. Bubbles popped quietly across the surface of the water. Steam rose from among them. Tom appeared in the doorway, holding an armful of fluffy towels from the linen closet. The softness looked almost ridiculous against his strong broad body. He set them down on the hamper and pulled me into his arms. We sighed together at the wonderful feel of skin on skin.

'Lots of bubbles?' he whispered.

'Yes.'

'Can we play hide-and-seek in there?'

'Probably.'

'Do you want to?'

I smiled against his chest. Even now, he had a way about him that left me feeling as though I was the one in control, the one who called all the shots.

'Please.'

Tom held my arm as I sank into the tub. He climbed in right behind me. The water made our bodies slick and soft. He tangled his legs with mine and his hand came up to my throat, pushing my head back against his shoulder. We lay together that way for the longest time as our bodies adjusted to the heat and the bubbles played on every inch of skin that was above the water. The flames on the candles swayed hypnotically.

'You make me feel so safe,' I said to him.

'That's my job,' he answered. Long moments of silence followed the words. We were sleepy, comfortable and aroused, but there was all the time in the world.

'What happened to you, Kelley?' Tom asked.

'What do you mean?'

'I make you feel safe. Who made you feel unsafe?'

I closed my eyes. The light of the candle was a pale red against my eyelids. I swallowed hard and focused on the sweet feeling of Tom's hand on my throat. He caressed me lightly and I thought again of how much I trusted him.

'No one hurt me,' I said. 'If that's what you're wondering.'

'Not physically, you mean.'

'No.'

'Then what?'

I shifted in the tub. The bubbles rose up over my shoulders. A bit of water splashed on the floor. Tom smiled against my neck and kissed my ear.

'I've never had a man who was faithful to me. I've never had a man who took care of me. I've always been on my own, even when I was with someone.'

I thought for a moment.

'My mother was the same way,' I said. 'One night my father called from work, about an hour before he was supposed to come home. I answered the phone. He told me he wasn't going to be coming home, that their marriage was over, and that he wanted me to tell my mother. He told me to keep her from doing anything stupid.'

Tom shook his head and pressed his lips against my neck.

'I learned that, even when everything feels fine, even when the world is entirely perfect, it can all change in the blink of an eye. I watched my mother fall apart and then slowly build herself back up. But she was never the same. She never trusted anyone. She never felt safe.'

'How old were you?'

I sighed and opened my eyes. 'Fourteen.'

'Right at the age when you start to hope for love and fairy tales,' Tom mused.

'I don't believe in fairy tales,' I whispered and, much to my surprise, tears stung my eyes. I took a deep breath and bit my lip, trying to keep the emotions under control. Tom knew me well enough to know exactly what I was doing, and this time he didn't allow it.

'That's why it is so important to you to be in control all the time. That's why you submit so completely to me. It's your way of controlling, not the other way around.'

Tears ran down my face. Tom took my chin in his strong hand and turned me towards him. He kissed the tears and suddenly I was bawling like a baby, or like a fourteen-year-old girl whose whole world has been shattered.

Tom wisely kept silent.

'I never dealt with it,' I said, when the tears had finally abated enough for me to speak. 'I just let things happen to me and I never dealt with any of them. I made up for it by trying to make everyone happy. I tried to excel in everything. I tried to be the best student, the best girlfriend, the best daughter. If I could do so well, maybe I could make up for everything else.'

I sat forwards in the water. Tom ran his fingertips down my spine. I grabbed at a towel and blew my nose on it. One of the candles sputtered and went out. The smoke curled towards the ceiling until it was obscured by darkness.

Until Tom and I stumbled upon each other, I hadn't really analyzed the reasons I acted the way I did. My mother had often told me she worried about me because I was too controlled, too careful, too calm. Nothing ever seemed to rattle me. I was the steady one, the one everyone else could depend upon to take care of problems. I prided myself on that and cultivated it.

The more time I spent with Tom, the more I realized those actions were a defense mechanism. I was still that young girl in so many ways, fighting against the unthinkable in the only ways I knew how. My trust in Tom had opened the floodgates.

'I will never make a promise I cannot keep,' Tom whispered against my ear.

Later as we lay in bed, our limbs intertwined and our breathing in counterpoint, there were no more words. His hands were reverent and his lips were everywhere. The trail of tiny nibbles from my chin to my ear made me smile. His fingers linked with mine and he pulled my arms up over my head.

Every last inch of him sank deep. His cock throbbed and I clenched him tightly, using my muscles to squeeze in a slow easy rhythm. His lips came down on mine and his tongue mimicked everything his body was doing. I was wet enough to drip on the sheets below us. When I moaned, the sound was caught by his mouth.

My legs wrapped themselves around his thighs, then his waist. Tom caught my legs in his hands and lifted them over his shoulders. He pushed my thighs back, bending me almost double, looking down into my eyes in the semi-darkness while he poised right above me.

His next thrust took him deep enough to hit bottom. I cried out once in surprise. The fucking was deep but it was gentle, and Tom made every thrust count. He pulled out so far I could feel the air lick between us, then pushed in so deep I could hardly breathe.

I reached between us to play with my clit. I matched his strokes, moving my fingertips up and down, and Tom finally looked away from my face to watch my hands. I played with my nipples while I fingered my clit, and that's when his strokes started to speed up. They weren't hard yet, but there was the promise of that in every tense muscle, every deep breath and low moan.

The orgasm rose up from my spine, tingling all the

way down to my toes. When I jerked under him, Tom sighed in approval. My pussy clenched rhythmically on his cock and he was coming right after me, pushing hard and filling me deep. The throbbing melted into pure sensation. Goosebumps covered my skin. I cried out loud with every wave of pleasure, and so did Tom, our voices bouncing together around the room.

Then he collapsed over me, pulling my legs down, wrapping his arms around me even though we were both covered in sweat. I shook in his arms and he kissed every place he could reach.

Eventually the heat became too much, and he lay on his back next to me, both of us staring up at the ceiling, touching only with our toes. Before he fell asleep he found my hand and linked his fingers with mine.

Long after he was snoring lightly beside me, I thought about the evening we had just had. I wiped tears from my eyes and stared at the ceiling while Tom breathed deeply beside me, his body twitching every now and then with whatever dream was running through his head.

Sleep took longer to come for me. I lay there and thought about my mother, the way she had been blind-sided by the fact that her husband no longer wanted her. I hadn't seen the parallels with my own life until that night. Michael had done the same thing to me, hadn't he? Had I been expecting it all along, if not for the way he had treated me, but for the way my own history had been? Did I expect every man to leave me?

I listened to Tom's breathing. Did I expect him to go away, too?

I was realizing that more and more of what I felt was coming from deep within, and had nothing to do with anything Tom might have said or done. The sexual explorations were opening up a lock on the trust I hadn't given to anyone until now. The further we went, the more I learned about myself, and I wasn't sure how I felt about those things.

But learning had awakened a sleeping beast inside me, a freight train of knowledge that was already running hard on the tracks. I couldn't go back and hide in the little shell I had created for myself. I had to go forwards.

I fell asleep with that thought on my mind, and I awoke to Tom's hands.

'We had what we needed,' he said. 'Now let me give you what we wanted.'

His hands closed on my breasts and squeezed. My nipples were instantly hard, and he scraped his teeth carefully over them. His leg pushed roughly between mine, opening me up for him. I dug my nails into his shoulders and he bit down harder. When I was gasping with the thrill of it, he abandoned my nipples and made his way down my body. He dipped his tongue into my belly button. He blew cool air over my skin.

Tom sucked my clit into his mouth and slid two fingers inside me. I was still wet from the combination of arousal and him, and he groaned in approval as we both heard the sensual sound. Tom thrust those fingers in and out, delving as deep as he could and then pulling back to touch that oh-so-sensitive spot.

He pushed in a third finger.

I rose off the bed towards him, my hips moving in time with the thrusts of his hand. He hadn't let up on my clit and, when he pushed deep and flicked his tongue over that sensitive button, I exploded. I saw stars behind my closed eyelids. I was coming down from the sensation when Tom surprised me by pulling his hand back and slowly sliding in four fingers.

'Shhh,' he murmured. 'Easy, little one.'

He slowly pushed those four fingers deeper. I was stretched wide, not to a point of pain, but to a pleasant tingle I had rarely felt before. He twisted his hand and the sensation changed, became sharper. The burn began low in my belly, spiraling all the way down between my legs, making everything feel heavy and full.

The small twinge of fear was quickly overcome by desire. I knew Tom, I trusted him, and I had the safe word tucked away in the back of my mind.

I wanted this.

Tom watched my face. I spread my legs wider and shifted just a bit, bringing my bottom up. Tom took the cue and put a pillow underneath me. The angle made it easier to move into each other.

He began to slip his fingers in and out, gently stretching me each time he pushed forwards. He moved his fingers first in one way and then in the other, feeling every inch of me, preparing me for what I knew we would do before the sun came up.

'More,' I said.

Tom chuckled and kissed the inside of my thigh. 'We'll get there, baby.'

I reached down to touch myself. I ran my hands over my belly, down my hips, up the inside of my thighs, where Tom stopped me long enough to kiss each fingertip in turn. When I slid my fingers up and brushed them lightly over my clit, Tom exclaimed in surprise. 'Don't do that!'

'Why?'

'It makes you way too tight. You clench down every time you touch your clit.'

I lifted my hands to my nipples. I pinched down on them and Tom nodded against my thigh, his hair brushing across my skin.

'Do that instead,' he said, and even in the semi-darkness I could see his wicked grin.

He worked his fingers back and forth, sometimes twisting them, sometimes pushing deep. He played me with his thumb, sliding it around his other fingers, pushing it in a little at a time. Soon I was covered in a fine sheen of sweat, my thighs aching, my pussy throbbing.

'Relax,' he murmured.

I closed my eyes and tried to do just that. I thought about things that were soothing – the way Tom's hand felt in my hair when he was feeling romantic, the way he held me when he drifted off to sleep, the sound of his truck pulling into the drive, the call of the birds in the early-morning hours before anyone else was awake.

As I relaxed into his touch, the heat of desire wound its way through my belly. My breath was fast and my heart was pounding, but my body was limp. It was a transcendental experience.

I came back to earth when Tom began to gently kiss the inside of my thighs. The stretching sensation was now a ring of heat, radiating outwards into every part of my body. My nipples were so hard, they hurt. Tingles of pleasure ran through my spine.

'Tom,' I whispered.

Tom twisted his hand and, with a sigh of satisfaction, pushed forwards one last time. This time the ring of heat became a ring of fire, but a second later his whole hand was sliding inside me. I started to tremble under him, shaken to the core by what he was doing to me.

His fingers moved slowly, exploring. His fingertips stroked my cervix and I jerked with the pleasure of it. Tom moaned as I clenched down on his hand. He watched my eyes from his place between my legs, hungrily soaking up every expression, every sigh and every moan. He twisted his hand from one side to another. His knuckles pressed against a certain spot that had never been caressed like that before. It sent me to the edge and back, over and over.

Then Tom leaned forwards and sucked my clit into his mouth.

The sensation was beyond anything I had ever

imagined. My pussy contracted hard, but I was stretched so tightly, the natural spasms were a completely new feeling. There was the slightest bit of pain, but it was the good kind of pain, the kind that makes pleasure so much more intense. The heat spread all through my body, and the tingles reached even to my fingers and the tips of my toes.

Tom did not move. His head rested against my thigh as he looked at me. His expression was one of total awe.

Slowly I came back down to earth.

Tom gently moved his hand. I was so tired I could barely keep my eyes open. The exhaustion was a surprise.

'Easy, little one. Be still for me.' Tom said, and carefully worked to slip his hand out. It was easier than putting it in, but it still took some time. I knew he was being careful not to hurt me, and I appreciated the kindness, but I was so tired I just wanted him to end it and lie down to sleep with me.

His hand came out of me with a rush of wetness. I slowly pulled my legs together. Much to my surprise, there was no pain. There was only a feeling of fullness and that pleasant tingle that I hoped would never go away, even as I knew it would go away much too quickly.

Tom disappeared for a moment, then came back with a cool washcloth. His gentleness lulled me into that place between consciousness and dreamland. He pulled the pillow out from under me and the slightest discomfort shot through my hips, the reminder that my muscles would be sore in the morning.

By the time Tom crawled up next to me and took me into his arms, I felt weak as a newborn kitten. I also felt powerful in a way I had never known. I had just done something I had always chalked up as a fantasy that would never be fulfilled, something I had never thought I could trust enough to really do. The whole experience had been perfect.

I smiled against his chest. My emotions were all over the place. One minute I wanted to cry, the next I was giggling like a schoolgirl. Tom took it all in stride, kissing my forehead and telling me with every touch that I was just as cherished as I felt.

'Sleep, little one,' he instructed, and I did.

9

As we lay in bed together the next morning, Tom cuddled me into his arms and kissed my forehead. I woke up sore, but not in the ways I had expected. Tom had taken his time with me and, as a result, the soreness was more of a pleasure than a pain. I was grateful for that, and I felt closer to him than ever.

'I have a job to do this weekend,' he said. 'The band I work for needs a crew.'

'Who are they?'

Tom snickered. 'Romeo Rage.'

'That's their name?'

He nodded and kissed my forehead. 'I think it's silly, but the people who pay those ticket prices don't seem to mind.'

'Can I go with you? See what you do?'

'It's boring. I stand there and watch people.'

'So can I stand and watch you?'

Tom shrugged and cupped his hand between my legs. He leaned forwards and kissed my belly. 'There are always ambulances standing by with a big crowd. So someone will be there when you expire of sheer boredom.'

'Hey, I won't be bored. I'm your biggest fan.'

Tom smiled and licked all the way down. I moaned as he spread my legs wider. He sat back and looked at me in the sunlight that streamed through the windows. His eyes took in every inch.

'You are still open,' he whispered. 'I can see inside you.'

Tom slipped a finger inside. I gasped at even more

newness. I was sure there were places inside my body that had been touched for the first time. He was the one who had done that, he was the one who had discovered so many new things about my body, and surely that made me closer to him than to anyone else.

Tom slid two fingers in. I was still sore but my body was waking up again, wanting more. I squeezed down on his fingers and, to my surprise, it was very difficult to do. My muscles didn't seem to respond as quickly as they should have.

'You're stretched,' Tom said. 'Everything will be normal again in a few days.'

He slid in a third finger and I arched my hips up off the bed.

'Again?' he asked.

Even as I whimpered with desire, I knew not to push things too much. My body needed time to recover.

'No,' I whispered, and Tom immediately slipped his fingers out.

'OK.'

'But you can do other things,' I offered with a wicked grin.

Tom crept up the bed until he was between my legs. One slow inch at a time, he pushed his way inside. I was open enough that his cock slid in easily.

Every nerve ending was alive, far too sensitive. Every thrust was a strange tingling sensation. It was pleasant, not painful at all, but it was also completely foreign. I felt as though I was fucking someone else.

'You feel so different,' I said.

'So do you,' Tom responded. His cock was rock hard, harder than I had felt him in a long time, and he was stroking with a speed that said he would last for a very long time, if I let that happen. 'You're not tight at all. It's a strange feeling.'

'Do you like it?'

'Oh, yes.'

'Does it feel like you're fucking a different woman?' I asked breathlessly.

Tom paused so slightly I almost didn't catch it. But I couldn't possibly miss the way his breathing sped up, or the way his voice dropped. 'Yes.'

'I want you to do that,' I whispered. 'While I watch.'

Tom did pause then, as surprise took over his libido. He pushed in deep and stayed there for a while, studying me. Little tingles shot all through me, and the muscles in my legs protested at the deep invasion. Soon his eyes drifted closed and he sighed deeply as he began to move.

'You feel so good,' he murmured.

I watched his face as he stroked in and out of me. I knew he was thinking of someone else, perhaps someone he had already been with, but more than likely a stranger. I also knew he was thinking about me, because his hands were all over my body in all the ways I liked.

'Do you like being watched?' I asked.

'Yes.'

'Do you like the way her pussy feels?'

Tom paused. The slightest smile crossed his face.

'Yes.'

'Tell me.'

'She's not nearly as tight as you are,' he said. 'She feels like she's been fucked by a dozen guys.'

'You like that, don't you? You like sluts.'

Tom groaned and pushed harder. I reached up and ran my fingers through his hair, caught it in my hands and pulled his head back.

'You like me watching it, don't you?'

'God, yes.'

'What's wrong with you? If you're going to fuck somebody else, you better make it worthwhile. You're not fucking her hard enough.'

That was enough to send Tom past the point of being careful. He slammed me with his next thrust and, though every muscle protested, I met him with just as much force. Soon his hands were in my hair and his hips were pistoning up and down, riding me hard and fast, pushing deep with every thrust. It might have been someone else he was thinking about while he rode me that hard but, when he came, the name he uttered was mine.

He collapsed beside me. I reached down to touch myself, to feel his desire seep out of me. Tom watched with sleepy eyes. I wasn't even close to an orgasm, but I didn't have to be. I was learning that with sex, just like everything else, the exploration was more important than the destination.

We didn't speak much, other than in sighs and giggles. Then we didn't speak at all, as a late-afternoon nap started to steal us away.

'Hey,' he said suddenly into the silence. 'Wanna shoot a gun?'

The smell of gun oil brought back the first time we kissed. I turned the gun over in my hands, marveling at the weight of it. It was fully loaded. I had watched Tom snap the bullets into the long black magazine, each of them making a lethal snicker.

'Forty-caliber rounds,' he said. 'They are definitely enough to stop somebody in their tracks. They go in and, when they hit bone, they ricochet. The path of the bullet is hardly ever straight in, straight out. That's why they do so much damage.'

'Is that what shot you?' I asked.

Tom snapped the gun closed and sighted down the barrel. 'No. It was an M-16 that shot me.'

'What happened?'

There was a long pause. When his answer finally came, it was very quiet. 'I got lucky.'

His eyes took on that far-away look, and I didn't ask any more questions.

'Are you ready?' he asked me now.

'No.'

Tom laughed and nestled the earphones around my neck. He pointed to the target, which had been pulled up rather close, befitting an amateur. I tried to aim but I couldn't seem to hold the gun steady. Tom adjusted my stance. His hands were strong on mine.

'Don't ever touch the trigger until you are ready to shoot,' he said. 'Keep your finger straight.'

I did as I was told. I tried to use the sight on the barrel and, every time I did, I felt as though I wasn't aiming properly. Tom told me to close first one eye, then the other.

'Which one keeps it on target?'

I tried one eye, then the other. Then I immediately got confused about what I had just done. Tom watched patiently as I went through the whole thing again. 'When I close my right eye, it stays there. When I close my left eye, it shifts.' I did it again to make sure, and nodded with certainty.

'Right eye is dominant, then. That affects the way you shoot. Always remember that.'

'Yes, Chief.'

Tom moved back and touched my shoulders. He slipped on the ear protection and moved out of the room. The door closed behind me and then the little light went on. I heard the whistle.

I pulled the trigger.

The gun recoiled hard. For something that looked so small, it packed a mighty punch. The first shot was better than I expected – I had hit just above the shoulder of the life-sized paper man. The target was still swaying with the shot.

I aimed again, remembering what Tom said about which eye was dominant. This time the shot went into the arm of the paper man. I was getting closer. I wondered how many bullets I had. Were they called bullets, or rounds? I fired again, and this time I didn't aim as carefully. To my surprise, I hit the paper man in the throat.

Tom's reflection was in the glass beside the booth. He crossed his arms and said something to the man beside him, then nodded back at me.

The next shot hit the paper man in the belly.

'Good one!' I saw Tom mouth at me through the glass.

The next one went astray, barely clipping the paper. I had just shot any credibility I had gained, so to speak. I aimed more carefully and this time the paper made a satisfying ripple as the bullet sliced right through the center. I couldn't contain a squeal of delight.

Tom flashed the thumbs-up sign.

There was a slight twinge in my forearms. I wondered if I was too tense. My shoulders didn't ache, but they were definitely feeling the impact of the weapon. So was my heart. It was racing with the excitement. Having so much power in my hands was a heady rush.

I emptied the pistol into the target. The paper jerked and shook. By the time I was done, it was in tatters. A whistle went off above my head. From another booth came the muffled thumps of someone else firing their weapon. Tom opened the door and stepped inside.

'Addictive, isn't it?' Tom asked, knowing damn good and well that he had got me hooked on the rush.

'I want to do more.'

'You can do as many as you want.'

I watched as he removed the magazine, carefully checked the chamber, and then reloaded the gun. Seeing my rapt attention, he assured me he would teach me all the parts, how to take it down and put it back together, how to clean it and how to load it myself.

Tom slipped out the door. I put on the ear protection. The little paper man slid into place, and I started to fire.

Later, when we were home and dinner was finished and the dishes put away, Tom and I sat down in the basement. He pulled the Glock out of its holster. He held it carefully, but with a certainty that said he was just as familiar with that gun as he was with his own body.

'This is the slide,' he said, as he started to take the gun apart. He named each part as he laid it on the table. There in the dim light of the basement, he introduced me to another part of his life as he taught me how to take care of a gun. He taught me to use a soft silicone-based rag to clean it, explaining that oil from a person's hands was one of the worst things for a gun. To keep it looking the way it was intended, it was necessary to clean it after every use.

By the time he was done, I could almost put it together myself. It was amazingly simple to do, considering how powerful a weapon like that was. I held it in my hands, aimed it at the wall, and pulled the trigger. It was bad for the firing pin, so I only did it once.

'It's not so scary now, is it?' Tom asked.

It wasn't. I knew what was inside it, I knew how it worked, and I knew how it felt when it was loaded. I recognized the power behind it, and how easily that power could be unleashed if it was used improperly.

I suddenly understood.

I looked over at Tom, and he smiled at me.

'You know exactly what you're doing,' I said. 'Don't you?'

He reached over to take my hand. The gun slid across the table between us, benign now that it was unloaded, powerful regardless of what it represented. I suddenly remembered a gun quite like that one being pointed at me the first time I met Tom, and the world seemed to tilt. Had it only been weeks since that moment?

'I'm falling in love with you,' he said.

The women were screaming, the men looked bored and the security looked tense. There were dozens of men dressed in the same way Tom was, but I wondered if all of them were packing as much firepower. I thought perhaps the ones in the crowd weren't, but those with the band certainly might have been.

Tom stood at the corner of the stage, watching everything through tinted glasses. He had a radio attached to his belt. In his ear was a tiny receiver and a small microphone snaked out of that, coming halfway down his jaw in the direction of his mouth. It was sensitive enough to pick up a whisper. He wore an unassuming suit and seemed to fade into the background as a businessman who was there to watch the band build up his bottom line. The suit hid the two loaded guns and two deadly knives.

I had watched him dress and, when he saw my eyes on the weapons, he shared more of his knowledge with me.

'This is an eviscerator,' he said as he flicked open a knife. The blade was curved like a talon. Light glinted from the lethal edge. 'You pull it out and the blade comes out with the same motion. Then you strike forwards,' he said, swooping it through the air, 'and it cuts and tears anything in its path.'

I stared at the knife. Tom's hand was firm and confident. 'You've used that before,' I said.

'It saved my life once.'

He said nothing more, and made the knife disappear into his pocket with a casual twist of his wrist.

Now I watched him from the sidelines, behind the curtain and down the stairs, away from the crowd and within easy distance of the bus perimeter. I watched the backstage happenings with interest – had he really said I would be bored? The roadies with their security clearance lanyards looked just as excited as I felt. I watched as they made a final check of the stage, chatted with each other and flirted with every girl they saw. The players slowly emerged from backstage. All of them looked tired.

Tom spoke into the little microphone. His lips barely

moved. Within seconds a man wearing cut-off jeans and a T-shirt casually walked up the stairs and stood next to Tom. Neither of them spoke, but I knew that, behind those shaded lenses, their eyes were searching the crowd.

Watching Tom at work gave me a whole new perspective. Now I understood where those moments of silence came from, that stillness that was almost eerie, the calmness that made even the squirrels on his front porch railing feel safe. He was trained as a soldier and spent time in war zones where the only way to survive was to become one with the terrain. Now that short lifetime of learning served him in good stead. The idea of heading up security in a venue so big was intimidating, but surely it was a walk in the park for Tom when compared to other things he had seen.

I watched the women. It was an interesting view. There were those dressed casually, usually with a boyfriend or other women around them, talking animatedly and watching the stage with interest. There were the ones who were beautiful and bored; those were obviously the ones with the band, the ones who had seen it all before. Then there were the groupies, those with too-tight clothes and too much make-up, those who preened in front of the stage and drooled like Pavlov's dogs at the slightest hint of a guitar string being strummed.

Right now, before the band took the stage, they were looking at Tom.

One groupie took particular interest in the security detail. She licked her lips as she looked Tom over. Her coquettish smile was ready every time he looked her way. She carefully shimmied her skirt up her thighs and wiggled her shirt down her chest. She was showing more and more skin. When she caught his eye again, she winked. There was no change in his expression, but he shifted his weight from one foot to the other and stared at her for a moment before looking away.

Was this what it had always been like? His pick of

women from the endless rows in the arenas? A woman in every port, that's what he'd said. After seeing the abundant possibilities, I believed him.

The lights went down. The crowd roared. Tom disappeared into the shadows.

The opening act was a band called Twisted Heyday. They were definitely a bit twisted; their music was an eclectic mix of everything from funk to bluegrass. The crowd didn't seem to know how to take it. They were bored and interested by turns. They were waiting for Romeo Rage.

By the time the band did take the stage, the crowd was so rowdy I wondered how any security guard could possibly know what was really going on out there. People were jostling each other for a better space. Venue security, dressed in their bright-yellow shirts, fought to keep the hordes of people away from the stage. The place was packed, everyone on their feet, hungry for that first chord to come out of the smoke.

When it did come, the place descended into a deafening roar.

I glimpsed Tom from time to time, usually as he walked around the corner of the stage. At one point I saw him among the crowd, quickly making his way towards another man in a suit. I wondered what the problem might be.

Soon I was bored with the band – it wasn't my kind of music. I amused myself by watching the roadies. They stood in small circles and talked quietly, the red embers of their cigarettes bouncing in the darkness. Occasionally one would fly in an amber arc, and then there would be the snicker and flare of a lighter as another was lit.

The band went out for the encore. A security guy ran by, his radio crackling. I searched for Tom but didn't see him. By the time the last drumbeat sounded and the lights went down, there had been no real security incidents, as far as I could tell.

As the last note sounded, the roadies swung into action. The security guys slowly relaxed, talking and joking even while still alert for the groupies who would do anything to fight their way backstage. The band was whisked away to the buses.

I wandered out to the SUV. It was a huge black Chevrolet with tinted windows, one of those vehicles usually seen in movies where the good guy is in the FBI and the bad guy is being chased by a fleet of identical black trucks like this one. I unlocked the passenger door and crawled in to wait for Tom. In the overhead light I could make out a glint of steel in the backseat, a CB in the front and all sorts of electronics devices on the dash.

He had explained all of the equipment to me in his slow methodical way. The more I learned about Tom, the more I realized there were avenues of his life that were completely closed off until they absolutely had to be opened. His secrecy didn't come from not wanting to share; it came from things that hurt him too much to be put on display.

I thought about the scars on his chest, the ones I couldn't see but could feel when I touched him, and the one on his leg, where that bullet from an M-16 had sliced through his skin. What was that look in his eyes when I mentioned it? Where did his mind go? What had really happened to him out in that foreign land whose name I probably couldn't even pronounce?

I watched the crowd thin out, the vehicles leave one by one, their tail-lights winking in the darkness.

When Tom opened the door, I was startled out of a light doze. He looked at me, then closed the door. He opened the one in the back.

'Get back here,' he said. 'And lock the doors.'

I did as I was told. When I climbed into the backseat, his hands were on me. His erection was almost as hard as the gun at his hip. He didn't bother with buttons; he ripped my shirt open instead. Buttons flew. My jeans were unzipped and slid halfway down my thighs before I fully realized what was happening.

'Fuck me,' he growled.

It took a moment to free myself from my jeans. Once I did, I didn't waste any time. Tom had freed his cock from that suit, and I slid onto it while he cried out against my throat.

'Is this what you want? Huh? You want a good fuck after the show?' I hissed.

The truck wasn't rocking yet, but it wouldn't take long at this rate. His gun dug into my thigh. He throbbed between my legs.

'Is this what it was like?' I spat at him. 'Was this it, you fucking Romeo? Huh? Fucking some stranger who would open her legs for your cock?'

Tom's hands clamped down on my hips. He laid me down in the seat and thrust from above me. I yanked the suit jacket down his arms and lunged forwards to bite hard at his neck. His hiss of pain was followed by a thrust that drove me up the seat. My head hit the door.

'Is that the best you can do?' I asked.

Tom pulled one of my legs up over his shoulder. The truck was rocking now, swaying on its wide wheels, and I wondered how many people outside could see it and know what was happening behind the tinted windows. I wondered how many times Tom had done this before, with how many different women who had eyed up the handsome security guard from the front rows and settled for him instead of a band member.

Inexplicably, the thought turned me on.

'Surely a whore like you can fuck me better than this,' I taunted.

The words were all too much for Tom. He came with one last thrust, growling into my ear. His hands dug into my hips so hard I knew he would leave bruises.

When it was over we were exhausted, panting and covered in sweat. The leather seat made an obscene sucking sound as I sat up. Tom pulled out of me, shrugged out of his suit jacket and draped it over his lap. We sat on opposite ends of the seat, looking at each other in the darkness.

'Is that what it was like?' I asked.

'Yeah,' he said, almost defiantly. 'Every damn night.'

I reached forwards and snatched the suit jacket away. His cock stood straight up in the air, glistening. Tom didn't try to move, didn't try to hide himself.

I climbed on.

One slick thrust and he was deep inside. He watched as I played with my nipples. I lifted one to my mouth and licked it; then I did the same to the other one. Tom didn't touch me, just watched everything I did.

I leaned forwards and pressed my chest against his. That wasn't enough, so I reared back and grabbed his shirt. I yanked it open, the same way he had done with mine. Tom didn't even flinch as the buttons flew. I leaned into him and only then did I kiss him – hard, deep and wet – while I ground down hard on him, intent on my own orgasm and not really caring much if he had one or not.

'You're mine,' I murmured into his mouth. 'You won't fuck any other woman from this point on. No matter how many groupies want you. If you ever want this, you'll come to me to get it. Won't you?'

Tom stared into my eyes as I rode him. 'Isn't that what I just did?' he asked.

My orgasm was close. Tom's hands clenched hard on the back of the seats. I bounced up and down on him, letting my breasts move with the motion, my hands braced on his broad shoulders. The orgasm flowed over me, from the center all the way out, the thrill filling me like light flooding into a dark room. Right after I came there was the deep and secret throbbing of him inside me, then the rush of wetness that said he was right there with me.

Only when it was over did he touch me. His arms came around me and he held me so tightly I could hardly breathe.

'I'm yours,' he said softly into my ear.

Suddenly I was laughing. The tension of the night, the possessive fuck, the undercurrents between us, it all erupted into a peal of laughter that took us both by surprise. Tom grinned up at me, his eyes bright with amusement.

'You are mine,' I agreed.

10

When I thought of Michael during those days with Tom, it was either with sadness and acceptance, or with a feeling of sheer panic, as though I was waiting for him to call. During those times, I didn't want him to find out what I was doing with Tom. My heart and my mind would go back to a time when Michael and I were happy, and the remembrance of that would bring all my hopes for the future to a screeching halt. I would wonder where he was, and especially if he was with her, and the jealousy would flood me until I could hardly breathe.

It made no sense. During our conversations in the months after the breakup it became obvious that a friendship with me was something he wanted very badly; however, a relationship with me was something he didn't want at all. Michael was moving on with his life and, though he swore he wasn't dating anyone, I knew it wouldn't be long until he did. I dreaded that day, because I knew it would bring back every feeling of inadequacy I had tried so hard to overcome.

It spoke volumes about my psyche that I felt I was the one who was inadequate. Somehow I believed I should have been enough to hold him, enough to make him forget the woman who had gotten so deeply into his heart. But she had become like a cancer, destroying him a little at a time and destroying us, too. It wasn't my fault, so why did I feel like it was?

The worst part was the unpredictability of the pain. It would slam me at the moments I least expected it and, even when I did anticipate it, it never seemed to come in the way I thought it should. I could now look at Tom's weight bench, even work out on it myself, and not feel a twinge of jealousy. I could look at certain things, read books that used to bother me, see something on television that reminded me of Michael, and not get upset.

It was the simplest things that rose up to attack me, like calm water turned into a tsunami from a deep underground tremor. I didn't know it was coming until it washed over me.

It was like that when I walked into the salon.

Premier Day Spa was in the heart of town. The building was so new the paint still smelled fresh. It offered massages of all kinds, yoga classes from beginner to advanced, and a full-scale gym with a cardio room and lap pool. The true appeal of the spa was the beauty treatments, a full menu of everything that exfoliated, toned, cleansed and beautified a body.

I was there for a massage. It had been years since I had one and, when Tom found out, he gave me a massage of his own, right there on his big bed, lying on towels and slathered with massage oil. But, even as he worked his magic, he insisted I go to a professional.

'Every woman deserves a massage,' he said. 'There should be a law.'

The pretty woman behind the counter directed me to a waiting room in the depths of the building. The furniture was opulent and comfortable. I sank onto a brocade sofa and picked up a fitness magazine from a polished table.

The door in front of me opened. A woman stepped out, looking rather warm in her white dress. She had a high color to her cheeks and smelled deliciously of tanning oil.

I watched her walk out. The door swung on silent hinges. Before it closed, I caught a glimpse of the glow of the tanning beds.

Suddenly, I couldn't breathe.

I had to get out of there. Panic rose up, a complete

surprise. I hurried to the front door, pushed it open and almost ran into a man who was on his way in. I stood outside against the wall, right in front of traffic and passersby and God and everybody, and took deep breaths.

I burst into tears.

The pretty receptionist ran out of the building and found me. 'Ma'am? Are you all right? What happened in there?'

I let out a few more sobs before pulling myself under control. She handed me a tissue. It was wrinkled from her pocket. I dried my eyes.

'My ex-boyfriend,' I said. 'He has a thing for tanning beds.'

She nodded with the light of understanding in her eyes. 'You took one look at them and remembered all sorts of things you didn't want to remember?'

'Yeah.'

She nodded again. 'For me, it was cantaloupes.'

Despite my tears, I smiled at that. 'Cantaloupes?'

'Going to the grocery store was a bitch,' she said sagely.

My laughter sounded foreign and forced.

'Thanks for checking up on me,' I said.

'It goes away, you know,' she said. 'Sometimes it takes a long time. But once you realize what he really was, not who you wish he had been, then it will start to go away.'

I stared at her. She couldn't be more than twenty, if that. She smiled and went back into the building, and I skipped out on the massage by getting in my car and driving out to the lake.

Once you realize who he really was, not who you wish he had been, then the pain will start to go away.

I stared at the water. I hadn't considered that I didn't know who Michael really was. But if a man could be so loving and so open with me, and then suddenly turn on a dime and announce he wanted someone else, was it really possible that I knew him at all?

I thought about things that had bothered me back then. Now that I was looking at those things in a different light – all the long nights at work, all the phone calls not answered, all the dodging of questions and the fights for no reason – I started to feel the sneaking suspicion that maybe not everything was OK after all. It was easy to look at what was on the surface and be happy with that. Was I so happy that I didn't bother to look deeper?

What else had Michael hidden?

I watched the water and thought about Tom.

How well do you ever really know someone?

Jet skis kicked up tails of water behind them. Men in swim trunks and women in tiny bikinis sat on the top of boats, letting the sun bake their skin. Kids played happily in the water near the shore. It was a world of families and couples, and I was sitting here in my car, alone, watching them.

What else was there? What else didn't I know?

I started the car and squealed out of the parking lot. Families, content in their togetherness, looked up in annoyance at my show of disrespect.

There were so many things I didn't know. There were so many questions rising to the surface. The things I didn't know would drive me insane if I let them, so instead I just drove. My speedometer hit sixty, then went far past it. I didn't care if I got pulled over. It would give me something else to focus on, something other than the horrible images in my head and the questions that kept my heart pounding just as hard as that engine under my hood.

I cried the whole way.

I almost ran out of gas. I finally pulled into a little service station, miles and miles away from where I should have been. I filled up and turned around, heading back for Tom.

By the time I got there, darkness was settling in. Tom was sitting on the front porch, waiting for me. As soon as he saw my car, he vaulted down the stairs and came running. He pulled the door open before I stopped the engine.

'Where the hell were you?' he asked, his voice barely on the sane side of panic. 'Where have you been? I've been worried!'

I looked at Tom helplessly.

'I needed to take a drive,' I said, knowing it was the absolute truth and knowing it also wasn't nearly enough.

Tom stared at me. He wasn't sure what to think and I didn't blame him. I wasn't sure what to think, either.

'I'm so sorry,' I whispered.

Tom knelt beside me and touched my thigh. 'What is happening, Kelley?'

I didn't know what to say.

'I want to help you, Kelley. But if you don't let me in, there's nothing I can do to help you. You have to meet me halfway.'

The sudden flare of anger was completely unexpected and entirely out of place. He was simply trying to help me. What was my problem, anyway? Why did I expect him to put up with my emotional bullshit without any input from me? Was he supposed to read my mind or something?

I took a deep breath and said all I could say. 'I'm sorry, Tom.'

'Get yourself together and come in the house. We need to talk.'

I sat in the car for a long while. Tom went around the side of the house, then inside the kitchen – I saw the lights flicker on. He waited for a long time, then came back out to the car. His concern had transformed into anger. Tom pulled the door open again. This time he wasn't nearly as nice as he had been earlier.

'Get out.'

I climbed out of the car, both sheepish at what I had done and angry for reasons I couldn't name. I was furious at Tom for being so solicitous towards me. I was furious with myself for letting Michael elbow his way into my life without even trying. I was angry with myself and sad over the whole situation.

I walked into the house. Tom was right on my heels. The remnants of dinner were all over the kitchen. I grabbed a plate and scraped the last bits of steak into the garbage disposal. I turned it on and listened to the grinding sound. It kept Tom from talking to me.

He watched from his place near the counter as I cleaned the kitchen. With each small chore, my anger dissipated a bit more. I tried desperately to hold onto it.

'Talk to me,' Tom finally said.

I dropped a plate. It shattered on the floor at my feet. Tom flinched hard, and I covered my face with my hands.

'Michael,' I said, and then the tears came.

Tom came towards me. Fine china crunched under his shoes. He took my arms.

'Walk this way,' he said. 'Careful. You've got a cut on your foot.'

I looked down and saw the blood. The world went hazy. Tom caught me before I fell, and then lifted me into his arms. His jaw was set in a hard line, but his eyes were filled with worry. He carried me through the house and set me down on the couch.

The sun had gone down long ago, and the living room was dark. I lay there while Tom went into the bathroom and came back with the things he needed to clean the cut. He spread a towel over his lap and pulled my foot onto it. We looked at each other from our opposite ends of the couch.

'Talk,' he said.

The peroxide was cold and made me jump. The bubbles made a white foam across my foot.

'I went to the spa today. There were tanning beds there. I took one look at them and I got sick, Tom. Physically sick. I thought about him and that woman, and the fact that he wanted her more than he wanted me, and I got sick.'

Tom patted my foot dry. He looked at it closely, then poured on more peroxide.

'What else?'

'I got in the car and went to the lake. Then I drove. I just drove.'

Tom looked up at me for a moment. He patted my foot dry again, then picked up a band-aid.

'I don't know why I did it. I didn't think, Tom. I just went, and then I came back, and now I don't even know where I am.'

'You don't know where you are?' He opened the band-aid with a tiny ripping sound.

'Emotionally.'

'Oh.'

'I want to be free of him, Tom. But I don't know how.'

Tom flicked on the lamp on the table. It was just enough of a glow to see each other clearly.

'You're not ready for this, are you? For you and me,' he said.

'I want to be.'

'What can I do to help you?' he asked. There was an edge of desperation to his voice, a fear that was barely in check. 'Tell me what I can do, Kelley.'

I shook my head. 'I don't know.'

'You need to talk to him,' Tom said. 'You need to ask him all those questions that are tearing you apart, Kelley. You won't move on until you have the answers.'

I shook my head. 'He won't give me a straight answer to anything,' I said.

Tom cupped my face in his hands. 'I love you,' he said. 'I know now isn't the most romantic time to say that to you. But you have to know how far it's gone for me, Kelley. I love you, and I'm here for the long haul.'

I kissed him, as trusting as I had always been. Try as I might, there was nothing nagging in the back of my mind, no reasons not to trust Tom. I was ashamed of myself for trying to find anything amiss.

'I'm sorry,' I whispered.

Tom kissed me for a long, long time. I pushed him to his back on the couch. When I reached for the buttons of his shirt, he stopped me.

'Not now, Kelley.'

I was floored. Sex was what we enjoyed and used generously at times like this. His rejection of the act felt like a rejection of me. Hadn't he just told me he loved me? And now he didn't want me?

I knew that wasn't the case, but it was the excuse I needed to find the anger again. I climbed off the couch. He didn't say a word, and he didn't move. I tramped down the stairs into the basement. I slammed the door so hard, the hinges rattled.

Tom didn't come after me.

I punched at the bag that hung in the corner. It hardly moved. I hit it again, harder this time. It moved even less. The force of my anger felt dangerously impotent, as though, if I didn't get it out, it would turn on me and tear me apart from the inside out.

I was so fucking tired of this.

I slammed into the bag with my full weight. It was like hitting a brick wall. I wrapped my arms around it and tried to move it, but nothing happened. I settled for punching it as hard as I could, over and over, until sweat was running down my body and my breasts hurt from bouncing with every punch. A thin line of fire ran up and down my spine. My arms burned from the pounding

I was giving the bag, but still I didn't stop until the pain was too much for me to handle.

I slumped on the weight bench. The leather immediately grabbed at my wet buttocks, making a sucking sound as I shifted. The room smelled like leather and sweat and hard work. I looked at the weights on the bench and the bolts on the floor, and remembered all the times Tom and I had made love – or simply fucked – on that bench.

I hated that bench tonight.

I kicked the weights with my foot. The flare of pain shot through my toe and I was grateful for it. It took away the attention from the pain in my heart.

I limped over to the mirror and stared at myself. I looked for so long that it began to seem as though I wasn't looking at a reflection at all, but another person, someone I didn't know. How audacious I had been, to believe Tom was the one with the serious issues.

The guilt finally swamped me, replacing the anger with a slow, sinking rush. Tom had just told me he loved me, and I had taken it all the wrong way. I shouldn't be down here, berating myself; I should be up there in the bedroom, making it all up to him.

The staircase seemed to be longer and steeper than it had been before. I expected to find Tom on the couch where I had left him, but he wasn't there.

I looked out the window. Both vehicles were out in the driveway. The four-wheeler was parked in the backyard. Moonlight glinted from the handlebars. The broken plate was still scattered on the kitchen floor. I ignored it and walked back to the office. The door was closed and no light was showing through the small space underneath.

I finally found him on the porch, standing at the corner of it and looking down into the yard. He took a long pensive drink from the stoneware mug in his hand.

'I think I'm going to build this porch further out,' he said. 'I know you like wrap-around porches. I could do that.'

I smiled. 'How do you know that?'

'I've been reading your books.'

I sat down on the swing. The chains made a comforting squeak as I moved back and forth. It was the sound of pure country, harking back to a time when life was simple.

'You're very observant,' I said. 'To know which parts are true and which parts are not.'

He glanced back at me suspiciously, as though he expected a punch line.

'Do you feel better?' he asked.

I shook my head. 'I feel horrible. For more reasons than you can imagine. I'm sorry, Tom.'

He waved my apology away.

I watched him as he watched the yard. From somewhere in the woods a bobwhite quail called, and Tom whistled back. After a puzzled silence, the bird answered, and Tom proceeded to carry on a conversation with him. The bantering back and forth was comforting.

I thought about how lucky I was to have a man who was willing to share so much with me, who had opened his home and his heart and laid them all out for my inspection. There were so many things about him I didn't know, but what could he really hide? When I was with Michael it was a long-distance relationship, and he had more than ample opportunity to hide things from me. Tom had no such luxury. So why was I lumping him into the same category as Michael when it came to honesty?

'I had no idea,' I said, 'how badly he damaged me.'

Tom surprised me when he answered: 'I didn't know, either.'

He came to sit next to me on the swing. Our thighs touched. He leaned forwards with the mug in his hands and stared at the liquid inside it. The bobwhite whistled again, puzzled now that his singing partner had suddenly fallen silent.

'You know what you need?' Tom asked quietly.

'Do tell.'

'You need a good, hard, savage fuck.'

I looked at him, but he didn't move. The swing gently rocked, the bobwhite called, and nothing seemed to have changed – but the electricity was there, in the air, practically crackling with heat. I almost expected to see fingers of lightning flash down from the sky.

How was it possible to go from such anger and despair to this thrill of anticipation?

'Yes,' I said. 'I do need that from you.'

'From me?' Tom asked. Even as the sharp edge of his doubt cut into my heart, the excitement surged, stronger than ever.

'I don't want anyone but you,' I reassured him.

Tom stood up. The swing moved more easily without his weight. He tossed the remainder of his drink off the railing. Moonlight flashed through the liquid as it flew in a gentle arc.

'I think it's time for something special,' Tom said.

He reached out a hand. I took it and followed him into the house. He led me through the living room, down the hallway, to the basement stairs. Tom flicked on the small light over by the whirlpool. It cast a dim light over the exercise equipment, threw shadows on the walls and made the basement look more like a medieval dungeon than a gym.

He looked at me. Without a word, I removed my clothes.

'Get on the bench,' Tom said.

I was trembling with anticipation by the time I reached the bench. The leather seemed to glow in the pale light from the corner. I touched the bar for a moment, looking down at the place where Tom wanted me. I slowly straddled the bench.

Tom carefully tied each ankle to the lower bar. Then he tied my hands to the support bars on either side of the bench. In that position my ass was up in the air, and I was entirely exposed for whatever he might choose to do to me.

'Do you remember our safe word?'

'Yes,' I whispered.

'Good. You don't say a word unless it's that one. Understand?'

I started to say yes, but then realized what he had just told me. I nodded instead. I looked up at Tom and he gave me a smile.

'Good girl,' he praised.

He stood over me for a long time. I thought he would touch me, but the pressure of his hand never came. He simply stood there, breathing deep and even, his eyes taking in every inch of me. Goosebumps rose on my skin and then went away. I blushed like fire, then that went away, too. I squirmed a little against my bonds, but eventually found a comfortable place where I simply resigned myself to the way I was bound. I closed my eyes and let my head hang down.

Only then did Tom move. I didn't open my eyes or look up. I concentrated on my breathing. I heard the cabinet door open, and I knew he was pulling something out of there – or many things – but I still did not move. Tom's calmness had infused me.

'You are so beautiful like that,' he murmured from right in front of me. 'You have no idea how you look now, Kelley. Trust is so damn beautiful.'

He trailed something made of leather down my spine. It was cool against my skin. I didn't even flinch; I just arched into it, welcoming it, feeling it grow warm.

Then the paddle followed the same trail. I knew what

it was from the shape and the hard edge. It touched every inch of my spine, almost as if Tom were counting the vertebrae. Then came what had to be the cane, a springy thing that was surprisingly warm already. Tom rolled it down my spine and back up, eventually using it to massage the back of my neck. I relaxed even further.

The first blow of the cane was surprisingly soft. My mind and body instantly focused on this strange new sensation. The touch was feather light, and the thought of what the cane could do versus what it was doing was a contradiction that kept my attention narrowed to a thin corridor of pleasure. The touch of it fluttered down my spine, tapping lightly on either side, never actually touching the center. There was a difference between the taps with the end of the cane and the ones that came from further up the shaft; those were harder, heavier, but still not hard enough to hurt. The small taps were like punctuation marks, illustrating the differences.

Tom went up and down, moving the cane slightly with every stroke. My back began to hum with warmth. I wanted to arch into it, to take more of what he was giving me, but a bigger part of me demanded that I stay very still and savor it all at his pace.

I was suspended in a place between being completely turned on and feeling completely comfortable. I couldn't stop smiling. Once I even giggled out loud, and Tom chuckled with me but didn't pause. The feather-light touches were harder now, and the tip of the cane was tickling at my sides, but still there was no pain.

The warmth slowly turned to a tingle. When the blows began to edge into the slightest pain, I took deep breaths and hung my head. I relaxed as much as I could. Even though the blows came harder, the pain began to edge away again, leaving only pleasure.

I was moaning quietly, a rhythmic sound that

matched the strokes of the cane. Tom was breathing harder from the exercise he was getting. The muscles in his arms were tense as steel bands. I watched him through half-open eyes and realized with a jolt that this was all about me. It had nothing to do with him. He was giving me the gift of trust in the face of all the emotional upheaval.

The moaning began to sound like his name, but Tom didn't reprimand me. He was entirely focused on what he was doing. Finally the blows were hard, almost overlapping and creating the illusion of a rough waterfall rolling down my skin. The giggles came without much warning, and Tom seemed to like those. He also brought the cane down a little harder, and what should have been pain was instead something very welcome.

By the time the blows did begin to hurt, I was too far gone in a sea of satisfaction to protest. It felt good to have the searing heat instead of the warmth. It felt good to watch Tom's muscles tighten as he brought the cane down harder and harder. It felt good to feel the stripes the cane was leaving, the tiny raised welts that heralded where it had been. By the time he had worked his way down either side of my spine and was focusing on my buttocks, I was so lost in the sensation that I broke the rules and spoke: 'Please, Tom. Please. More.'

Tom didn't respond with words. He worked the cane over my ass, leaving marks that burned so sweetly I wanted to cry with the pleasure of it.

In that moment, Tom had all of me, and he knew it.

The touches of the cane became stronger and, for the first time, I cried out with the pain. Tom lashed across my buttocks, each stroke barely overlapping the last. By the time he paused, my cheeks were on fire, there were tears in my eyes and I was gasping for air. But the deep trust and thrill of it all surpassed everything else.

Tom went over my body again, this time with strokes

that became gentler. It was the reverse of what he had just done. He had built me up to a crescendo, and now he was slowly bringing me down.

The last touches of the cane were so light, they tickled all the way through me. Though it was my back he was touching, I could feel the jumps of pleasure all through me, especially in my belly. I laughed out loud.

Tom laughed with me.

Then the cane was gone and, in the absence of it, I drifted with my eyes closed. Tom straddled the bench behind me. He didn't touch me, didn't make a sound, but he was there.

Waiting.

I didn't move, breathing hard, my mind slowly starting to move again. I was aware of him behind me, and of what he must be seeing – the redness of my back and my buttocks, the way I was tied down to the weight bench, entirely vulnerable and ready for anything he might do.

And then I was ready, because the warmth of the rest of me had settled between my legs. I needed Tom to work me over the inside just like he had worked me over on the outside.

The hunger was immediate and almost desperate. I had to feel the kindness of him tempered with the wild passion I knew he was capable of showing. I wanted the two extremes. I wanted every contradiction that defined the man.

Tom slowly worked his way in, even though he could have slammed me with all his strength. He kept it slow and steady, driving me to a crescendo of need. I was swollen. I was dripping. I was on the verge of begging. My nipples were hard and my legs were trembling and my moans were automatic, something I could no longer control. I was entirely at Tom's mercy, and he knew it.

By the time he did push all the way home, I was thrusting back against him, trying to take as much of him as I could. Tom held my hips steady and rocked deep, sometimes moving in circles, but never letting up with the pressure. He shifted just a bit and pushed harder, stroking me from another angle, trying hard to touch every part of me.

He slowly pulled out after long minutes of sweet torture. He held very still, his dick pointed right at the entrance of my pussy. He caressed me with slow circles. A drop of desire dripped down my thigh.

I gasped at the sudden shock of lube dripping between my cheeks.

Tom slid into my pussy slowly, all the while caressing between my cheeks with a finger, working the lube into me. Words sprang to my lips, things I was dying to say, but the only rule he had given me was to keep my silence. All I wanted to do was break into a litany of begging. By the time Tom was all the way in and his finger was teasing that tight little hole, I was biting down hard on my bottom lip, trying to keep the words from spilling out.

Then came the surprise of something pressing against the base of my spine: It was cold, and smooth, and obviously metal of some sort. I knew exactly what that was. Tom flipped a switch and the low hum rocketed through me.

'Remember what you told me you wanted? When we first became lovers?'

Tom slipped the vibrator through the wetness of the lube and teased my ass with it. He pulled his cock slowly out of me, until he was teasing both holes – one with himself, one with the toy. I caught my breath as he slowly slid the tip of the vibrator inside. He moved it around, stretching me with it, before he slowly pushed. Every slow inch was accompanied by an equal inch of himself. He was filling both holes, and I was delirious with the pleasure.

He pushed all the way in with one final thrust. I

shouted as the first orgasm gripped me. My whole body throbbed. Tom held very still until the sensation began to fade.

Then he drew back, pushed the speed on the vibrator up and began to fuck me with long hard strokes. The gentleness in him was rapidly disappearing. He could feel the vibrations of that toy all through his dick. He was closely watching what he was doing to me. I knew he wasn't going to let up.

Tom began to thrust harder. One hand dug into my hip, holding me steady – the other pressed against my ass, holding that toy in, moving it around whenever he got the urge. Soon Tom's thrusts were hard enough to rock my whole body. The ropes that bound my ankles and wrists began to tighten, to strain with the effort.

Suddenly, the whole bench rocked. The momentum of his thrusts was moving it underneath us. Soon the bench was straining against the bolts in the floor, protesting at the pressure that kept it in one place. Tom paused long enough to move closer to me, to brace himself – and then the next thrust came, and I couldn't even moan. It was hard enough to take my breath away.

Tom fucked me harder than he ever had.

I don't know how many times I came. Each one of them was a sudden burst of pleasure with no buildup before it. It was an endless stream of peaks and valleys, over and over. Tom thrust so hard the weight bench was letting out groans of its own.

Tom slowly pulled out of my pussy. He pulled the toy out as well. Another toy – some sort of dildo – slipped into the place Tom had been.

Tom pressed his cock against my ass and pushed. He slid straight in. The small flicker of pain barely registered before Tom was fucking me again.

This was what I had asked for weeks ago, while I rode him on this bench and asked him to replace all the negative memories with ones of our own making.

He held the toy in my pussy while he rode me. The weight bench rocked with every thrust. My ass burned. My pussy burned, too. My breasts bounced. The weights chimed merrily with the rhythm. My wrists and ankles were chafed from the ropes. Tom was completely lost in his own world even as he fucked me, and for the first time I wondered: if I used the safe word, would he even hear me?

Tom's final thrust was deep and solid. The bolts on the floor squealed in protest. Tom came without a sound, but I felt him – it was hot and wet and almost burned deep within me. He ground against me for a long moment, then slumped down on the bench with startling suddenness. I called his name.

'Tom? Are you OK?'

'I'm OK,' he whispered. He slowly slipped the toy out of me. His hand came up to caress my thigh. My whole being was focused on the gentleness of his fingertips. Tom lazily reached forwards and loosened the bonds around my wrists until I could slip out of them myself.

There was no hurry. What we had done was deserving of patience, now that it was all over. I pulled my wrists free and, instead of untying my ankles, I lay down on the bench, pushing back against Tom. He rested his head on the small of my back. Together we lay there in the dim light, breathing hard, our hearts pounding.

'I love you,' I said softly.

Tom chuckled against my back. 'You had better,' he said.

Now that the adrenaline was ebbing away, the aches and pains were evident. I thought about the first time he tied me to it, the things he did then, and how sore I was when we were finished. I was becoming accustomed to his body, to the things he liked. Things felt different now; I knew Tom better, and I knew my own body even better than that.

'Bullet for your thoughts?' he asked.

'I was just thinking that I might be able to handle this hard-core submission thing.'

Tom laughed then, a weak sound that told me just how tired he was. 'You've always been able to handle it. You just needed somebody to show you.'

I slowly untied my ankles. Tom kissed my spine, one inch at a time, until he was hovering over me. He kissed my neck slowly, lingering, until I was tingling from head to toe.

'You are full of contradictions,' I whispered. 'You can be so gentle and then you can be almost violent. I love that about you.'

He kissed the back of my head. 'You just love me for the sex.'

'That, too.'

He stood and wrapped his arms around my middle to help me up. I was shaking and my knees were weak, but I was more than able to stand up under my own power. Tom looked down at me for a long time.

'You've changed,' he said.

'Yes.'

'It's your fault.'

He snickered as he kissed my forehead.

'Let's go to bed,' I said.

Up there in the bedroom, I curled into him. He stroked my hair. We both slipped into sleep, and the last thought on my mind – the only thought on my mind at all – was that I was a very lucky woman.

11

It was two weeks of absolute bliss. Tom worked on the weekends, gone from Friday to Monday, and I spent that time glued to my computer, working more than I had ever worked in my life. I was suddenly inspired. The words flew from my mind onto the page and sometimes I would wake in the morning and not remember a certain turn of phrase or paragraph. It had flowed that easily. Tom's devotion deserved much of the credit, for my work improved in direct proportion to my sensual confidence.

During the weekdays, we were like a couple that had been together for years. We did little things together, took small trips, spent time watching television and occasionally went out to dinner, but more often than not we were in the kitchen, making something at home while listening to the evening news. My clothes had found their way into his closet, and my home hadn't seen much of me at all. We were both more comfortable out in the wilderness.

And the sex – it was better than it had ever been.

Then came the phone call.

I was at my home on a sunny Tuesday afternoon, putting a few necessities into boxes. Tom and I were gradually moving everything over to his house, even if neither of us had put it into words. We could hardly stand to spend a night apart, so when he was home I was always right there with him, lying in his bed, cooking in his kitchen, wandering in his forest. His home was the more comfortable one, and I fit into it as though I had always been there.

I was almost done, almost out the door, when the phone rang.

Michael.

I knew who it was before I looked at the caller ID. In the same way I had always had a sixth sense when it came to Michael, I knew. It was something I had once joked about, how strange it was that I could anticipate his calls. This time I wished I was wrong.

I picked up the phone before I could convince myself otherwise.

'Where have you been?' he said warmly. 'I've been worried about you.'

Despite my admonitions to myself, my heart leaped in my chest.

Stop that, I warned myself. Stop that right now.

'I've been busy,' I said. It wasn't a lie. 'How have you been?'

Hearing his voice was like a lifeline to a world that I knew was almost dead and gone. Even as he talked, telling me about his son and his truck and his job, I was wondering where he really had been. Had he been with her? Had he been seeing anyone? Had he been trawling those Internet dating sites, like he used to?

It was none of my business, but I wondered anyway.

'You're too quiet,' he said to me after a while. He was reading my mind in that maddening way he always could. 'Talk to me, Kelley.'

I didn't mean to ask. It just popped out. 'Are you dating anyone?'

The silence was so complete, a pin drop would have sounded like a gunshot. Michael cleared his throat. 'Would it matter?' he asked.

The old frustrations welled up in me. Why couldn't he ever answer a question head-on? Why did he have to do that thing he always did, the dodging, the question answered with a question, the half-truths that were never a lie, but never quite accurate, either?

'It matters,' I said calmly, giving away nothing of the anger I felt.

'No, I'm not dating anyone,' he said. His voice took on a sanctimonious tone. 'But we're not together any more. You broke up with me, remember?'

'I think it was the other way around,' I said.

'No, it wasn't. You asked me a question, I answered honestly, and you didn't like what you heard. You told me it was over.'

The anger flared up, and this time I couldn't hide it. 'I asked you if all the problems we were having were about her. I asked you if you would fuck her again. And you said yes. Did you expect me to just roll over and take that?'

Michael sighed. 'No. But I was honest.'

'You should have been honest with me from the beginning. You weren't over her. Why did you break my heart? Was I an experiment to see if you could move on? Is that what it was?'

I knew the anger was quickly approaching the point of breaching emotional levees. I wanted to hurt him with my words, as badly as he had hurt me with his confessions. He knew it, and so was careful with his answers.

'No. That wasn't what it was. I thought I was over her.'

'Are you over her now?' I asked, and damned myself immediately for doing it.

'No.'

The anger overflowed. 'How you could trade me in for a whore like that –'

Click.

Michael had hung up on me.

I stared at the phone in sheer surprise. He had hung up on me?

Then the reason occurred to me, and the anger became raging fury. He hung up on me because I had said something bad about his precious bitch-on-a-pedestal. He was too caught up in his fantasy world to see her for what she really was.

And he was attacking me for telling the truth. My goodness, wasn't that the pot calling the kettle black?

I dialed his number.

'What?' he snapped on the first ring.

'Don't you ever hang up on me for saying how I feel about that woman,' I growled.

'She's not a whore. I don't appreciate you calling her one.'

'You just can't see her for what she really is.'

'Look,' he said, exasperated, 'I've got to go.'

'How could you do this?' I asked. I was falling back through time, remembering that night he had torn my world apart. I was remembering the pain that was like a physical blow, the way he had never apologized, not once, for leading me on for months and months. It all came back in a vivid rush.

'I want my life back, dammit!' I hollered.

Michael sat on the other end of the line in stunned silence.

'I was so happy,' I said, trying hard not to cry. 'I was never as happy as I was then, when I was with you.'

'You're not as happy now, with Tom?' Michael growled, and a furious blush flooded my face. It was confusion and anger and sadness and shame, all rolled into one. He knew how far things with Tom had gone? No. No, he couldn't possibly.

'You don't know what it has been like,' I said.

'I really have to go,' Michael said then, and his voice was filled with jealousy. The shock of that rocked me to my core. Jealousy? Where had that come from?

'Michael?'

'Look. If I say anything else we will both regret it.'

I sat in silence. A tear slid down my cheek.

'I'll call you later,' he said, and then I was listening to the empty dial tone.

I dropped the phone. It clattered on the floor, flipped over on its face, and obscured the caller ID that would still have his name on it. I covered my face with my hands and slumped into the chair.

He was jealous. It was more than evident in the dripping anger that laced his words. And if he was jealous . . .

'Stop that,' I said out loud. 'Don't go down that road. You're too smart for that. You know it's over and you know you need a man who will put you first. You need a man like Tom.'

Tom's name seemed to hang in the air. The first shards of guilt wormed their way into my head. How could I want Michael back after all this? Why did I let his voice get to me the way he always had? Why didn't I have more respect for that man in the cabin across town, the one who was waiting patiently for me to come back?

The tears came then, and I didn't know which one of us I was crying for – Michael, Tom, or myself.

I cried the whole time I was packing that box, preparing things to take to Tom's house. I cried as I coiled the water hose in the backyard and brushed leaves from the picnic table. I ignored the hellos from the neighbors and instead went back into the house, locked the door, and slid down it until I was sitting on the floor. I buried my face in my hands and cried, this time with an edge of hysteria that frightened me.

'This has to stop,' I said out loud. 'This has to stop.'

That is the same thing Tom said later that night, when I told him what had happened. Sitting there on the porch as dusk made its way towards us, I told him everything, certain now that full disclosure was the only way to get past this and make our relationship work. I spilled the whole story and, when I described that edge of hysteria that had frightened me so badly, he reached forwards and took my hands.

'You need to go away,' he said.

'God, Tom, it can't be that bad –'

He shushed me with a fingertip. We both knew our relationship would begin to deteriorate even before it had a chance to truly begin, and that was thanks to the man I couldn't get out of my head. The parallels between Michael and me were becoming clear. He had sacrificed our relationship for a woman he couldn't forget; was I now going to do the same thing with Tom? Was I going to put him through the same kind of pain?

I absolutely could not do that.

'Maybe I could take a vacation,' I said through my tears. 'To a beach somewhere. To clear my head. What do you think?'

Tom nodded, and there were tears in his eyes, too.

'Why do I feel like this is a separation?' I asked.

'Because it is.'

I moved into Tom's arms. The kiss for comfort soon became a raging fire.

I couldn't get his shirt off fast enough. He ripped it over his head and before his hands came down, I was halfway out of my own clothes. The swing moved too much, so we abandoned it for the hardness of the porch floor. My jeans were caught on one leg and Tom's jeans were still on, but neither of us cared.

He bit down hard on the back of my neck as he slammed into me from behind. I braced myself on the wide boards, my knees burning against the unfinished wood as I rocked back against him. His hand tangled in my hair and he yanked hard, making me squeal in something halfway between protest and delight. I reached underneath us and stroked him every time he pulled out. Our bodies made lewd sucking sounds. I played with his balls and finally squeezed them, silently urging him to give me what was in them.

Tom uttered words that made no sense while he fucked me hard enough to force the breath out of me. His final few thrusts drove me to the floor, and then he was above me, thrusting straight down while my fingers found my clit. I was ready to go off like a rocket. I just needed him to go off first.

'Shoot that load inside me,' I growled. 'You know how bad I want that big cock to explode deep in me, don't you? Give it to me, you son of a bitch!'

Tom cried out when he came. The throbbing of it went through me and set my heart racing. Even as my own orgasm tipped me into the realm of pleasure, I ground against him and reveled in each pump of his cock.

Neither of us spoke for a long while. Neither of us moved. By the time my breathing was back under control, Tom was ready for more. Every muscle was primed and ready, and he was thrusting shallowly. His cock felt as though it had no intentions of giving up.

'Go down on me,' I demanded.

Tom didn't hesitate. He grabbed my hip and pushed me over onto my side. I spread my legs for him and he dove right in. There was no foreplay and no teasing – he went straight to my center and latched onto my clit. I gasped and wriggled, far too sensitive to simply lie still under his attack, but Tom patiently followed my every move. He licked and sucked and then he delved deeper.

'Do you like the way you taste?' I asked.

Tom looked up at me in the growing darkness. 'I like the way we taste together,' he said.

'Show me.'

Tom slid up my body and licked my lips. I tasted both of us there, and the thrill of it turned me on enough to wrap my legs around him and guide him into me again. One thrust and he was home, and then we were at it hard and fast again, with no mercy in sight. Tom was slippery with sweat. My hands were hard on his back, and my nails dug in. Though my spine protested against that wooden floor, I didn't dare tell him to stop. He braced himself and went at me like a raging bull, and I met him with every ounce of strength I had.

There were no words – there wasn't enough breath for words. But there was the low grunt of satisfaction when I raked my nails down his chest and growled out his name. The sound of our fucking was loud and somehow hearing the evidence of what he had just left inside me turned us on even more. When I thought it would take a long time, Tom surprised me with a quick orgasm, a sudden shuddering moan. I held on and let him ride it out, kissing his slick shoulder and whispering naughty words in his ear.

Tom lay back and pulled me over on top of him. I looked down at him in the thin light of the moon. The stars were out by now, and the night birds had begun to call to one another, a litany of excitement in the darkness.

'I'm impressed,' I teased. 'You're acting like a teenager.'

'Fuck me like one,' he challenged with a grin.

I slid off him. I licked my way down his chest, pausing at each nipple to tease it until he squirmed, then my tongue slid down his belly. I swallowed him into my mouth with one long suck, not taking any time or finesse, attacking him with the same kind of sexual vigor he had used on my clit. There was my own musky and sweet taste, blended with his darker one. I bobbed up and down on him and he responded instantly, thrusting up into my mouth and moaning.

'Fuck me, oh, God, Kelley. Fuck me,' he chanted, over and over.

Amazingly, he was approaching orgasm again. His cock was throbbing harder in my mouth. His body was shaking. His muscles were tensing, and his hands were fists of pleasure above his head. Being still was a struggle, and he was losing.

I slid my lips down his cock and sucked hard as I pulled up. I scraped his head with my teeth. Tom erupted into my mouth with a shout of surprise. He tasted different this time, strangely bitter, but I swallowed every drop while he panted there on the porch floor.

I licked my lips and sat up. Tom lay very still, catching his breath and watching me with dark, satisfied eyes.

'Three times,' I mused, and shook my head in amazement.

He surprised me when he said, 'I'm not done yet.'

'You're not?'

'Not by a long shot. And, when I can't fuck you with my body any more, I'm going to use my hand. Or a toy. Or a cucumber out of the garden. I'll pick it myself.'

I smiled sadly. 'I will be back, Tom. I'll come back home.'

The silence hung between us for a few long moments.

'Home,' he repeated softly.

I lay down beside him. His chest was broad and hard under my head as I rested on him and listened to his heartbeat.

'Home,' I agreed.

'You had better come back, Kelley,' Tom said, and this time the tears were very clear in his voice. 'You had better come home. You belong here now, and I'm not going to let that bastard take you away.'

It was the first time Tom had ever said anything negative about Michael. I turned my face into his chest and breathed deeply of his skin. He smelled like cotton and clean sweat. He smelled familiar. How I cherished that man – but, until I was free of old ghosts, there was no way he would ever know how much.

'I love you,' I whispered.

Tom's arm tightened around me, and he let out a sob. 'Oh, Jesus – Kelley – come back to me.'

'I promise, Tom. I promise.'

That night in bed, we didn't make love again. What

we did was much more fitting to what we were going through. We lay together and watched the moon move across the sky, and we talked.

Our discussions weren't the romantic kind. They were somehow more important, because we were now talking about things that had molded us. I told him more about Michael, about how we had met, about the things we had done together before the negatives began to creep into our relationship. I told him more about my mother and father, and the way their relationship had affected every day of my life since. I told him everything, the good and the bad.

For the first time, Tom told me about his tours in the military. He told me about his time in a place he either would not or could not name, and the hellish few days there, when he was cut off from all supplies and half his unit, while the rest of them were held down by enemy fire in a bombed-out building. Snipers were everywhere, and there came a moment when he was so weakened by hunger he considered just making a run for it – but two of his buddies were already down, and he was the one left in command.

'Is that where you got the scar on your leg?' I asked.

Tom nodded against my forehead.

'What happened?'

Tom lay very quietly for a long while, almost so long I thought he had fallen asleep. When he spoke, his voice was hollow, and I knew a very big part of him was no longer with me, but back there in that country on the other side of the world.

'One of my guys – his name was Richard – the stress was too much. He snapped. He was jumping at shadows anyway. We all were. But this was different. Something fell in another room, a brick maybe, or a piece of wood, something simple like that, not a threat – but Richard just started shooting, and he didn't stop.'

I took his hand in mine. The world Tom was talking about was as foreign to me as the storybooks about unicorns I had read when I was a little girl.

'He shot you,' I said, prompting him to go on.

Tom was silent for a long time. 'I wish I had a cigarette now,' he said. 'I used to smoke, you know? In the military. Everybody did. When I came back here, the cigarettes tasted wrong. I stopped cold turkey and I never even crave one, until I'm talking about things like this.'

I rose from the bed. I was familiar with Tom's house by now, and I knew what was in the top drawer of the dresser. I found the pack of Marlboro Reds and the lighter, and brought them back to bed with me.

Tom sat up and smiled. He shook one out of the pack and I held the lighter. The first drag made him cough.

'Told you it had been a long time,' he said. 'That damn pack is probably three years old.'

I watched as he tapped ashes carefully on the back of the box. Watching Tom smoke made him seem like a stranger. He finished half the cigarette before he spoke again.

'I shot back,' Tom said.

I didn't understand.

'What do you mean?' I asked, though, as soon as the words left my mouth, I realized that I already knew.

'He had hundreds of rounds,' Tom said slowly. 'He was firing at everything that moved. He killed Saunders, and then he hit Dempsey in the arm, almost killed him too. Dempsey. That's my friend Jake's daddy. You need to meet Jake one day.'

Tom drew on the cigarette. He held it in front of him and watched the amber glow as it burned down.

'It was him or me, you know? I was OK with that as long as the other guy wasn't an American named Richard, from some little town in Indiana with a wife and two kids at home.'

I pulled my knees up to my chest and buried my face in my arms. Tom exhaled towards the ceiling and watched the smoke dissipate into the darkness.

'He was my best friend over there,' Tom mused. 'It's hell to see your best friend go down because somebody else shot him. But it's beyond hell to have to do the shooting yourself.'

I shook my head, uncertain of what to say.

'We got out of there four hours later. Four hours. Can you believe that? Richard goes nuts and I put a bullet in him and then four hours later the choppers arrive, and they are blasting the whole place to kingdom come. They mowed it flat to get us out. Four hours,' Tom said again, and this time he looked at me with a haunting so deep that it made me shudder with something very much like fear.

'They gave me a medal,' he said. 'Should I be proud of that?'

Tom crushed the cigarette savagely on the bedside table, leaving a black mark.

'There were questions, of course. And everybody said the same thing, of course. Dempsey made it, but he lost his arm, and you know damn good and well what his take on the whole situation was. The military decided I had done something brave and good and they gave me a medal for saving the lives of the other guys in the unit. That's when I learned that most medals don't mean a damn. Nobody ever truly knows the story behind them, and the ones who do know don't tell.'

Tom set the box of Marlboros on the table.

'I got out. Medical discharge, thanks to the bullet in the leg. I came back home and went crazy for a while. Then I strapped on a gun and started protecting people.'

Now I understood.

'That's why Melissa left you,' I said. 'That's how it happened.'

'I went crazy for a while,' he repeated. 'It wasn't her fault.'

'But it wasn't yours, either,' I said.

Tom pulled me into his arms.

'You come back,' he growled. 'You hear me? I know what demons are. I know better than you can ever imagine. You get rid of that man and then you come back to me. I don't want to pay for someone else's sins, Kelley.'

Long after Tom had fallen asleep, I lay awake. I stared at the Marlboros on the bedside table.

The next morning, Tom drove me to the airport.

The last-minute flight was booked by an understanding travel agent, and there I was, holding my computer printout in one hand and my carry-on bag in the other. Tom and I stood near the ticket counter, looking at each other while the minutes ticked away.

'Are you sure you have everything?' he asked.

'I don't need much.'

'You can buy things there, if you forgot to pack them.'

'Yes.'

'Do you have a calling card?'

'Won't you let me call you collect?'

'Kelley –'

I shushed him with a kiss. By the time we were done, we were both breathing hard and fighting back the tears.

'I have to do this. I have to make the hurt go away,' I said, repeating the same thing I had said over and over during the drive to the airport.

'I know.'

'You do, don't you?'

He nodded and braved a smile.

'Please be here when I get back. Please.'

'How could I not be here?' he asked.

One more kiss, then I turned to walk away before I

changed my mind. Every step felt like a separation from some vital part of myself. What had I been thinking? Was I crazy? How could I walk away from him? Wasn't he enough to help me work through this?

I turned around.

Tom had vanished.

12

The plane touched down right on time. Instead of a busy condo, the travel agent had lucked into a small house available for rent by the day. Secluded on its own inlet, the house was still within walking distance of small seafront bars and a few shops that carried necessities. It was an island paradise – and I was here alone.

I was determined to leave there alone, too. I would leave Michael there on the beaches, and come back to Tom with a clear and free heart. He deserved no less.

Soon after leaving the plane, I climbed into the small boat that would take me to the outer reaches of the island. The man at the helm looked at me with knowing eyes. He was deeply tanned from a life under the hot island sun. His eyes were dark, almost black, and his hair was so long it was shaggy, bleached white from the rays. The muscles in his arms bulged as he turned the oar in his hand and dipped it into the water.

'Welcome,' he said.

We didn't speak on the way to the house. He looked out at the water as he rowed. When the water became too shallow he climbed out of the boat – and suddenly stopped, staring at the horizon. He gestured out to sea, and I followed his gaze.

A dolphin rose from the water and let out a snickering call. The gray body shimmered in the light.

'They usually don't come this close to the island,' he said. I stared at the place where the dolphin had vanished. 'Do you know what we say about dolphins who come that close?'

I looked back at him. His eyes were serious.

'What?'

'We say that they are coming to care for someone. Dolphins are very protective, you know. They are very loyal as well. We say, when a dolphin comes this close, they have intentions of protecting. Imparting wisdom, perhaps.'

I smiled. 'You're making that up.'

'Am I?'

He hauled the boat closer to the shore. I waded up onto the beach. The sand was white, and the house up on the small bluff was weather-beaten, the old boards of the porch almost as mellow as the sands below it. It wasn't much larger than an apartment, but it was secluded and quaint and exactly what I needed.

'What is your name?' I asked the man. He was climbing back into the boat.

'Adrian.'

'How do I contact you? When I want to leave the island?'

He pointed down at the bar, a small structure barely visible from where we were. 'The man at the bar, he knows how to get me. You go down there and call for me, and I will come back and get you.'

'Just like that?'

'Yah,' he said, and for the first time I heard the native island accent. 'Just like that.'

I watched him maneuver the boat out into the water. He gave me a small salute. 'Watch for the dolphins.'

I studied Adrian until he was a dot on the far horizon. I looked for the dolphins long after the tiny boat was gone, but they never showed themselves.

The house was unlocked, the key on a string beside the front door. I had paid in advance, and probably wouldn't see the owner of the house at all.

I opened the door and stepped inside.

The small house was cozy, furnished with weather-beaten furniture that would be as much at home outside near the ocean as under the roof. The floors creaked as I walked over them. Wide and low windows faced the sea, covered with a thin crust of sea spray. The world outside looked grainy and distant. The roar of the water filled the little rooms.

I found the single bedroom with a small bed, perfectly white sheets and a bedside table that held a lamp and a stack of books. The pillows were generous and abundant. A small chair in the corner was worn and the cushion in it was frayed. The kitchen was small and old-fashioned, but the fridge was stocked with beer and other beverages, plus a huge box of Popsicles. I smiled and picked out an orange one before I ventured onto the porch and looked out at the waves.

Birds wheeled overhead, calling to one another. They landed on the roof with a scratching sound. The swing creaked ominously when I sat down on it, but it held my weight. The armrests were worn smooth as silk. I wondered how many people had been here before me.

I slipped off my sandals and put my foot on the railing. The sun peeked out from behind a cloud and the birds sang from above me.

I missed Tom.

It was a good sign, that I was missing him instead of missing Michael. It meant I was focusing on the man I had instead of the man I had lost.

I sat there until the sun started to lower itself in the sky. The colors sprang forwards, vibrating with life and flooding the whole world with color. The blue faded into red and the red faded into deep purple. The birds began to silence themselves. The ocean roared even louder when purple faded to black, as if celebrating the passing of the sun.

A distant and throbbing beat came from the strip of bars just down the beach. Not a single soul had disturbed me out here, and I assumed it was because everyone else on the island was over there.

I began walking in that direction.

The bar was surprisingly small for the number of people who were attracted to it. The bartender had a friendly banter for everyone, laughing and joking in his island lilt. He slipped my money into his pocket, slid my longneck across the bar and gave me a jolly wink.

I found a table almost by itself, sitting in the sand off the boardwalk. There were two chairs. I sat in one and stared at the other as I sipped the beer. The first sip, so rich and heady with flavor, made me almost light-headed.

'Would you like some company?'

I looked up at the man standing at my table. He didn't have strong features. He was the kind of man who would fade into the background. But he did have an intriguing look about him – a certain shape of his face and look in his eyes that made you wonder exactly where he was from, and just how exotic a place that might be. His hair was black, and his eyes were almost as dark. He was richly tanned and fit in the way of men who don't work out because they don't have to. He was lean but not muscular, handsome but not overtly so.

I realized I was staring. The blush lit up my cheeks, and I was grateful for the moonlight.

'I'm not sure,' I said. 'I think I might need some time alone tonight.'

He smiled down at me, showing a flash of perfectly straight white teeth. 'Next time, then.'

He walked away and the darkness swallowed him. I took another sip of my beer and watched the people at the bar. There were young couples who couldn't keep their hands off one another. There was a woman who kept staring at the shiny ring on her finger, as if she couldn't believe it was there. Newlyweds. When they looked my way, I saluted them with my beer, and they saluted right back.

There were men with tan lines where their wedding bands had been. There were women with long sad faces who were drinking a little too much and a little too fast. There were businessmen with phones anchored to their ears, working overtime even here in paradise. For a few minutes I watched a man doing paperwork on a wide wicker table in front of him. His briefcase was open, papers of all colors peeking out from the corners. His face looked tense in the light from the small lamp in front of him.

I drained the beer while I watched him. He glanced up once and caught my gaze. I was rewarded with a scowl before he went back to his work.

The bartender appeared beside my table, materializing as if by magic. He set down another longneck, and I put down my money. It was gone and then he was too, going from one table to another with the speed of a seasoned bar veteran.

The first sip of the second beer made me feel pleasantly buzzed. I was probably going to get drunk. And why not? The house was within walking distance. I had nowhere to be. I drank half the beer in one long drag.

It was much later – and several beers later – when he came back. Mr Exotic. I smiled up at him as he looked down at me. He wasn't all that tall, but from this vantage point he looked like a tower of temptation.

Tower of temptation? I giggled at my own thoughts.

'You're drunk,' he said.

'Yep.'

'I'm getting there. Would you like some company now?'

I shrugged. He gathered two more beers from the bartender and came back to the table. His long body slumped in the chair as he looked at the world through dispassionate eyes. He ran his fingers through the sand beside him – swish, whirl, do it all again.

He wasn't wearing a wedding band.

'Where are you from?' I asked.

He took a long drink of the beer in front of him. 'Brazil.'

I nodded, as if I had known this all along. 'What's your name?'

'Daniel.'

'That doesn't strike me as a Brazilian name. I suppose I expected something else. Like Ronaldo.'

'The soccer player?'

'Is that what he is?'

Daniel smiled. 'Maybe you're drunker than I thought.'

'I doubt I can walk back to the house without drowning.'

He nodded in sympathy. He was drinking those beers as though there was no limit. I watched as he drained the second one and signaled the bartender for a third. His eyes wandered across everyone and everything. He stared at a bikini-clad woman as she walked by. He seemed to be taking in everything and impressing it on his memory.

It suddenly reminded me of Michael.

'What do you do for a living?' I asked.

He thought about his answer for a moment. 'I could lie,' he said. 'You would never know.'

Now he reminded me even more of Michael.

'Then don't tell me,' I said to Daniel. I pushed the rest of my beer away.

'I'm a painter,' he said. 'Not famous yet. Notorious, perhaps.'

'Notorious for what?'

He answered me with his eyes. He took a long pull of his beer and watched me over the bottle. I deliberately looked away and followed the moon with my eyes.

'I could paint you,' he said.

'You could, or you will?'

He smiled. 'I will. But with your permission, it could be a work of art instead of a memory.'

'You want me to pose for you?'

'I want you to sit for me. You pose for a photographer. You sit for a painting.'

'Ah.'

'I would love to put you on a canvas,' he said.

He was studying me in the moonlight, his eyes sliding over me and making me blush, even with the heat of the alcohol. Excusing himself, he went to the bar. He came back with a pristine white napkin and a stubby pencil. He started to draw. Still I refused to look, even though I knew what he was doing.

'You are so pretty,' he murmured.

The stars seemed to twinkle here, free from pollution clouding the way. The skies were alive with those stars, even with the intense light of the moon. Had I ever seen the moon so bright?

Daniel tossed the napkin to my side of the table. I looked down when it brushed against my bare arm. What I saw made me stare.

That was definitely me, carved onto the white napkin in careful pencil strokes. I was laughing up at someone, my smile big and my eyes sparkling. My hair was lush and full, spreading out behind me in rich waves.

I looked up at Daniel. He tipped his beer at me.

'That's amazing,' I said.

'That's you.'

I picked up the napkin and studied it. He even had the eyebrows right. 'You really are an artist. I believe you.'

'You're lovely,' he said, and I blushed at the earnest note in his voice. 'You have neat compact features. You're not a classic beauty. Classic beauty is cold and refined. You're more approachable than that. I like looking at you.'

I stood up from my chair. The world swayed. Daniel took another drink of his beer.

'Thank you,' I said. 'I think I should go home now.'

He reached out and touched my arm. The touch was gentle, a caress, as light as the strokes on that napkin. 'You think about sitting for me. I'll be around here tomorrow. I would love to paint you in moonlight, the way you look right now.'

He pressed the napkin into my hand. 'Incentive,' he said.

Daniel's eyes followed me all the way down the beach.

The walk to the house seemed much longer than the walk to the bar. I prudently stayed away from the water. I berated myself for the evening. I was supposed to be here to think things through, thinking about Tom and me and, most of all, how to get Michael out of my head – and instead I was getting drunk and spending too much money and wandering around alone at night, thinking about the water and the beach house and illustrations and eyes so deep brown they appeared to be black. What was wrong with me?

I climbed the porch steps. It took more of an effort than I wanted to admit. When I paused to look over the railing, I saw them – the couple down on the beach.

The moonlight shone on their bodies but obscured their faces. Their few scraps of clothing were discarded on the sand beside them. They were rolling around down there, the water sometimes coming up to lap at them, threatening to steal the bikini that glowed pink in the evening light. She was on top of him. Her breasts bounced with every motion. Her soft cries echoed over the water. He was thrusting up to meet her every now and then, putting more power into the fuck.

The image of Tom flooded my mind. I remembered the marks I had left on him, the marks of my teeth on his skin, the way he loved to look at those places in the mirror when he thought I wasn't watching. I thought of the thin pale scratches on his back, and the way he shuddered with pleasure every time I drew my nails along his skin.

I should have gone in the house. I should have left them to their privacy, their intimate moment with the sand and the moon and the sea and each other.

I sat down on the porch and watched.

His hands came up to cup her breasts. They were high and tight, smaller than mine. I wished I could see more of him. Did he look like Tom? Was he just as muscular? His skin was dark, even in the moonlight.

The couple rolled over. He rose above her and lifted her legs to his shoulders. The wet slapping sounds carried all the way up to my place on the porch. He drove into her, hard and fast. I squeezed my legs together, trying to ignore the ache of my body. I needed a fuck like that. I needed Tom here with me.

The man looked up at the moon and growled deep in his chest. The sound was faint, but unmistakable, the sound of a man completely lost in pleasure. The woman responded with her own faint cry. When she bucked under him, he pitched forwards over her, breathing hard.

Soon they were on their feet, giggling. He raced naked towards the water and grabbed the bikini top she had almost lost to the ocean. I watched without any shame at all as they got dressed there on the beach. The man tossed his head and brushed the sand from his hair, and with a jolt I realized I had seen him before.

It was the man who had brought me here from the plane. The man who had pointed out the dolphins. Adrian.

I chuckled quietly and buried my face against my knees. I had just watched him have sex, and in a few days he would come back to this very beach to pick me up in his little boat and carry me across the island to a plane. What would I say to him when I saw him? Hey, dude, good job out there?

I got up as quietly as I could and let myself quickly into the house, lest my laughter give away the fact that they had an audience. In the bedroom, I kicked my travel

181

bag to the floor. My clothes went the same way. I fell into bed seconds later, suddenly exhausted despite what I had just seen on the beach.

I was asleep almost instantly.

The morning sunlight woke me. It was a cruel moment, lying there in paradise with a headache the size of the island itself. I reached blindly for the window, feeling for the shades, or the curtains, anything to cut off the light that dared fall across my bed. I opened my eyes a small crack and looked up. The window was completely unadorned. Not even a shutter to close. I rolled over and stuck my head under the pillow, but sleeping again was impossible. The drumbeat in my head had taken care of that.

I rolled over – slowly, carefully – and looked at the clock. It was nine in the morning. I instinctively began to look for a phone, but I knew even as I started to do it that there wasn't any point. There was no phone service here. My cell phone certainly didn't work.

I couldn't call Tom.

I looked up at the ceiling. Someone had painted stars over a deep-blue background. Why hadn't I noticed that the day before? I studied them until the white spots began to merge into each other. I closed my eyes.

Tom would be working right now, in a venue in some far-flung town, wandering the site and finding all the security nightmares. Tonight he would be wearing his suit and his earpiece and moving so carefully and quietly among the people that hardly anyone would notice his existence.

Except the groupies.

My eyes popped open. My head throbbed harder than before.

This was part of why I had left, why I had come here alone. It was a test, not for Tom, but for myself. He had never given me a reason not to trust him, and now I was forcing myself into a situation where I couldn't call to check. I couldn't go to his house and find him. I couldn't get on a plane and get there before the show was over. I had to trust him. There was no other choice.

But there were so many groupies.

'Stop it,' I said aloud.

Tom had been faithful from day one. In fact, he had been faithful during a time when he didn't have to be, during a time when we were nothing more than fuck buddies who were hoping for something more down the road. I could have just as easily fallen into bed with someone else during that time, and Tom couldn't have said a word. Since we had become a couple, he hadn't given me any reason to doubt him. Even in a situation with so much opportunity, he had come home to me. He had done it consistently, every single time.

There was no one else.

So why couldn't I get that through my head?

My fears concerning relationships were going overboard. What had happened with Michael shouldn't have damaged my trust that badly, should it?

But then I remembered the shock of knowing he wanted someone else, that he would have her if she gave him the slightest chance, that he would disregard our relationship for what would be nothing more than a fuck with no strings, no promises – and the betrayal of that was just as bad as if he had truly had her.

I deserved better than that.

The drumbeat in my head sped up. My stomach heaved. I lunged for the bathroom, every step shaky. I thought I would throw up, but I didn't. Thank goodness for small mercies.

The bathroom floor was cool as I sat down and looked up at the windows. I thought about the couple on the beach. My thoughts turned to the painter. A spike twisted in my forehead when I did it.

I found my shorts on the floor in the hallway. In the

pocket was the napkin. The woman in the illustration looked so happy. Was that really what he saw? Or what he wanted to see?

I turned the napkin over. There was a number. I stared at it for a while.

That afternoon, I had recovered enough to wander out on the beaches. I walked through the scrub brush and scared a small animal, a pretty little thing that looked like a chipmunk. It reminded me of the forest around Tom's cabin, and made me smile even while it made me miss him more than ever. This was turning out to be a very long trip, and it was only the second day.

I spent many hours there on that shore, going over things in my head. I rehashed all the arguments Michael and I had, all the things he had said that cut to the bone, all the things I had tried not to think about. The old sense of panic welled up in me, the old fear of losing him – and then I remembered that I already had lost him, and someone else probably had him now.

I wondered what else there was. What else didn't I know? I even let myself consider the possibility that he had been fucking around the whole time we were together. He had ample opportunity to do so. How could I know if everything else was true?

I skewered myself with the memories. I dove into the most horrible fights, the longest nights, the crying jags that made me sick before I wound up crying some more. I remembered those long nights of lying in bed and wondering where he was, knowing he was free to do what he wanted, while all my dreams had been shattered.

The loss of the dream was what hurt the most. I had so wanted to be the other half of the couple sitting on his porch decades later, in matching rocking chairs, looking out over his beloved mountains. I dreamed of having a lifetime with him.

Would I have a lifetime with Tom?

If my relationship with Michael could end so quickly, could I lose Tom so quickly, too?

I sank to my knees on the sand. I watched small sea creatures wandering just below the surface of the water.

I had to accept it: there were no answers. There were no certainties. It wasn't about trust any more; it was about a leap of faith.

Could I do that?

I stood up and walked back towards the bar.

I called Daniel from the small phone the bartender handed to me. It was a different man from the night before. This one was more businesslike, and barely gave me a glance as he slid the phone across the polished surface of the bar. I dialed the number and looked out over the water.

'Do you still want me to sit for a painting?' I asked.

I had decided, somewhere between the beach and the bar, that I would do something special for Tom. Maybe he would see it as a way of sharing in the experience of being down here in paradise. I would give it to him with a smile and tell him that, the whole time that painting was being created, I was thinking of him.

Daniel readily agreed, and asked where we should do it. I invited him to the little house, and he arrived within minutes.

'This is a beautiful place. The light is perfect. The windows are just high enough. Sit there, and don't move unless you have to. And, if you do, tell me first.'

Daniel was sitting in a chair in the middle of the living room. I had expected an easel, a case of paints and all the trappings of a painter, but he arrived with a small ornate box and a thin black folder. In the folder was thick high-quality paper. In the box were pencils of every color imaginable, charcoal that had been worn down to nubs, and fingerprints all over everything. He sat back in the chair and watched me as I moved around the house. Then he began to direct me, told me how to sit and where, drawing all the while, flipping through paper as though it cost nothing.

Finally he settled down to draw with an intensity that was almost unnerving. I wasn't a woman in the room any longer; I was a subject, one that had to be picked apart and put back together on that sheet of paper. His gaze was filled with creativity that bordered on passion, but it wasn't sexual in the least. I watched him right back, fascinated. This was a man at work.

I relaxed into the pose. I was lying down on the couch, one leg bent, one hand on my belly and the other above my head, twined into my hair. My dress was a simple sheath of the lightest blue. The light from the high window fell directly over me, a little too bright for my eyes, warming my skin.

Daniel paused in his work. He came forwards and arranged my hair with a gentle hand, moving the locks here and there. He looked at me with a critical eye.

'Smile,' he demanded.

Surprised by the sudden order, I did as he asked. He winked.

'Perfect.'

Then he sat down on the chair and made only small comments about the light and the pose and the fact that he loved the color of my hair. The scratching of his pencils on the paper was sweet and comforting.

'This is good,' he said after long minutes of work.

'Is it?'

'Oh, yes. You were made to be captured.'

I smiled at the romantic sound of that. Daniel's eyes were alight with the thrill of what he was doing. He leaned forwards and studied me intently. His pencil was in constant motion.

I looked out the window. The ocean was rolling hard out there, heralding a storm that would probably come about sunset. I was looking forward to it. How would the world sound, in the middle of a storm out here, where the roar of the ocean would be so loud?

I wondered where Tom was right now. Was he thinking of me?

'OK,' Daniel said, and stood up.

I was shaken out of my thoughts. Birds called and wheeled outside. The ocean slammed harder against the shore.

'OK, what?'

Daniel smiled down at me. 'OK. I have enough for the day. I'm going to go back to the condo and paint a bit. I will be back tomorrow, if that is all right with you.'

I nodded, still somewhat dazed by the abrupt change in circumstance. 'Yes.'

'You are lovely to draw,' he said. 'Now I must go, and start to paint you as well.'

I watched as he packed up his little box with all the utensils of the artist. 'Can I see what you have done?' I asked.

'Tomorrow.'

When he should have headed for the door, he hesitated. He stepped over to the couch and looked down at me.

Daniel stood over me for a long moment, looking at my face. He was cataloging my features one at a time. A red blush stole over my face. He lifted a hand and arranged my hair one more time. His hand brushed mine and he let it linger there, finally looking into my eyes as he did it.

'You're beautiful,' he breathed.

The air between us suddenly crackled with tension. Daniel traced each one of my fingers with his calloused fingertips. He never took his eyes from mine. I was very aware of the length of his body, the heat of him standing so close to me, and the fact that, with just one small motion, either one of us could set something more into motion.

And no one would ever know.

As soon as that thought crossed my mind, the guilt flooded me. At the same time, as if on cue, Daniel leaned down and kissed me.

His lips were soft, his touch reverent. The guilt disappeared and what replaced it was a flare of desire that was on the verge of rage. I lifted my hands to his shoulders, and within seconds we were both on the couch. His leg immediately pressed between mine, riding that dress up my thighs. I ran my hands into his hair. His body felt entirely foreign and wickedly tempting.

I kissed him and forgot about everything – Tom and Michael and the ocean and the bar and what in the world I was going to do when I got back home.

Daniel's lips made their way down my throat. He wasn't gentle. Every inch was a nibble, then a pinch, then a small bite right there over my collarbone. Even as I arched into him, I pushed him away, afraid of evidence that would tell Tom what I had been doing here on this island. Daniel unbuttoned my dress and licked his way down the center of my chest. I was desperate for more, and spread my legs when he slipped his hand between them.

Then, something – perhaps it was a sound from outside, or the particular fall of sunlight, or the way Daniel moaned when he found me naked beneath the cotton – whatever it was, it stopped me cold. My heart began to pound with something other than desire. I pushed Daniel hard with my hands on his shoulders. He wasn't nearly as big or as strong as Tom, and the force was enough to push him off me.

'What's wrong?' he asked.

I shook my head, tears already starting, and bit my lip hard to keep from sobbing outright.

Daniel didn't move for a long moment. He looked down at me, watching my face, wondering what in the world he had done wrong. I hadn't tried to stop him; in fact, I had been a more than willing participant. And now I was crying?

'You didn't do anything wrong,' I whispered.

He sat up slowly, giving me time to pull my dress together. We sat on opposite ends of the couch and looked at each other. His eyes were concerned. I was sure mine were filled with a raging war.

'I don't know if I should apologize or not,' Daniel said helplessly, and then I felt even more guilty than I already did.

'No. Don't apologize. You did nothing wrong,' I said. The tears were already gone, replaced with a numbness that scared the hell out of me.

Daniel didn't know what to say, and I didn't blame him. He stood up from the couch and looked at me, uncertain where to put his hands, unsure of how to treat me now that the events had taken such a sudden turn.

'I'm all right,' I said, and my voice seemed to come from a far-away place, hollow and distant. 'I'm fine. Just go, please? I'm sorry I started something I couldn't finish. It isn't you. It's me.'

Daniel didn't move. 'You just gave me every cliché in the book,' he said.

'But they are all true.'

He nodded and picked up his box of instruments. I watched as he walked to the door and stepped outside without a second glance.

I curled up into a ball on the couch. This disconnected feeling was completely new to me.

So this was it. This was how it felt to cheat.

'It was just a kiss,' I said aloud. Some people might consider that less than cheating, but I knew myself and my heart. I knew what I had done.

I lay there until the sun went down. The storm blew into shore, and I listened as it rocked the house. My eyes were red and dry from the crying. My body ached, but it wasn't the sweet tender aching I was accustomed to feeling from Tom's hands. It was a deep heart-wrenching kind of ache, the kind that I thought might never go away.

I walked into the bathroom and looked at the mirror. The woman there was someone I didn't recognize.

Was it really that easy? Was that really how quickly it could happen?

So much for the pedestal I had put myself upon. I had always held up my faithfulness like a virtue no one else could touch. I had looked down upon those who found it impossible to be faithful – as though I had a monopoly on righteousness. I blushed scarlet at the thought of how pompous I had been. While I touted the fact that life was painted in shades of gray, I hadn't let that apply to myself. I had seen everything in hypocritical shades of black and white.

Some things were nothing but gray. Some things had no reason.

As soon as I realized that, I forgave Michael. Just like that. The pain and the anger and the hurt were still there, but it was all seen from a different perspective. How easy it was to make a mistake. How easy it was to walk into something you didn't expect. How easy to wade into the water and get unexpectedly caught in the hidden undertow.

I stared at myself in the mirror for a very long time. Then I walked out onto the porch and down the steps, into the rain, even though the lightning cracked overhead and the ocean roared its way halfway up my secluded beach. I stood there in the downpour and breathed deep, the air heavy with mist, my lungs catching too much of it, making me cough and gasp. The drops woke me up from what felt like a very long sleep. With every passing moment I felt more like the person I came here to find.

I stood there until the storm was over. My feet were

buried in wet sand. It was heavy, threatening to hold me there forever. I watched the skies until the clouds became softer, and eventually the moon came out, bathing everything in pale light. The stars were upside down here, different from the way they looked from Tom's porch. But they were still the same.

It was time to go home.

13

Just as it had in the islands, the plane landed right on time. The sun beat down on the runway. There hadn't been a single cloud in the sky during the whole flight. It was a good day for being out on the four-wheeler, or for taking the boat out on the water. I had thought of little else on the flight back, but now the doubts assaulted me.

Would Tom be there to pick me up?

What I had done there in that island paradise would hurt Tom so badly. I wasn't the kind of woman to cheat, and what I had done was enough to flood me with constant guilt. But what had happened in the islands was proof of what I really wanted.

I wanted Tom.

I sat in my seat while those around me pulled their belongings out of the overhead compartments. I had only the small bag on my lap. When there was a clearing in the aisle, I took a deep breath and made my way to the front, trying not to look over at the parking lots one last time for the sight of Tom's truck.

The flight attendant said goodbye with a plastic smile, and then I was walking down the ramp to the brightly lit terminal, where children were happily reunited with parents and busy executives headed straight to the luggage carousel. Lovers met each other and with kisses and hugs threw themselves into reunions. The occasional traveler wandered slowly towards the doors, in no particular hurry and with no one to meet.

I stood in the middle of the terminal. Alone.

Slowly I scanned every corner of the place, looking hard into the bookstores and the coffee huts, watching for any sign of Tom. I tried not to panic. He knew today was the day I would be back, but his voice over the phone had been so clipped, as if he already knew what I had done – though of course that was impossible. But the doubts still slammed me. Perhaps he wasn't going to be there to pick me up after all.

'Hey, stranger.'

I whirled around to see him walking towards me. His eyes were hidden by a baseball cap. His shirt was wrinkled, as though he had just woken up from a nap in the recliner. He strode towards me quickly, without an ounce of hesitation, and swept me up into his arms.

The guilt threatened to overwhelm me.

'I missed you so much,' I wailed, and Tom kissed me. I had to fight for breath. Other passengers walked past us and most smiled, seeing what they thought was a joyous reunion of two lovers who had been apart for far too long. And maybe it was that for Tom, after all – but for me it was an exercise in torture. I had the man I wanted, the man I had missed so much, but my actions on that island meant I could lose him before the night was over.

I wondered suddenly if there were any marks on me, any bruises that might give me away. I had berated myself in the bathroom mirror for so long, surely I would have seen them, but still there was a slim chance.

Tom hauled me hard against him and kissed my throat. I closed my eyes and listened to the conversations of thousands of people around us, the booming sound from the overhead speakers, the whine of planes outside the thick glass windows. Most of all I heard the tremble in his voice when he told me how much he had missed me.

'Let's get you home,' he murmured.

We held hands on the way out to the truck. Tom carried my bag and with his other hand kept his fingers linked so tightly with mine that my fingertips tingled.

We both remembered the way things had been left between us, and I was determined to make things right. It appeared he was, too.

I wondered how much forgiveness Tom had in him.

He kissed me at the truck, pushing me hard against the side of it, bracing himself with both hands on the bed. He kissed me with all the passion he had in him, and his body echoed the motion of his tongue. He was primed and ready and, if I would let him, he would have me right there, right in the middle of that massive parking lot, and bystanders be damned.

When I climbed into the truck, I pulled him in with me. The door slammed shut behind us. He had brought my truck, the one with the wide bench seat, and I slithered all the way up the leather. He settled right between my thighs.

'Just kiss,' I whispered.

And we did, his leg pressed high between my thighs and my hands all over him, necking like teenagers who had just gotten away from the parents. He kissed every inch of skin he could reach, every part of me that wasn't infuriatingly covered with clothing. He touched me underneath the fabric but didn't delve too far, knowing that the thrill was in the anticipation and the sweet desire, not in the race to get to the finish line.

'I missed you so bad,' Tom murmured. His breath was harsh and what was in his pants felt hard as a rock against my thigh. Spirals of pleasure shot through me, tightened my belly and made my heart race.

I slid my hands under his shirt. He groaned in approval. Already we were drawing stares from passersby and, though I really didn't care much, it was probably time to get moving before security came to investigate.

'Let's go home,' I whispered.

Tom chuckled against my throat before he rose up and let me wiggle out from underneath him. He slipped the keys into the ignition and took a deep breath to get his libido under control. His jeans were noticeably tight, and his face was flushed with the anticipation of getting home and getting into bed. I smiled at the way he looked.

'You look so young,' I said to him.

He revved the engine. 'You make me feel young,' he said.

I looked out the window and smiled, trying to fight back sudden tears.

'What's wrong, baby?'

I shook my head and looked at him. I didn't try to hide the emotion. Tom would look at them and think I was just that glad to be home. Surely he wouldn't see the guilt.

'I'm glad to be home,' I said, and it was the truth. I sidled up next to him, foregoing the seat belt for the touch of my thigh against his.

I thought about Michael as we rode. I knew it would be one of the last times I let him take my thoughts away from Tom. This was the kind of thing Michael had done – he had kept a secret from me, a secret quite like the one I had, until it had choked away everything that mattered. It had torn us apart from the inside out.

I would not do that to Tom. I had to tell him.

Soon.

But not right now.

'Listen, baby, I have to tell you something,' he said, and he sounded so excited that for a while I completely forgot about what had happened on the island. I gave Tom my full attention.

'Tell me.'

'I talked to David yesterday,' he said. 'I mean, really talked. We hadn't talked like that in a long time. He showed up to ask me for money again, and instead of just shouting at him I asked him to sit down and talk about it. And he did.'

I tried to envision Tom and David sitting at the

kitchen table, discussing things rationally. It was something I couldn't picture. I slid my hand over his knee and Tom patted my hand distractedly while he went on.

'We really talked, Kelley. We haven't done that since he was a kid.'

Tom shrugged and smiled.

'I guess he's not a kid any more. He's messed up, yeah, but he's got potential to fix it.'

My heart swelled with pride. 'And you're going to help him.'

'He's my son,' Tom said.

We rode in silence for a while.

'Kelley?'

'Hmmm?'

'I think he will get accustomed to you. He is used to women just floating in and out of my life. He knows you're different.'

Taken by the sweetness of the man, I laughed out loud. I leaned over and kissed his throat. Tom sighed, and his hands tightened on the wheel. I kissed him again. Then again. Tom swerved and cursed, but he was smiling.

Being reckless felt good. I slid my hand down his belly and he sucked in his breath. I unbuttoned his jeans. His cock was hard and thick as I pulled it free of the denim. Tom bit his lip and looked straight ahead.

'Do you still taste the same?' I asked.

Tom groaned and shifted in his seat.

'You feel the same,' I whispered as I stroked him.

The thin wetness at the tip of his cock was already enough to make my hand slick. At that moment, Tom was merging into heavy airport traffic. He stared at the road but only a small part of him was paying attention to the drive. The rest of him was focused entirely on what my hand was doing.

I stroked harder. Tom gasped and glanced at me once, then shot his eyes back to the road. A ghost of a smile crossed his lips.

'You bad, bad girl,' he said.

I kissed my way down his throat, then planted soft kisses in a line down his chest. His T-shirt was a nuisance. I wanted to touch bare skin. And then I did, when I sank my mouth down over his cock.

Tom shuddered. I looked up to see his jaw set, his teeth clenched, his eyes on the road and his knuckles white on the steering wheel. I bobbed up and down, not bothering with foreplay of any kind. I licked his cock every time I slid down. I sucked hard every time I pulled up. I made my lips a hard ring around him and slid just the head of his cock into my mouth, caressing it with sharp hard strokes.

'Fuck,' he uttered once, but made no other sound.

Tom warned me with a small moan right before he came. He sucked in a sharp breath as the first shot of semen filled my mouth. I swallowed all he gave me, then carefully sat up and looked right at him. Cars and trucks were zooming past us on either side. Tom stared at the windshield for a moment, then glanced over at me. He blushed scarlet. The rush of power was heady.

'Touch yourself for me,' he ordered, as if he was the one with the upper hand. I smiled and slid across the seat until my back was pressed against the passenger-side door. After a moment's thought, I reached up and locked it. Tom chuckled. I unzipped my jeans and slid my hand inside.

'I want to see,' Tom protested.

I didn't push my jeans down. I teased him with the knowledge of what my hand was doing there between my thighs. Tom kept glancing over at me and then looking back at the traffic. It was a busy day at the airport. When a trucker drove by, I knew he could probably see us from his higher vantage point – but I still didn't stop. I thrust my hips up to meet my hand. Tom stared at me for a moment, licked his lips, then suddenly looked back out the windshield, as if he had forgotten he was supposed to be driving.

'This is dangerous,' I murmured.

Tom shook his head in frustration but didn't say a word. I rested one foot on the dashboard and pushed the other one right under Tom's ass. He looked at me in surprise. With my legs spread like that, I slipped both hands down the front of my pants.

The truck swerved. 'Jesus Christ,' Tom swore.

'Uh-huh.' I was wet enough to make lewd sounds that Tom could clearly hear from the driver's seat. I rested my head against the window and bit my lip. A car honked – whether in response to what I was doing or in response to Tom's increasingly erratic driving, I had no idea.

I stared at Tom for a long time, watching him try to navigate both the road and the fact that his cock had more control over him than his brain. I was ready to fuck right there in the middle of traffic. I would give anything to see Tom pull off an exit ramp, drive to the shoulder and pound me right there on the seat of my old pickup.

I studied him, especially the muscles in his arms, the way they bulged and moved under his T-shirt as he drove, and I began to compare him to Daniel, the long and lanky painter who probably had a painting of me up on an easel right now, somewhere down under the equator where the stars were upside down.

What the hell was wrong with me?

My ardor disappeared just as quickly as it had come, but I didn't stop moving. I closed my eyes and focused on the sensation and wondered what to do. I couldn't fake it – Tom knew me too well, knew all the little cues I couldn't possibly create out of imagination. If I stopped now, he would know damn good and well that there was something wrong.

And maybe that was best?

I sat up in the seat. Tom looked at me curiously as I

zipped up my pants. I was sticky and messy and guilty as sin.

'What's wrong with you?' Tom asked as soon as he merged out of traffic and onto the exit.

'I'm glad to be home.'

I moved across the seat and curled up next to him even though it was hot as hell, even though the air conditioning wasn't working right, and buried my face in his shoulder. He was so strong. So broad. So understanding.

Had I done something unforgivable?

Tom didn't seem to read my mind this time. He chuckled and patted my hand.

'I missed you,' he said.

I zipped up his jeans. He was hard again, even after a strong orgasm, but with my sudden change in temperament he wasn't raring to go any more. I kissed him and my lips slid off the side of his as he looked at the side mirror and changed lanes.

'Tell me about the island,' he said. 'What did you do there?'

My laugh was a short and sudden sound that almost frightened me.

'I got drunk,' I said, and then I was laughing so hard I couldn't catch my breath. I lowered my head between my legs. I laughed hard enough to make my ribs hurt, to make my eyes water.

It seemed to take forever, but I got myself under control. One last giggle bubbled to the surface and quickly went away. Tom was looking at me, incredulous. He had pulled over to the side of the road and there we sat, the truck occasionally rocking when the wind from an eighteen-wheeler whistled over it. Beyond him I could see the cars whizzing by, sometimes slowing down, sometimes curious.

'Kelley?'

I had to tell him. 'I got drunk and then I went home

and I slept it off, and that next morning I was so sick, and I thought so much about too many things, and by the time I was sober again I did something I should never have done, and I am so sorry, Tom.'

Tom stared at me for a long moment. There was no understanding in his eyes. He hadn't a clue what I was talking about. None of it had really registered.

'You're sorry you got drunk?' he asked.

His tone was like a knife twisting in my belly. He was so trusting, he never would have dreamed I could have turned to someone else. He reminded me so much of me, back when I believed everything Michael told me.

I would not let that happen to us. I would not let a ghost reside between us.

'I'm sorry that I did something I shouldn't have done,' I said, and again, I knew Tom didn't understand. His eyes were almost blank.

'You were drinking –'

'I almost slept with somebody else,' I blurted out.

Tom looked at me for a long moment. Then he looked straight ahead, staring out the windshield as the cars zoomed past. He blinked a few times. He took a deep breath. I watched his hands as he carefully opened them, making a conscious effort not to grip the wheel with all his strength. One little muscle at the corner of his mouth twitched.

'Were you drunk?' he asked carefully.

Until that moment, it hadn't occurred to me that forgiveness would be more likely if I had been under the influence of something. Then he could say that I wasn't acting like myself. He could say that I had been seduced. He could say anything but what he really didn't want to believe, that I had done such things while I was completely in my right mind.

For the first time, I considered lying to Tom. But my silence stretched out too far, and, before I could form the words that would absolve me from the heaviest guilt, Tom spoke again.

'Your silence says you weren't drunk.'

I leaned against the dashboard and shook my head from side to side, over and over, wondering how we wound up here – in this truck on the side of the road, removed from everyone who was going about their busy and productive lives, watching our own suffer through an earthquake that very well might leave us in ruins.

I started to cry. I tried to keep it under control – I was the guilty party, after all, and if anyone had a right to cry it would be Tom, not me – but control vanished with every moment of silence from Tom. There was no tenderness from him, no touch on my back, no kind words that would make the burden easier.

'I want to know everything,' he said. 'No. On second thought, I don't want to know everything. I just want to know the basics.'

I sniffled and sat up in the seat. 'The basics?'

Tom stared out the window. His jaw was clenched tight. It crossed my mind that his history could lead him to violence at a moment like this, and I was also very aware that he was determined not to let that happen.

'I should make you tell me every last detail,' he said. 'I should torture you with making you remember every last bit of what you did.'

I nodded and tried to look at him, but I couldn't find the strength to do it.

'But that would be torturing myself, wouldn't it?' Tom turned to me so abruptly that I flinched away from him. 'Did you go all the way?'

Tom's eyes were darker than I had ever seen them. Tears shone at the corners – whether from pain or from anger, I didn't know.

'No.'

'Did you want to?'

I choked back a sob. I thought about lying with Daniel on the couch. We hadn't gone too far, but had I wanted more?

'I don't know,' I said honestly. 'But I don't think so.'

'What stopped you?'

I looked at Tom then. He was looking right at me, and now those tears were obviously made of something much deeper than anger. They went straight to my heart.

'You. You stopped me.'

Tom slammed the truck into drive. He roared off the shoulder, throwing gravel and dirt behind us. The force threw me back in the seat. Cars honked wildly. A truck swerved and I caught a glimpse of the irate driver, flipping Tom off while he braked. Tom roared up to sixty as he dodged cars on the road, then pushed the speedometer even higher.

I buckled the seat belt. Tom noticed and slowed down, but still not enough.

'We're going home,' he said, as if I had asked.

Tom tore down the interstate with little regard for the other drivers around us. He was making enemies with every mile. He shot into the exit and in the process cut off a little red compact car. The woman behind the wheel was yelling. I could see her doing it, but all I could hear was the squeal of tires as Tom laid rubber all the way up the ramp.

'Slow down,' I said softly.

'Don't you dare tell me what to do, you understand?'

Tom's voice was filled with venom. I sank back against the seat as the scenery flashed past. The road hummed underneath us, then whined as he turned onto a secondary road. When he turned into the driveway, the crunch of gravel wasn't comforting – it was ominous, as the wheels threw tails of the little white stones. They tinked hard against the underside of the truck. Tom slammed on the brakes but not quickly enough – I instinctively grabbed the dash and braced myself as Tom ran into his own privacy gate.

'Fuck!' he shouted.

Tom climbed out of the truck and stalked to the front. He unlocked the gate and pushed it open. The dent in it was clearly visible. The gate was ruined. I didn't want to think about what the front of my truck looked like. Tom stood there for a long moment and stared at it, then walked back to the driver's side door with a surprisingly calm stride.

'Take the truck up the house. I'm going to take a walk.'

Tom's eyes were bright with tears, and there was something else on his face – something that looked like fear.

'Tom?'

'Start dinner, if you don't mind. I don't know if either of us can eat, but we should at least have the option.'

I started to speak again but Tom held up his hand. He shook his head and looked towards the gate. He stared at the damage. He looked back at me. 'I don't want to do anything either one of us would regret and, if you speak to me again, I can't promise I won't. So trust me one more time, Kelley.'

The mention of trust twisted straight into my belly. I nodded and slid behind the wheel. After I put the truck in drive, I looked over at Tom. He hadn't moved. Though I wanted to say something, anything, I held my tongue and simply looked at him until he stepped back from the truck, giving me the room I needed to drive forwards.

I didn't move, and neither did he. Finally, Tom spoke. What he said was the last thing I expected.

'We will get through this.'

Before I could answer, Tom slammed the door and walked across the yard. He moved into the woods without a second's hesitation, and I stared at the place where he had been. He seemed to have vanished.

I drove up to the house, wiping tears out of my eyes to see the way.

Tom hadn't done much cleaning while I was gone, so there was plenty to do. I swept the floors and cleaned the counters and put in a load of laundry, stopping only to pull one of his shirts up to my nose. It smelled like the wilderness, like trees and grass and black soil. There was the slightest hint of campfire smoke. I breathed deep of all those good things and suddenly felt lightheaded, assaulted by all I had taken for granted. I leaned against the washing machine until the feeling abated.

By the time Tom came back, dinner was bubbling on the stove and I was finishing the last of the dishes. I turned to look at him as he came in, but I didn't stop what I was doing. I needed somewhere to put my hands, something to do to keep an emotional distance between us.

'What are we having?' Tom asked carefully.

'Beef Stroganoff,' I said, trying to keep a normal tone, too.

'It smells delicious. You're a very good cook.'

'Thank you,' I whispered. The tears were right under the surface. I hid them as well as I could but, when Tom stepped behind me and wrapped me in his arms, there were no defenses left.

The plate I was washing slid back into the water. I suddenly remembered our first kiss. We were doing dishes together then, and there was nothing between us but anticipation and possibilities and the slightest hint of a former love to be overcome. The future was laid out, and all we had to do was accept it as it came.

'We need a dishwasher,' he said inanely. 'I need to get you one of those.'

Tom kissed the back of my neck. I let out one sob, then stood silently as Tom's lips played over my skin.

'Kelley.'

I was silent.

'I want to say things to hurt you. At the same time, all I want to do is take you to bed,' he whispered. 'Isn't that insane?'

We stood there so long that the Stroganoff began to burn. Tom finally let me go long enough to turn the heat off underneath it, and within seconds he was against me again, his chest pressing hard against my back, so hard I had to brace myself against the sink to keep from bending under his weight.

'Please,' I murmured.

The admission of what I wanted slipped from me without any warning. If someone had told me an hour ago that I would have asked for Tom to take me to bed, I would have said they were, as Tom had so aptly put it, insane.

'I'm very angry,' he said.

'You won't hurt me,' I said right back to him, and I knew it was true.

Tom sighed. 'I'm not a saint,' he said, and I knew then that he was scared, perhaps even more scared than I was, of what was happening here between us. I didn't know what to say, so I said the thing that was most obvious.

'Do you want dinner?'

Tom kissed the back of my neck. The touch was sudden and unexpected. I jumped when he did it. When I turned to look at him, he was already walking away, heading down to the basement. The way he closed the door, with a slow and decisive slam, said clearly that I was not to follow. Within moments I heard the clatter of the weights and the rhythmic sound that said he was working out on one machine or another.

An hour later, as I lay in bed alone, I listened to him pound the punching bag. Sometimes I listened to him cry. I lay awake until the sun came up.

14

For days there was very little discussion from Tom. He slept on the couch. He spent time in the woods, and hit the punching bag in the gym more often than I wanted to think about. His friend Jake called, fresh home from an overseas tour of duty, and, more than once during their long phone calls, I heard my name mentioned. Once I heard him crying in his office while Jake was on the other line and, even as I was embarrassed that someone else knew what I had done, I was glad Tom had someone to talk to.

I once begged him to come to bed with me, to simply hold me while we talked things over. He glared at me with such intensity I took a step back and caught my breath.

'I'll be in there when I'm damn good and ready,' he said.

I hesitated for a moment, uncertain whether I should say anything at all.

'Maybe I should leave,' I finally whispered.

Tom stared at me. 'Is that what you want?'

'No.' Tears sprang into my eyes. 'I came home to you.'

Tom shook his head and, though his attitude and his stance didn't change, his voice was softer than it had been in days. 'We will talk this out soon. But not now, Kelley. I can't do that yet.'

'Maybe I shouldn't be here,' I repeated.

'You came home, Kelley,' he said. 'I want you to stay.'

The questions finally came to a head, and I couldn't help but blurt out what I had been so afraid of all this time. 'Are we over?'

Tom didn't answer for the longest time. I was ready to break away, to bolt and run and pack all my things, when he finally responded.

'No. We're not over. We're just in suspended animation, Kelley.'

'But –'

'Go to bed,' he said, and his tone made it clear the discussion was over.

In the big bed that was so comfortable for the two of us, I tossed and turned. I listened to him snore from the living room. How could he sleep at a time like this?

It was four long days before Tom came to me.

'Tell me how it happened,' Tom finally said. 'I don't want details. I don't want to know what you did with him. I just want to know how one thing led to another.'

We were standing in the kitchen. Tom had crept up behind me and wrapped his arms around me before I had a chance to realize he was there. It was almost the same as the night we had come back from the airport, the same stance, looking over the same scene. I had been doing dishes, the same as before. It was like the last four days hadn't really happened – like we were back in the same place we had been on that day when I told him what I had done. The ambush set up a well of longing in my heart. My chest was heavy with unshed tears.

I told him. I told him everything, from the moment I got to the island, starting with the dolphins. I told him about the bartender, the businessman who was working so hard, the couple on the stools who weren't noticing anyone but each other – and then I told him about the painter, and the drawing on a napkin.

Tom rested his chin on my shoulder while I talked. The pressure of his hands never wavered. His breathing didn't change. I would have thought he was asleep, if he hadn't been standing up. I expected a reaction of some kind, but I didn't get a single one until I was finished.

Then: 'Is that all, Kelley?'

'That's all. I swear to you, Tom. That's all.'

One of his hands slid up. It rested lightly against my throat. His touch was possessive and gentle all at once.

'What about Michael?'

'Michael is not a problem any more.'

'Why not?'

I took a deep breath and hoped I wouldn't offend Tom with my answer. Even though it was the honest truth, in light of the circumstances it could be seen as an excuse.

'Because I understand how easy it can be to do the wrong thing.'

Tom's arms tightened around me. We stood there in silence for a very long time, until the sun began to drop and the room became dark. Finally Tom pulled my T-shirt off my shoulder and kissed the bare skin he uncovered there.

'Come to bed,' he said. 'It's over now.'

All the strength ran out of my knees. I slumped in his arms, and he held me up as though he was expecting this sort of breakdown. The sobs came, and I didn't try to stop them. I leaned over the counter and, instead of trying to control myself, I just let it go. There was nothing left to hide from him any longer.

Tom leaned over me and pulled my hair away from my face. He cooed to me, as if I was a child in need of comfort. He whispered into my ear. 'Hush, little one. It's all right. I understand, and it's all right.'

I sobbed until there was nothing left in me. Tom cried, too. His tears were silent, but I could feel them as they fell onto my back, seeping through my shirt, leaving small circles of pain that evaporated to coolness in the air.

'Come to bed,' he said again, when the tears were all gone.

'Are you sure?'

My voice cracked. My throat was sore from all the crying I had done over the last few days. My self-esteem was at an all-time low, and Tom was the only one who could pull me out of that downward spiral. I needed to know he accepted me still, even after all this, with all my shortcomings and mistakes.

'I'm absolutely sure,' he said and, though his words were strong, his voice faltered just like mine did.

'I almost lost you,' I said, hardly willing to believe that I was forgiven.

Amazingly, Tom laughed out loud. The sound wasn't filled with mirth – rather, it was a sound of relief. His words were balm to a tortured soul.

'No. You couldn't lose me. You never even came close, Kelley.'

He carefully wiped the tears from my eyes with his fingertips. He trailed his hand down my throat, that familiar touch I knew so well.

'Come to bed,' he said the third time.

Kissing Tom after those long lonely days felt like coming home. He eased my fears with the first touch, when he moaned in that way that only Tom did. His breath was short and his heart was thudding hard under my palm. It was just like that first night in his basement, when he was so afraid he wouldn't satisfy me. Same story, different time – but it all seemed to blend into one.

'I love you,' I whispered against his skin.

'I know you do,' he said, and this time his voice was broken by tears.

'I'm so sorry,' I said.

'I know that, too.'

Tom's hands were everywhere. I watched his face as he abruptly pulled away from me and his eyes trailed over the curve of my jaw, the soft dips of my collarbone.

'I want to be better than he was.'

The words were a shock, even if they shouldn't have been. This was the same thing I had felt – this was the same thing I had gone through. This is what Michael had done to me.

Suddenly, what Michael had done was a gift of sorts. There was a silver lining in the heartbreak after all. This had been done to me – and what had I needed to recover? What were all those things Michael hadn't given me? I could now give those things to Tom. I could make up for what was done to me by making everything up to him.

The relief of it made my body weak, but my determination was strong.

'He is nothing compared to you,' I said vehemently, not sure whether I meant Daniel or Michael. Either way, I knew it was the truth. 'Nothing, Tom. Do you hear me? Nothing.'

Tom nodded. He closed his eyes.

'I will do whatever it takes to show you,' I said. 'Just give me a chance.'

Tom took a deep breath. 'I'll give you my whole life,' he whispered.

I pulled him down onto the bed with me.

Every moment there in the darkness felt surreal, as if we had fallen through a rip in time. Every touch was like the first between two lovers who were afraid of what they might find – afraid of being rejected, of being torn apart with the wrong word or the wrong glance. It was everything I had wanted when things ended so harshly between Michael and me. It was everything I needed to give, now that I had jeopardized the love of a man who meant the most to me. One moment bled into another, the past moved into the present, and it all became a new beginning.

Tom lay back on the bed. The moonlight fell over his body. His breathing was deep and steady, but the throbbing of the pulse in his throat told me he was scared.

I touched his throat. I cupped my hand around it, touching him lightly, the same possessive way he loved to touch me. His lips opened but he didn't say a word. I slid my fingertips along his skin, until I reached the fabric of his T-shirt. I traced the line of it, all the way around his neck, across his shoulders, all the way around his arms. By the time I got to the end of it, he was breathing a little harder.

I tugged on the shirt. He sat up just enough to let me pull it over his head. His hair was in disarray as he lay back against the pillows.

I started with his jaw and worked my way down, touching every inch of him. He lay very still underneath me. His eyes moved quickly behind his eyelids and I knew exactly how he felt – every instinct was telling him to cut and run. It took all the energy he had to just lie there and let me touch him.

'I know what you're thinking,' I whispered.

Tom flinched slightly, but nothing else about him changed.

My lips followed the trail my hands had made. Even when I kissed his ribs and he flinched away from my touch, ticklish now that his entire being was focused on the sensation, I didn't stop. I just let his body ease before I laid another kiss down, right beside the one before it. By the time I got to Tom's belly button, he was breathing hard and his whole body was covered in goosebumps.

I unbuttoned his jeans. The zipper came down so slowly it didn't make a sound. I slid the jeans away, one slow inch at a time, kissing my way down his legs. Tom moaned once when I kissed the inside of his knee. By the time I was done, there was only one place that hadn't been kissed or touched or caressed.

'You are everything I have ever wanted,' I said against his skin.

He was hard as steel. His cock throbbed in my hand. The veins were hard and pulsing. I had never seen him so aroused. He moaned lightly as I slid my hand up and down, from side to side, like a corkscrew going up and down his shaft.

I leaned forwards and licked that most sensitive spot, the place right underneath his head that always made his cock move as if it had a life of its own. It jerked in my hand and Tom's moan was louder. I teased that spot with the tip of my tongue, coaxing more wetness out of him, until he bucked once into my hand, asking silently for more.

I slid my tongue over the head of his cock. The effect was electric. His dick jerked hard, and I squeezed him at the same time. Tom's hand came down and tangled in my hair. There was tentativeness in his touch, but it wasn't enough to stop him. He was giving himself over to the pleasure.

The head of his cock throbbed wildly as I sucked him into my mouth. I settled my teeth right underneath the ridge of his crown. I didn't bite down, but I gave the hint of what I could do if I chose, and the question of it – will she or won't she? – pushed Tom to an even higher pitch. I gently scraped my teeth over the head, and Tom's shudder told me how much he liked it. I did it again. The third time his hand tightened in my hair, and he thrust his hips up. When I finally sucked him deep into my mouth, he groaned in approval.

Now that my mouth was busy, I had both hands free. I ran them up his chest and played with his nipples, rolling them between my fingertips, making them hard as little rocks. Tom suddenly let go of my hair and grabbed the headboard.

'Don't stop,' he said, almost desperately, as if he didn't know I wanted this just as much as he did.

Tom's knuckles were white on the headboard. Still he hadn't opened his eyes. I watched his face as he jerked between my lips one last time. His orgasm flooded my mouth. His low cry was something like a sob. Then he was reaching for me, pulling me up to his side even before his release was over.

'I was so scared,' he whispered against my neck. My fingers laced through his hair and held on tight while he rocked back and forth on the bed, trying to pull me closer, almost as if he could fold me into himself.

'There's nothing to be scared of now. Not any more.'

Calmness came by slow degrees. He took deep breaths, one after another, until his body was gripped with a different kind of urgency. He began to remove my clothes, one slow inch at a time, until I was just as naked as he was.

Tom didn't touch me with his fingertips, or his tongue, or his body – only with his breath. Cool trails meandered over my skin, from the tip of my chin to the hollow of my throat, along my collarbone, down each arm, then over to my belly, where he worked in widening circles until he was back up at my lips.

He gently blew air over my lips as I opened them and reached for him. I took his breath into myself, sucked it down, took every wisp of air he offered. My whole body was trembling, my mind was wiped clean, my very soul was aching for him to make love to me – and he hadn't even touched me yet.

'Touch me,' I begged, and he smiled down at me.

'I am,' he said. 'Can't you feel it?'

Tom worked the same magic along my legs, on each of my feet, over my ankles and back up. By the time he reached the center of me, I was sure he would stop the teasing and give me what we both needed, but he didn't. It was still only his breath, coming harsher now, faster, against my heated skin.

Unable to take any more, I lifted my hands to my breasts and started to play with my nipples. Tom looked up at me with eyes that were hungry and wanton, and I realized what he had wanted all along.

His breath led my touch. He showed me what he wanted with every exhale. When he finally blew cool air over my clit, my fingers were right behind it, stroking into the wetness. The rush of passion was so sudden, so intense, that it shook me into utter silence.

'That's it,' he said. 'Show me.'

Tom and I worked in counterpoint, his breath and then my touches, until it was nothing but my touches and his words, encouraging me, telling me how beautiful it was to watch me, asking me to come, to show him everything.

The orgasm swept through my whole body, from the tingling of my toes to the dizziness that made me close my eyes. My stomach quivered with butterflies. I arched up under Tom's gaze, letting him watch every moment as the pleasure wracked my body and left me breathless.

Only when it was over did he touch me. He laid a hand on my belly. My muscles jumped under his touch. He looked down at me as my body calmed.

'That was beautiful,' he said softly.

When I reached for him this time, he didn't hold back. He crawled between my legs and, before the last of my orgasm faded away, he was slipping inside me. We both sighed in appreciation at the snug sweet fit. We were perfect for each other. I told him this. He brushed my hair away from my forehead and kissed my nose.

Then he started to move, and I was lost in the thrill of it. My arms wrapped around his neck. My legs wrapped around his hips. I knew he wanted it faster, but he held back until I was begging underneath him, pleading and bucking into him. Only then did he reward me with the first hard thrust, the one that took my breath away and lit a raging fire that demanded we not make love. It demanded a good hard fuck.

'Take what is yours,' I said to him.

Tom paused and looked down at me. The light of anger suddenly flashed in his eyes, and I knew he had crossed a very important hurdle. His confidence in my love had been restored – now he needed to restore other things, too.

That next thrust rocked the bed. The thrust after that was hard enough to send a small shaft of pain through my spine, hard enough to make the bed squeak with the effort. Soon Tom had set up a rhythm that made the bed sing. The rails squeaked. The headboard thumped against the wall. The bolts protested. The mattress itself bounced with the effort. I wrapped myself around him and closed my eyes, taking in every ounce of power as he rammed into me.

It wasn't punishment, and it wasn't desperate. It was a reclaiming.

Tom came with a shout. The force of his orgasm was such that he struggled to keep from collapsing on top of me. It seemed to last forever, so much longer than any other I had watched him have. He called out until he was out of breath, thrust until he was out of power, and then fell to the bed beside me, leaving a slick trail of wetness across my thigh.

Somehow I had expected a discussion afterwards, talk about what we had done, a conversation about what would happen from this point on, and how it would all be different. But, as Tom fell asleep beside me without saying another word, I realized that there was no need for words, not right now. There was no hurry. The wounds would heal in time, and we had all the time in the world.

I touched his face. He smiled in his sleep.

15

It was a month later when Tom introduced me to Jake.

Jake was the son of one of Tom's former army buddies. Over time, Tom had become a mentor and friend to Jake. The young man had gone into service and a month later, terrorists destroyed the World Trade Center. Jake went overseas within weeks. Tom had worried about him constantly, and confessed that he breathed a sigh of relief when Jake first called him several weeks ago, safe and sound somewhere in Georgia, and announced that he and Uncle Sam had finally parted ways for good.

'He's home. He won't be going back,' Tom said. 'I can't tell you how relieved I am.'

'Jake helped you quite a bit,' I said softly, remembering those nights when Tom cried over the phone to his friend.

'He helped me understand,' Tom admitted.

'I'm grateful for him,' I said, and we smiled at each other.

'I want you to meet him,' Tom said. 'Why don't we have him over for dinner?'

Since Tom and I had reconciled after my trip to the islands, he had become much more open about introducing me to his friends. He seemed almost eager, as though he wanted to show me off. I was learning that Tom inspired loyalty everywhere he went. Those who knew him couldn't help but love him.

'You find out when he can get here,' I said, 'and I'll cook whatever he wants.'

'Tonight?'

I laughed at his eagerness, then headed for the kitchen to figure out what to make for dinner.

Jake pulled into the drive at six sharp. By the time I got to the door to greet him, Tom was already vaulting off the porch. Jake turned and smiled at Tom, and I was surprised by how young he was. He couldn't have been more than 25.

The men embraced in the driveway with lots of back slapping and hand shaking. I smiled at them from the porch, waiting out their reunion. Jake reached into the car and pulled out a small wooden box, which he handed to Tom. He also pulled out a clutch of wildflowers.

Jake approached me with a broad smile and good manners.

'Good evening, ma'am,' he said, and held out the flowers. 'I'm so glad to meet the woman who settled Tom down. These are for you.'

I was instantly charmed. His eyes were deep brown and seemed to take in everything with one glance. His hair was too long, shaggy now that he didn't have a military barber to keep it trimmed. He was clean shaven, with just the slightest hint of five o'clock shadow. He looked at turns like a young man and then like a much older one, depending on the way the light touched him, and I wondered if that was a result of the things he had seen over the last few years. But his smile was infectious, his openness a delight.

Tom followed Jake into the house. I had rarely seen him so relaxed and happy. The men stood in the living room and Jake encouraged Tom to open the box. 'You're going to love it,' he said, and smiled at me proudly.

Tom lifted the lid. For a long moment, he said nothing. There were tears in his eyes when he lifted the hatchet to the light and turned it over in his hands, studying every side of it. Light glinted from the sharp edge. The handle was inscribed with some small sentiment that made Tom laugh out loud.

'I saw that and for some reason, I thought of your flintlock rifle,' Jake said.

Tom was nodding before the sentence was finished. 'Damn straight. It's perfect. Thank you, man.' Tom reached out and Jake took a step, and they embraced in the living room while I watched.

'Thank God you're safe,' Tom said quietly.

Jake clapped him on the shoulder and a look was exchanged between them, the kind of look that said they understood where the other had been, and that coming home safe was something neither of them had expected. It was the kind of look I only saw when Tom was talking about the military.

I loved watching this new side of Tom with his friend. Over the last several weeks, the gentleness in Tom had slowly edged out the anger. He wasn't just different with me; he was different with everyone. I liked this new man, who wasn't afraid of the things he felt.

The men wandered the house as I worked with dinner. Roast leg of lamb, asparagus and broccoli, and all the trimmings I could manage to fit into the oven. It was going to be a huge dinner, with leftovers that would probably last for days. Tom had assured me Jake would eat more than his share. 'He's a growing boy,' Tom said.

I had no idea how true that was until I watched Jake eat dinner. The man could put it away as though he was a bottomless pit. We sat at the kitchen table and talked over wine. Oil lamps burned in the center of the table, making the setting intimate but not romantic. Jake closed his eyes with the first bite and leaned back in his chair.

'Wow,' he breathed.

I smiled at him, and he blushed. 'I'm a bachelor. Fast food is usually what's on the menu.'

'There's plenty. Eat as much as you want, and we'll send some home with you for later.'

I watched Jake while he ate. His body was long and lanky, a contrast to Tom's built and solid frame. Every time he smiled, he flashed perfect teeth. The men talked about everything from cars to guns to families. When the conversation turned to me, Jake asked intelligent questions that made it clear he was really interested in getting to know everything about me. Tom watched me with love in his eyes.

'She's the best thing that ever happened to me,' Tom praised.

'I believe it,' Jake said.

I blushed. They both laughed.

Then Jake asked for seconds.

Later we stood on the porch, talking while the sun went down. The men had beers in their hands, and I was finishing up a glass of wine. Jake smoked a cigarette while standing a short distance away, politely keeping the smoke from blowing in our direction. I watched him as he smoked, the way he held the cigarette between his fingers as if it was an extension of him, the way he chased every drag with a sip of beer.

Jake was shorter than Tom. I noted this with interest as they stood side by side in front of me, talking as though I were not there at all. I didn't mind that in the least. It was good to watch Tom get so lost in conversation.

When I turned to go to the kitchen, both men noticed. Tom grabbed at my hand. 'Where are you going?' he protested.

'I'm going to clean up while you guys talk out here.'

A strange look passed between the two – if I had blinked, I would have missed it.

'Stay,' Tom said. 'We want you to stay.'

The pressure on my wrist did not go away. Tom pulled me back against him and sipped his beer. The condensation from the bottle dripped onto my shoulder and seeped through my blouse. Tom kissed the spot. Then he kissed my neck. I tilted my head to make it easier for him.

Jake watched every motion. He didn't try to hide his interest. He slowly drank his beer while he stared at the place where Tom's lips met my skin. I looked right back at him. My interest in him had to be the wine, I thought. There was no other explanation. He was simply a kind sweet man, and he was Tom's friend. It was safe to think he was drop-dead gorgeous, wasn't it?

Tom carefully set his beer on the porch railing. His hands slid down my arms. He held my wrists firmly by my sides.

Jake took a step forwards, watching my eyes all the while. The silence became awkward. Tom nuzzled my neck, seemingly oblivious to everything else.

Jake tipped up the bottle and drained the last of his beer. He twirled the bottle in his fingers and let it drop to the porch floor. There was a dull thud, then the clattering sound of glass rolling across wide floorboards. Tom didn't even flinch.

Jake stepped right up to me. He ran his hand into my hair. Tom's hands tightened on my wrists, but he didn't make a single move to stop Jake. It suddenly dawned on me what was happening – and then all thought seemed to cease, because Jake was pressing his lips to mine, kissing me softly while Tom held me.

Tom's lips slipped up to my ear. 'Do you like him?' he asked.

My mind raced wildly as Jake pulled away. He gave me that smile, only this time there was a rakishness to it that spoke volumes. So much for the innocence he projected. I wasn't sure what to say to Tom, or how to act, or even if I should kiss Jake back. Surely Tom was giving me permission if he was just letting it happen like this.

But was it a test? Did this have something to do with what happened on the island?

Tom bit down gently on my earlobe. Jake kissed me again, more urgently this time. I learned exactly what Tom wanted when I took a chance and opened my lips, kissed Jake back as he slipped his tongue into my mouth. Tom groaned in approval.

'Good girl,' he murmured.

My amazement was quickly turning to arousal. The rush that sank through my body was much more than the wine. Tom's body was hard against me, his hands like steel bands around my wrists, holding me still for whatever Jake might want to do. Jake himself wasn't shy about what he wanted – he kissed me until we were both breathless, and all the while his hands were trailing all over my body. Those hands finally stopped at the buttons of my blouse.

'Tell him to do it,' Tom whispered into my ear. He was watching every move.

I hesitated.

'Right now,' Tom ordered.

'Please,' I said, and Tom chuckled.

Jake flicked open one button at a time, watching my eyes. When the shirt was undone, Jake took both sides in his hands and spread it open. He took his time and let his eyes wander my body. The heat of my blush rose to my face and made my skin tingle.

Jake slid my bra straps down my shoulders. Tom kissed the places where the straps had been. Jake pushed my bra down until my breasts were free. My nipples stood out proudly, betraying how turned on I really was. Jake watched my face as he caught my nipples between his fingertips and rolled them around.

I moaned and leaned back harder into Tom. His erection was evident. It pressed up against me, straining in his jeans. Jake squeezed harder as Tom watched.

Suddenly Jake bent his head. His brushed one nipple and then his lips closed over the other one. The sensation was foreign – he didn't do it the way Tom did. Jake swirled his tongue around my nipple and sucked harder with each stroke. Then he scraped his teeth across the swollen tip. I was shaking and on the verge of whimpering by the time he finished with both of them. He looked up at me with a wicked grin and, for the first time in a long while, he looked over my shoulder at Tom.

'Do you want her?' Tom asked Jake, and my knees went weak.

Jake looked down at me. The polite gentleman was completely gone, replaced by a wild reckless man who didn't give a damn for propriety.

'Hell, yes.'

Without another word, Tom pushed me towards the door. My breasts gently swayed as I walked. My nipples were straining against the night air.

The door thumped behind us. Tom led me to the spare bedroom. I stood very still as he unsnapped my jeans and pulled them down my legs. Soon I was naked, and Tom was still fully clothed. Climbing onto the bed, Tom rested against the headboard and pulled me up against him, so that my back was pressed against his chest, his legs were cradling me. His cock was hard as a rock inside his jeans.

'Tom?' I asked once, and he shushed me with a fingertip over my lips.

'You know the safe word.'

I nodded.

'Trust me, Kelley.'

Jake watched us from the doorway.

Tom slid his hands down my thighs. He cupped my knees. Then he slid his hands up, pushing my thighs apart, until my legs were spread wide. I was lying there in front of Jake, naked and open and waiting.

The message was unmistakable. Tom was offering me to him.

'Damn,' Jake said in a rush as he let out the breath he had been holding.

Tom kissed my ear.

'She likes it deep,' Tom said. 'Isn't that right, Kelley?'

The heat of desire flooded me. Every inch of my body was alive.

Jake studied me as he walked to the bed. He stripped his shirt over his head. Every motion looked sexual. Jake slid his jeans down and hesitated before he removed his boxers. His cock was already poking through the slit in the front. My mouth started to water as I looked at it.

'You want that cock in you. Don't you?' Tom asked me.

I didn't answer, so he lifted one hand to my face and turned me to look at him.

'Do you want it?' he asked again.

'Yes,' I whispered.

'Louder.'

'Yes, Tom. Yes.'

'Tell him.'

I looked at Jake. He was naked and stroking his cock slowly with first one hand, then the other. Tom's hand tightened in my hair.

'Tell him, dammit.'

I poured out the confession. 'I want you to fuck me,' I said, looking directly at Jake. 'I want your cock as deep in me as you can go.'

Jake groaned aloud. He squeezed his cock hard. Tom's hands slid up and he squeezed my nipples. They were sensitive from what Jake had done to them on the porch, and Tom's touch made me gasp aloud. He chuckled against my neck, an almost sinister sound. Jake climbed onto the end of the bed and Tom ground his erection against my ass.

Jake crawled up between my legs. He kissed me. Tom

squeezed my nipples harder, until I cried out against Jake's mouth. Jake's dick was hot against my thigh. Tom was breathing hard as he let go of my nipples and cupped my knees in his hands. He pulled my legs wide apart.

'Fuck her,' Tom said.

Jake slowly slid his cock into me. I cried out as he touched me, then moaned as he impaled me. He was shorter than Tom but thicker, just enough to notice. Jake buried his head in my shoulder while Tom whispered in the other ear.

'Do you like the way he feels? Do you like that cock in you?'

I bucked up against Jake. His words were in my other ear, a counterpoint to Tom's:

'Your pussy is so sweet – so tight – damn, you're so wet.'

Jake kissed me while he fucked me. I already knew he loved to kiss, and I obliged, letting my tongue dance with his while Tom watched. I ran my hands into Jake's hair. It was thick and lush, soft under my fingers. I ran my fingertips down his chest and both men moaned in approval.

Jake pushed closer to me, until our bodies were touching almost everywhere we could, and he fucked me with deep and short strokes, getting the most out of every one of them. He was gliding right across my clit each time, and the orgasm was upon me before I knew it, before I could utter even a whimper of warning. I shuddered and Jake stopped kissing me long enough to murmur against my lips.

'Naughty,' he said, as he felt my pussy clenching around his cock.

Tom grabbed a handful of my hair and pulled my head back, breaking the kiss. He turned my face to his and kissed me himself. I expected something hard and demanding, like Jake's thrusts had become. Instead it was gentle and careful. It was the perfect contrast – the hard fuck and the sweet kiss, from two very different men who wanted very much the same thing.

Jake slowed down and watched me kiss Tom. Then he growled a warning, low in his throat: 'Where do you want it, baby?'

'Where?'

'Where do you want my come?'

I groaned in anticipation. Much to my surprise, so did Tom. He thrust up behind me, pushing me harder into Jake. I watched Jake's eyes as he plunged deep and gave up asking. He suddenly didn't care where I wanted him to come, because he was too far gone.

Watching him come was as much of a thrill as watching Tom do it. I reveled in the differences. Jake closed his eyes in the beginning, to savor that first rush – as it faded, he opened his eyes and looked right at me. He bit his lip and moaned deeply. He shuddered once, and the sexy sight of that was enough to make me moan right along with him.

'I know you like the way that feels,' Tom whispered into my ear.

I tore my eyes away from Jake and turned to Tom for a kiss. His manner was incredibly loving even as he thrust up from under me, his erection so hard it had to be painful.

'Is it your turn yet?' I asked breathlessly.

Tom climbed out from under me. I lay on the bed with Jake, who couldn't keep his hands to himself. He was touching everywhere he could reach. He couldn't stop kissing, either. I finally had to beg for some room to breathe, and Jake laughed as Tom climbed back on the bed, naked this time. He crawled up between my spread legs. I reached for him and welcomed him in.

Jake lay beside us and watched everything. Tom thrust hard that first time, and with a shock I realized what he was feeling – I was entirely wet, dripping with both my juices and the remnants of what Jake left in me. I locked my legs around his waist.

'Do you like what I did to her?' Jake asked. 'Did you like watching me fuck her?'

Tom answered by going over the edge of control. He thrust into me so hard the bed shook. Jake watched and stroked himself and occasionally encouraged us, but he mostly kept silent. He watched as though he was learning from everything we did.

Tom was almost at the edge when Jake spoke: 'Did I get her wet enough for you?'

That's what it took to send Tom to an orgasm that almost knocked him unconscious.

I watched them in the aftermath. They sat side-by-side on the bed and shared a cigarette. I watched the smoke curl up towards the ceiling in the dim light of the bedside lamp. They didn't speak at all. After long moments of comfortable silence, Jake knelt up and turned to me. His cock was rock hard. Tom looked back at me and smiled.

'Where do you want this?' Jake asked. He was looking at me, but the question was directed at Tom. Tom watched me for a while.

'Suck him,' he finally said.

I crawled over the bed towards Jake. He looked down at me with that smile that was no longer innocent at all. I teased the hell out of him, trying to get the most out of every small flicker of my tongue, every small nip of my teeth. Jake stroked himself as I worked my way around his hand, licking his fingers and his shaft and the head of his cock, until he grabbed a handful of my hair and shoved himself deeper into my mouth.

'Yeah,' Tom breathed. 'That's what she needs. She likes being taken.'

'Does she, now?'

I lay on my back, for the better angle, to take him deeper. He pushed relentlessly forwards. I swallowed on his cock, taking him in deeper. Jake groaned when he touched the back of my throat.

Tom was standing beside the bed by then, stroking his own cock as he watched me deep-throat Jake. I was too busy swallowing what Jake was giving me – I didn't notice what Tom was doing until he slammed into me with one long thrust. My pussy was so wet he slid in without any resistance whatsoever.

'Fuck, yes,' Tom groaned.

He fucked me with long smooth strokes. He pulled my legs up over his shoulders. Soon he and Jake were in a rhythm that took them both in deep at the same time. I was being speared at both ends. Jake grabbed my breasts and squeezed my nipples. Tom touched everywhere else but especially my clit. The fuck was rough and the deep-throating got even rougher as Jake got closer to an orgasm.

I knew from his moans that Jake was getting close. Tom did, too. He reached up to touch my throat, that same reverent touch that was always so possessive, and I realized what he could feel: the thrusts of Jake's cock as he slid in and out of my mouth. The fact of that was enough to set me off. I bucked and moaned and struggled against them both as the orgasm rushed up hard and fast.

Jake came at the same time. I was surprised by the hot flow of his come down my throat – it was so much more than I had expected.

'Swallow,' Tom demanded.

I did as I was told. Jake held his cock deep in my mouth, cutting off my air, until the last drops were gone. When he pulled out I sucked in a deep breath and looked at Tom.

I opened my mouth and let him see what was left. I let him watch me swallow it.

'Oh, fuck,' Tom cried out, and came hard with the next thrust.

I was exhausted. I needed rest. Somehow, I knew I wouldn't get much. Jake was showing no signs of leaving, and Tom was showing no signs of asking him to go. But I did get a brief respite when Jake went to get a shower.

When we were alone, Tom took me into his arms. I curled against him gratefully.

'Are you OK?' he asked.

'Yes.' I really was. I thought for a moment as I listened to the shower start.

'I considered using the safe word,' I confessed.

Tom surprised me when he said, 'So did I.'

'When?'

'When we were lying on the bed. Before anything had really gone too far.'

'I thought about it then, too.'

'Why didn't you?'

'I wanted to give it to you. Why didn't you?'

Tom smiled and kissed my nose. 'Same reason.'

'We're really quite the pair, aren't we?'

Tom laughed and cuddled me closer. I laid my head on his chest and listened to his heartbeat.

'Tommy?'

Tom laughed. 'Who's Tommy?'

'Are you really OK with all this?'

He sighed and ran his fingers through my hair. 'Yes.'

'Why?'

'Because it's my choice,' Tom said, almost defiantly. I closed my eyes against the pain I heard in his voice, that same edge that crept in at the most inopportune and unexpected moments. 'It's my decision. It's something we are doing together, not separate.'

We lay in silence and listened to the water running in Jake's shower.

'I'm sorry,' I said, and wondered how many more times I would have to say those words before there was no reason left to say them.

'You're long forgiven, baby girl. But I won't forgive you for calling me Tommy.'

I smiled against his chest and twirled my fingers through the tiny black and gray hairs I found there. His hand in my hair was gentle. I was almost asleep when Jake came back into the room and spoke quietly to Tom.

'Tom, man – I'll leave if you guys want me to.'

'No. No way. You stay here.'

'Where do you want me to crash?'

'Right here.'

I was surprised at that. I looked up at Tom and he patted my thigh.

'Move over and give Jake some room, baby.'

That's how I wound up with both men in bed with me, Tom on one side and Jake on the other. I fell asleep with the feeling of Tom's breath on my forehead and Jake's breath on my back. It certainly wasn't something I had ever imagined happening in my lifetime, but here it was, and it felt absolutely right.

I felt closer to Tom than ever.

16

Our relationship changed after that night, in most ways for the better. There were still problems, of course. Any couple has them. But they weren't earthquakes that rocked our foundation – they were simply storms here and there in an otherwise perfectly clear sky. Tom and I spent more time talking about the way inviting Jake into bed made us feel. We talked about what might come next. We both decided we had gone far enough for the time being, and that more would come later – much later. Right now, we were content with each other and occasionally with Jake.

The morning after the first threesome was a slow and easy awakening. I made love to each of them while the other watched. There were no crazy positions and no wild extremes. We were simply getting comfortable with each other. Since then, Jake had shown up every few weeks for dinner, and spent the night in bed, fucking me in every way imaginable. Tom and I seemed to come closer to each other after every time with Jake.

There came a morning that autumn, right about the time the leaves began to fall, when the decisions swirling around in my mind had finally been put to rest.

'I'm going to take a drive,' I said. 'There's something I need to do.'

Tom looked at me with understanding eyes. 'Exorcising old ghosts?'

I smiled at how well he knew me.

'Something like that.'

'I'll be here waiting,' he assured me.

'I will come home.'

'I know,' he said immediately, and the conviction in his voice was strong.

I drove to the lake highway and headed east. I drove for hours, until I saw the mountains in the distance, and then I sped up. Saying goodbye was never easy, but the sooner it was done, the better. I had a good man waiting back home.

Darkness fell as I navigated the streets in the shadow of the mountain. I was a bit surprised at how easy it was to find my way in the dark, even after all this time. I pulled off onto the sweet-smelling grass at the side of the road and killed the engine.

I sat there in my truck and laid my head on the steering wheel. Crickets started to sing. One of them had somehow got into my open window and was underneath the seat. It occasionally chirped while I watched Michael's house from across the street.

I sat there quietly, taking it all in. I knew it would be the last time. When I left here I would go back to Tom, and I would start our new life in earnest. I would move forwards, the wounds would turn to scars, and like most scars they would be forgotten until something happened to remind me it was there, and then it would become a nostalgic remembrance, a story to tell the friends who asked me where it came from, what happened to me to leave that mark?

But tonight, right now, I could sit here and remember.

I sank down in the seat. The radio played a soft slow tune. The house was silent and dark. Michael was at work, I knew, sweating in a noisy factory while his head filled with dreams. He was always like that – grounded and practical, a dreamer whose thought took flight while his life held him back. He had often said that he was born in those mountains and he would die there in them, without a chance to get out of that small town he called home.

I sat there in the truck and looked at the house he had lived in since he was a child, the mountains nestled right up against his back door, and the quiet serenity of knowing where you were going to be for the rest of your life. What wasn't there to be grateful for?

A few tears fell as I thought of the way things had been, and how one or two different turns would have led me to a life with him in that house he loved so much. But those tears were of remembrance, not of pain, and this time I was grateful for Michael – because, without Michael, there wouldn't have been Tom.

I finally knew where I belonged.

I had just put my hand on the key to fire up the truck and head out of town when I saw the headlights turn into the road. Quickly I sank back in my seat, hoping no one would see me and wonder why in the world I was sitting there in the darkness so far from home. I had intended to drive by Michael's factory, to take the road out of town that would lead me past the lake he loved so much, and then I would be gone for good.

The headlights slowed. There was no turn signal. The truck pulled into Michael's driveway and up into the carport. I watched as the driver cut the engine and the lights flickered into darkness. Only one person would have driven so confidently into that carport – the person who had lived there all his life.

Fresh tears stung my eyes when Michael stepped out of the truck. He looked almost the same as I remembered him. His hair was a bit longer under that baseball cap he wore. He was just as muscular, as broad and powerful as he always had been. He walked with the same kind of stroll. He looked about him with the same kind of attentiveness.

When he saw my truck, he stopped.

Even though I knew he couldn't see me in the deep shadows, I froze right where I was, almost unable to breathe. I thought about opening up the door and getting out to let him see who was waiting there for him, to walk towards him and say hello. But I also knew that doing such a thing would undermine the hard work Tom and I had put into our relationship over the last several months. I was a stronger person now, and part of that strength was in knowing what my weaknesses were – and my big weakness was still, and might always be, that man standing there in the driveway.

I let out the breath I had been holding. Michael kept watching, but finally decided there was nothing there to be concerned about. He turned for the house.

His phone rang.

I could hear the tone from across the street. Michael flipped open the phone and started to talk. His demeanor changed. His shoulders relaxed. He smiled. His voice was different from what I was used to hearing, and I realized with no small jolt of surprise that it was the voice I had known in the beginning – it was filled with the tenderness he once reserved for me.

There was someone else in his life, after all.

At that same moment, I realized that I was glad.

I watched him walk into the house. The lights came on, one at a time, until he was upstairs in the bedroom. After a few minutes, that light went out. I sat there in the darkness for a long time, thinking.

I hoped Michael was happy. I hoped he wouldn't treat her badly. I hoped he had found someone who was meant to be with him, someone who would make him feel all the things that he should feel. I no longer felt like a failure in that regard. I had done the best I could. I hoped this new woman would do it all better.

I started up the truck. I stared at the window of Michael's bedroom, knowing it would be the last time I would wonder what might have been.

When I flicked my headlights on, they shone across the front of the house. Two empty rocking chairs sat there on the porch, side by side.

'Take good care of him,' I said, to someone I would never know.

I put the truck in drive and headed home.

The sun was already up when I pulled into the driveway. The first thing I heard was the sound of the hammer ringing out into the trees every time it struck a nail. The faint scent of sawdust was on the air. The squirrels scampered out of the way of my truck. Leaves and gravel crunched under my tires. I came to a stop and looked out the windshield at Tom.

He was standing over a long section of wood, hammer in hand, nails clenched between his teeth. He didn't acknowledge my presence, though we both knew he heard me come up the drive. I watched as he drove one nail after another, the muscles in his bare back working with every stroke, the new deck becoming sturdier with every nail driven. Sweat rolled off his shoulders, even though the brunt of the autumn heat hadn't rolled in yet. The sunlight touched his back in dappled waves. He stood up once to wipe the sweat from his brow, and I tapped the horn to get his attention.

He looked at me through dark sunglasses, but his lips were curled up in the faintest smile.

I leaned out the window. 'I've been looking for a place around here – a nice little cabin to move into. I need some space and some wilderness. If it comes with cable and a fireplace and a dishwasher and a handsome hunk of a man already installed, that would be nice. Would you happen to know of any place like that?'

Tom squinted up into the sun, as though he was thinking about the request. He looked back at me and spoke around the nail that was held between his lips. 'Don't have a dishwasher here, sorry.'

I laughed. Tom flipped his hammer in his hand and, with two strokes, drove in another nail.

'So, if I could live without a dishwasher, what do you think?'

'Dunno. Tough to live without a dishwasher.'

He drove in another nail.

'What if I said I was willing to trade in the dishwasher for a four-wheeler?'

He tapped his hammer against his thigh and wiped his forehead with the back of his hand. 'Four-wheeler costs extra. But we could dicker. What can you bring to the table?'

I chuckled. 'Sex?'

Tom shook his head. 'Well, well. We might have something to talk about after all.'

I climbed out of the truck and walked towards him. He didn't turn around, but he did sigh when I wrapped my arms around him and laid my head on his back. Sawdust tickled my cheek and made me sneeze. The smell was sharp and pungent, a reminder of good things and hard work.

'Are you looking for a home?' he asked.

'I'm looking for a home,' I agreed.

Tom considered his answer for a long while.

'I've been thinking about getting a dishwasher,' he mused.

'I could live without one.'

'So you're just looking for a home, huh?'

'Yep. Know of where I might find one?'

'You've already got one,' he told me.

I smiled against his back. 'Do I?'

Tom chuckled. The sound rumbled up through him.

'You know you do. Are you ready to accept it now?'

I let go of him and took a step back. When he turned to face me, I stared into his eyes. What I saw there was promise.

I dropped to my knees.

Tom dropped the hammer. It made a thunking sound

on the new wood. The small impact shuddered through my legs. Nails fell from his hand, one by one, and ticked merrily against the boards.

'Will you marry me?' I asked.

Tom's hand shook as he touched my hair. He slowly sank to his knees before me and together we looked at one another, surrounded by singing birds and lumber and sawdust and the promise of a future with no ghosts.

'Yes,' Tom said.

Our wedding was like everything else in our life: we kept it simple. It was just us and a few of those closest friends – Jake, and Ronnie, and his wife. They were waiting with the preacher on the shore. The squirrels were there, too, chattering at us from the trees.

There were speedboats on the lake. Jet skis kicked up wakes. A boy rode by on an inner tube, hollering all the while. The sun beat down through the trees and it all appeared the same as it had been a year ago, but it was all different.

Tom took my hand and led me to the water.

Epilogue

'There's something I want you to do for me,' I said while switching on the bedside lamp. 'It's a matter of trust.'

Tom shifted in the bed. He lifted his hands playfully above his head. 'Bring it on, baby.'

I smiled down at him. 'I'm serious.'

Tom immediately sobered. He looked at me for a long moment.

'OK,' he finally said.

I slipped a small stone into his hand. It clicked against his wedding band. He looked at the stone, turned it over in his fingers.

'That,' I said, 'is your safe sound.'

'My safe sound?'

'When you've had too much, you drop the stone. It will hit the floor. It's hardwood – I will hear it. When I hear it, whatever is happening stops.'

Tom's expression was one of pure surprise.

'Who is the dominant one here?' he asked.

I smiled and reached over to the bedside table. I ran the silk scarf over his chest.

'How much do you trust me?' I asked.

Tom lifted his hands to the headboard. I tied first one hand, then the other. I used the knots he had taught me, the ones he couldn't possibly free himself from, the same ones I could release in an instant with one sharp tug. He yanked hard on the bonds as soon as I was done. They tightened almost painfully on his wrists. He smiled in approval.

I pulled the small package out of the bedside drawer and laid it on his chest. Tom looked down at it for a long time. Finally he looked up at me with understanding in his eyes.

'I never would have thought of this,' he said simply.

His hand moved slightly as he fingered the stone. I watched his face as he thought things over. I dangled the scarf in front of him, and he raised his head. When it was comfortably around his eyes, I leaned down and whispered into his ear. 'If you want anything to stop, you drop that stone. Understand?'

'Yes,' he answered.

I slid the second scarf over his chest. He was already breathing hard. I wound it carefully until it was a long, compact strip of fabric, then slipped it into his mouth. He obediently took it in. I tied the gag, effectively cutting off anything other than his moans.

Then I opened the package I had laid on his chest. Tom shifted in the bed. Without seeing his eyes I had no way to read his expression, but his body language told me he was nervous. I smiled at the fact that I had actually found something such an experienced man had never experienced before.

I slipped the earplugs into his ears. They were the soft comfortable ones that could be worn for long periods of time. They were guaranteed to block all sounds.

I slid off the bed and watched Tom.

Losing almost all his physical senses had a curious effect. He moved for a moment and then stopped suddenly, as if he was afraid to move at all. He slid his feet to either side of the bed, feeling for where I might have gone. His head turned from side to side, as if he were trying to hear – then he did it more deliberately, and I knew he was trying to see something from under the blindfold. But I had been taught well by Tom himself, and there wasn't the slightest way he could see out from under the fabric. He pulled on the bonds around his wrists and gave up on that quickly, as he realized that he had taught me that part, too.

Finally he lay still, his whole body tense, his mind racing.

How much could Tom really handle?

I waited until I knew he was becoming uncomfortable. The edge of fear had crept into him. I could see it in the way his hands clenched on the bonds, the way he shifted on the mattress. I knew that man better than I knew myself.

When I placed one hand on the center of his chest, he immediately relaxed.

I climbed on top of him, slipped his hard cock into me, and began to ride. I rode him until sweat ran down my body. I rode him until sweat ran down his. I rode him through one orgasm, then pushed him to the edge of another one.

And then I climbed off, leaving him breathing hard, his cock pulsing.

I looked at the man who was sitting in the corner and watching every move I made. He stood and started to unbutton his shirt. He looked at me and then at Tom. His eyes were bright with discovery. He flashed me that not-so-innocent smile.

'What's next?' Jake asked.

LOOK OUT FOR THE ALL-NEW BLACK LACE BOOKS – AVAILABLE NOW!

All books priced £7.99 in the UK. Please note publication dates apply to the UK only. For other territories, please contact your retailer.

LURED BY LUST
Tania Picarda
ISBN 978 0 352 33533 3

Clara Fox works at a prestigious art gallery. One sweltering summer's day she receives an email from a stranger who calls himself Mr X. Clara is curious, and begins to involve herself in a world of experimentation and adventurous games.

Can she juggle her kinky liaison with Mr X with all her other intense relationships? And when her former boyfriend Paul tries to win her back, what will he do when he finds that Clara has become a total perv?

Coming in February 2008

A GENTLEMAN'S WAGER
Madelynne Ellis
ISBN 978 0 352 33800 6

When eighteenth-century young lady Bella Rushdale finds herself fiercely attracted to handsome landowner Lucerne Marlinscar, she does not expect the rival for her affections to be another man. However, the handsome and decadent Marquis Pennerley has desired Lucerne for years and, when they are brought together at the remote Lauwine Hall for a country party on the Yorkshire Moors, he intends to claim him. This leads to a passionate struggle for dominance – at the risk of scandal – between the highly sexed Bella and the debauched aristocrat. Ultimately it will be Lucerne who will choose the outcome – and his decision is bound to upset somebody's plans.

POSSESSION
Mathilde Madden, Madelynne Ellis, Anne Tourney
ISBN 978 0 352 34164 8

Three otherworldly short novels of shape-shifters and possession.

Falling Dancer: Kelda has two jobs: full-time bartender, part-time exorcist. She meets vengeful spirits and misguided demons wherever she goes. She wishes the spirit world would leave her alone so she could have a relationship that lasted longer than 24 hours, but when she's contacted by a sexy musician who wants her to solve the mystery of his girlfriend's disappearance, she can't help getting involved . . .

The Silver Chains: Alfie Friday is a werewolf. For seven years he has controlled his curse carefully by locking himself in a cage every full moon. But now he's changing when it isn't full moon. His girlfriend Misty travels to South America to try to find a way of controlling Alfie's changes, but discovers the key to the problem lies in Oxford. The place it all began for Alfie and the place he has vowed never to return to.

Broken Angel: After stealing a copy of an ancient manuscript, Blaze Makaresh finds himself being hunted down by a gang of youkai – demons who infiltrate human society in order to satisfy their hunger for sex and flesh. When Talon, an elitist society of demon-hunters, come to his aid, he's soon enmeshed with the beautiful Asha, and the dawning of an age-old prophecy.

THE SILVER CAGE
Mathilde Madden
ISBN 978 0 352 34165 5

Iris and Alfie have been driven apart by the strongest forces in the werewolf world – the powerful thrall of the Divine Wolf – the mother of them all. Now Iris needs to win Alfie back, not just for herself, but because the fate of the world could rest upon it.

But the only way to free Alfie from the power of the Divine Wolf is to kill her. Something that could end the lives of all werewolves. Including Alfie himself – Iris's true love.

Coming in March 2008

CASSANDRA'S CONFLICT
Fredrica Alleyn
ISBN 978 0 352 34186 0

A house in Hampstead. Present-day. Behind a façade of cultured respectability lies a world of decadent indulgence and dark eroticism. Cassandra's sheltered life is transformed when she gets employed as governess to the Baron's children. He draws her into games where lust can feed on the erotic charge of submission. Games where only he knows the rules and where unusual pleasures can flourish.

PHANTASMAGORIA
Madelynne Ellis
ISBN 978 0 352 34168 6

1800 – Three years after escaping to London with her bisexual lovers, Bella Rushdale wakes one morning to find their delicate ménage-a-trois on the verge of shattering. Vaughan, Marquis of Pennerley has left abruptly and without any explanation. Determined to reclaim him and preserve their relationship, Bella pursues the errant Marquis to his family seat on the Welsh Borders where she finds herself embroiled in his preparations for a diabolical gothic celebration on All Hallows Eve – a phantasmagoria! Among the shadows and phantoms Bella and her lovers will peel away the deceits and desires of the past and future.

Black Lace Booklist

Information is correct at time of printing. To avoid disappointment, check availability before ordering. Go to www.black-lace-books.com. All books are priced £7.99 unless another price is given.

BLACK LACE BOOKS WITH A CONTEMPORARY SETTING

☐ ALWAYS THE BRIDEGROOM Tesni Morgan	ISBN 978 0 352 33855 6	£6.99
☐ THE ANGELS' SHARE Maya Hess	ISBN 978 0 352 34043 6	
☐ ASKING FOR TROUBLE Kristina Lloyd	ISBN 978 0 352 33362 9	
☐ BLACK LIPSTICK KISSES Monica Belle	ISBN 978 0 352 33885 3	£6.99
☐ THE BLUE GUIDE Carrie Williams	ISBN 978 0 352 34132 7	
☐ THE BOSS Monica Belle	ISBN 978 0 352 34088 7	
☐ BOUND IN BLUE Monica Belle	ISBN 978 0 352 34012 2	
☐ CAMPAIGN HEAT Gabrielle Marcola	ISBN 978 0 352 33941 6	
☐ CAT SCRATCH FEVER Sophie Mouette	ISBN 978 0 352 34021 4	
☐ CIRCUS EXCITE Nikki Magennis	ISBN 978 0 352 34033 7	
☐ CLUB CRÈME Primula Bond	ISBN 978 0 352 33907 2	£6.99
☐ COMING ROUND THE MOUNTAIN Tabitha Flyte	ISBN 978 0 352 33873 0	£6.99
☐ CONFESSIONAL Judith Roycroft	ISBN 978 0 352 33421 3	
☐ CONTINUUM Portia Da Costa	ISBN 978 0 352 33120 5	
☐ DANGEROUS CONSEQUENCES Pamela Rochford	ISBN 978 0 352 33185 4	
☐ DARK DESIGNS Madelynne Ellis	ISBN 978 0 352 34075 7	
☐ THE DEVIL INSIDE Portia Da Costa	ISBN 978 0 352 32993 6	
☐ EDEN'S FLESH Robyn Russell	ISBN 978 0 352 33923 2	£6.99
☐ EQUAL OPPORTUNITIES Mathilde Madden	ISBN 978 0 352 34070 2	
☐ FIRE AND ICE Laura Hamilton	ISBN 978 0 352 33486 2	
☐ GOING DEEP Kimberly Dean	ISBN 978 0 352 33876 1	£6.99
☐ GONE WILD Maria Eppie	ISBN 978 0 352 33670 5	
☐ HOTBED Portia Da Costa	ISBN 978 0 352 33614 9	
☐ IN PURSUIT OF ANNA Natasha Rostova	ISBN 978 0 352 34060 3	
☐ IN THE FLESH Emma Holly	ISBN 978 0 352 34117 4	
☐ LEARNING TO LOVE IT Alison Tyler	ISBN 978 0 352 33535 7	

BLACK LACE BOOKS WITH AN HISTORICAL SETTING

☐ THE CAPTIVATION Natasha Rostova	ISBN 978 0 352 33234 9	
☐ DARKER THAN LOVE Kristina Lloyd	ISBN 978 0 352 33279 0	
☐ WILD KINGDOM Deanna Ashford	ISBN 978 0 352 33549 4	
☐ DIVINE TORMENT Janine Ashbless	ISBN 978 0 352 33719 1	
☐ FRENCH MANNERS Olivia Christie	ISBN 978 0 352 33214 1	
☐ LORD WRAXALL'S FANCY Anna Lieff Saxby	ISBN 978 0 352 33080 2	
☐ NICOLE'S REVENGE Lisette Allen	ISBN 978 0 352 32984 4	
☐ THE SENSES BEJEWELLED Cleo Cordell	ISBN 978 0 352 32904 2	£6.99
☐ THE SOCIETY OF SIN Sian Lacey Taylder	ISBN 978 0 352 34080 1	
☐ TEMPLAR PRIZE Deanna Ashford	ISBN 978 0 352 34137 2	
☐ UNDRESSING THE DEVIL Angel Strand	ISBN 978 0 352 33938 6	

BLACK LACE BOOKS WITH A PARANORMAL THEME

☐ BRIGHT FIRE Maya Hess	ISBN 978 0 352 34104 4
☐ BURNING BRIGHT Janine Ashbless	ISBN 978 0 352 34085 6
☐ CRUEL ENCHANTMENT Janine Ashbless	ISBN 978 0 352 33483 1
☐ FLOOD Anna Clare	ISBN 978 0 352 34094 8
☐ GOTHIC BLUE Portia Da Costa	ISBN 978 0 352 33075 8
☐ THE PRIDE Edie Bingham	ISBN 978 0 352 33997 3
☐ THE SILVER COLLAR Mathilde Madden	ISBN 978 0 352 34141 9
☐ THE TEN VISIONS Olivia Knight	ISBN 978 0 352 34119 8

BLACK LACE ANTHOLOGIES

☐ BLACK LACE QUICKIES 1 Various	ISBN 978 0 352 34126 6	£2.99
☐ BLACK LACE QUICKIES 2 Various	ISBN 978 0 352 34127 3	£2.99
☐ BLACK LACE QUICKIES 3 Various	ISBN 978 0 352 34128 0	£2.99
☐ BLACK LACE QUICKIES 4 Various	ISBN 978 0 352 34129 7	£2.99
☐ BLACK LACE QUICKIES 5 Various	ISBN 978 0 352 34130 3	£2.99
☐ BLACK LACE QUICKIES 6 Various	ISBN 978 0 352 34133 4	£2.99
☐ BLACK LACE QUICKIES 7 Various	ISBN 978 0 352 34146 4	£2.99
☐ BLACK LACE QUICKIES 8 Various	ISBN 978 0 352 34147 1	£2.99
☐ BLACK LACE QUICKIES 9 Various	ISBN 978 0 352 34155 6	£2.99
☐ MORE WICKED WORDS Various	ISBN 978 0 352 33487 9	£6.99
☐ WICKED WORDS 3 Various	ISBN 978 0 352 33522 7	£6.99
☐ WICKED WORDS 4 Various	ISBN 978 0 352 33603 3	£6.99
☐ WICKED WORDS 5 Various	ISBN 978 0 352 33642 2	£6.99

BLACK LACE NON-FICTION

To find out the latest information about Black Lace titles, check out the website: www.black-lace-books.com or send for a booklist with complete synopses by writing to:

Black Lace Booklist, Virgin Books Ltd
Thames Wharf Studios
Rainville Road
London W6 9HA

Please include an SAE of decent size. Please note only British stamps are valid.

Our privacy policy
We will not disclose information you supply us to any other parties. We will not disclose any information which identifies you personally to any person without your express consent.

From time to time we may send out information about Black Lace books and special offers. Please tick here if you do <u>not</u> wish to receive Black Lace information. ❏

Please send me the books I have ticked above.

Name ....

Address ....

....

....

....

Post Code ....

Send to: Virgin Books Cash Sales, Thames Wharf Studios, Rainville Road, London W6 9HA.

US customers: for prices and details of how to order books for delivery by mail, call 888-330-8477.

Please enclose a cheque or postal order, made payable to Virgin Books Ltd, to the value of the books you have ordered plus postage and packing costs as follows:

UK and BFPO – £1.00 for the first book, 50p for each subsequent book.

Overseas (including Republic of Ireland) – £2.00 for the first book, £1.00 for each subsequent book.

If you would prefer to pay by VISA, ACCESS/MASTERCARD, DINERS CLUB, AMEX or SWITCH, please write your card number and expiry date here:

....

Signature ....

Please allow up to 28 days for delivery.